Ingrid Alexandra is based in Sydney. Her work has previously been long-listed for the Ampersand Prize and while living in London, she had the privilege of being mentored by the Guardian First Novel Award shortlisted and Nestlé Prize winning author Daren King. THE NEW GIRL is her first psychological thriller.

You can find Ingrid on Twitter @ingridwrites

D1110724

THE NEW GIRL

INGRID ALEXANDRA

avon.

Published by AVON
A division of HarperCollins*Publishers* Ltd
1 London Bridge Street
London SE1 9GF

www.harpercollins.co.uk

A Paperback Original 2018
3

PB ISBN: 978-0-00-829381-9
TPB ISBN: 978-0-00-831095-0

Set in Bembo by Palimpsest Book Production Limited,
Falkirk, Stirlingshire

Printed and bound in Great Britain by
CPI Group (UK) Ltd, Croydon CR0 4YY

MIX
Paper from
responsible sources
FSC www.fsc.org **FSC™ C007454**

For Vidar,
for everything.

Prologue

20th August 2016
4.17 a.m.

The smell of blood lingers. It's on my clothes, though they have been washed clean. On my skin, though I've scrubbed it raw.

Light is shining through a crack in the door. The yolk-orange glow steals across the bedroom like an intruder, illuminating the white, pinstriped shirt that hangs from the clothes horse. The empty sleeves dangle, twitching now and then in the breeze from the window.

I tune my ears to the sounds in the next room. He's pacing, thinking. '*Mary,*' he mutters. '*Mary, Mary.*'

As I curl against the cold wall, my skin tingles with adrenalin. He always said I couldn't be trusted. Now,

1

he's right. In the closet, under a pile of dirty laundry, there's an overnight bag. It's an old one of my mother's with white daisies embroidered on dark green canvas. A toothbrush, some make-up and a few items of clothing are all it contains. They've been waiting there, waiting for the right moment.

Footsteps sound in the hall and stop outside the door. I hold my breath. The tide is rising, and I can hear the waves as they swell and crash on the nearby shore.

The door opens and he stands, silhouetted by the hall light.

'Mary, Mary, quite contrary,' he slurs, the hint of a sneer in his voice. 'What are we going to do with you?'

Chapter One

Three months later

I heave over the basin, but there's nothing left to come up. I spit, turn on the tap and splash my face. It's bad this time, worse than usual. But I know it won't stop me. I'll only do it again.

Gulping a mouthful of stale water from the mug on the sink, I take a deep breath and tiptoe out of the bathroom. Sunlight streams through the floor-to-ceiling windows that lead to the balcony, making me squint. The sky glares sapphire blue, the overzealous shrieks of children and families drift up from the shore below. People out and about, doing whatever it is regular people do on a Sunday afternoon.

Cat is in the open-plan kitchen by the counter, bent

forward and shaking out her shower-wet hair. Her fingers comb the long, raven-black strands and fat beads of water drip onto the kitchen floor.

'I'm still freaking out about that accident,' she says through her hair. 'You could have been killed.'

I watch her upside-down face, forcing down my irritation. I could slip in the puddle she's making and crack my skull on the tiles. Then I might *really* be killed. 'It's nothing, just a dent.'

'It's not the car I'm worried about.' Cat tilts her head, one perfectly shaped eyebrow arched. I wonder if she knows I lied about how much I'd had before getting behind the wheel.

I sip the coffee she's made me but it tastes too bitter. 'The car barely hit me. Nothing a little buffing can't get rid of.'

'Which I'll sort out,' Ben interjects, winking at me over his shoulder as he nudges past Cat to get to the kitchen sink. He pours himself a glass of water and swallows it back in three large gulps. 'Once the hangover wears off.'

'Ugh. I guarantee mine's worse than yours,' Cat moans, flipping herself back upright and pushing her wet hair over her shoulder as she leans against the kitchen counter. She looks fine to me. I'm positive I'm the most hung-over. 'Whose idea was it to crack open the vodka?'

Ben and I exchange a look, but before I can be found guilty, Cat's phone rings and she jumps, knocking over the empty cocktail pitcher. It clatters loudly into the sink and my head pounds in response. 'Shit. I'll get that in a sec. This could be about the room.'

Retrieving the pitcher, I make a half-hearted attempt at clearing some of the house-warming collateral while Cat takes the call.

Ben steps over a squashed lime wedge and right into the puddle on the floor. He slips and yelps, arms shooting out, hands finding my shoulders and clamping on. His fingers dig into my flesh.

I gasp, my chest contracting. Ben's laughing, his feet skidding on the floor. Suddenly the ground slips out from under me and my spine connects with something hard. Spots of light dance before my eyes.

'What are you two doing?' Cat shakes her head, one hand on her hip, the other holding her phone in the air. 'You both look retarded.' She looks at me and her brow furrows. 'Mary?'

I shake my head, ducking to hide the tears. When I look up, Ben's there, his face close. His irises are a strange colour – not quite brown, not quite green.

'I'm sorry. Did I hurt you?' he asks.

I can't answer; my throat is too tight.

'Sorry . . .' Ben says again, but his kindness is too much. I turn away. Ben lets me go, clears his throat. 'You know,' he says, addressing Cat, 'it's actually your fault we're in this . . . situation.' He points to the tiles, which are now more grubby and smeared than wet.

Cat ignores him. 'Good news! I think we might have a candidate for our new roomie!'

'Seriously?' I say. The last few applicants have been less than desirable, particularly the creepy middle-aged guy who wouldn't stop staring at Cat's cleavage.

'Yup. She's our age, I think, doing some kind of arts degree at uni. She works part-time and she's available right away.'

'Another *girl*?' Ben moans, then pauses. 'Did she sound hot?'

Cat narrows her eyes. 'You have a *girlfriend*. And I only spoke to her on the phone. How the hell should I know if she's hot?'

Ben shakes his head sagely. 'You can tell. And Gia isn't my *girlfriend*. She's just a friend.'

'Does *she* know that?' Rolling her eyes, Cat turns to me. 'What do you think? Are you okay to meet her later?'

'Sure,' I say with a shrug, but anxiety whispers across my chest at the thought of meeting someone new. I try to ignore it.

'Great!' Cat squeals. 'I'll just text her to see when she's available, okay?'

'No worries.' I step out of the kitchen and take a moment to breathe.

Eagle-eyed Cat pauses in her texting and slings an arm around my shoulder. 'You okay there?'

I manage a smile, though I'm still edgy.

'It's better here, isn't it?' Cat gestures to the high-security intercom system with its intricate array of buttons. 'I'm glad we're here. I feel safer, don't you?' She smiles in that goofy, affectionate way that only an old friend can and wraps me in her arms.

As I inhale the smell of coconut shampoo and childhood, the waves of the past whoosh and roar in my ears.

Chapter Two

22nd November 2016

Dear Journal,

I guess that's how you're supposed to start a journal entry, isn't it? I've never written a journal before. Or I might have, as a kid at school or something, but I can't remember that far back.

I suppose I should introduce myself. I'm Mary. Hello. It's a while since I've written anything, actually. I used to write a lot, I found it cathartic. Anyway, here I am, making a start. I might not be doing everything Doctor Sarah advised in our last session, but at least I'm doing this. Mark used to say I never followed through with anything. 'Slacker,' he'd call me, as though he was one to talk. Doctor Sarah said keeping a journal will help to record my thoughts and feelings, so I can catalogue my moods and 'compartmentalise my issues', or whatever it is she calls it. She wants me to keep track of any changes. It helps to put things in words sometimes; it makes things seem smaller when you can fit them into a little box. At least, that's what Doctor Sarah tells me.

There's a quote I've got stuck in my head. I can't remember where I heard it, but it goes: 'The only constant is change.' A profound truth summed up in a paradox. It's pretty fitting to my current situation. Nothing is permanent, so you'd better not get too attached to anything, right? I mean, why waste your energy? But we do. It's human nature. People, possessions, ideas – we latch on like molluscs, suctioning for what we crave, whatever we think is going to get us through. The good news? Whatever terrible situation you may find yourself in, it will pass. The bad news? The things you depend on – really depend on – pass too. Often when you least expect it. Often before you realise you're dependent to begin with.

But I digress. So, changes. Where to begin? The biggest one. I've left.

I got tingles just writing that. Though not good tingles – yet. I'm hoping that will come in time. Yes, there was that initial euphoria – freedom! The world had opened up and suddenly I was able to be a part of it. I wasn't hiding anymore.

But then something happened, I don't know what. It shrank back, I guess. Into a claustrophobic bubble I can't escape. It's as if reality is elastic sometimes; it can expand and contract, or change shape depending solely on how you view it.

My old fears have crept back in, as though they'd been waiting until there was room for them. And now, there is. They say the world gets smaller the more you see of it . . . perhaps that's what's happened to me. I'm exploring more of the world now, so it's more accessible, less immense. I say that now, as if I'm the confident, brave person I'm supposed to be, but the truth is I struggle to leave the house most days. The world in here feels so much safer, like I have reign over it, while the world out there reigns over me.

It's funny, the 'heebie-jeebies' (Doctor Sarah uses some of the lamest terms) kick in at the strangest times. Right now, for example, I can smell his cologne, as though he's just been in the apartment. Which I know is impossible – it's probably a waft of the cheap deodorant Ben douses himself with after a shower – but I still get a jolt. Sometimes I'll see him in the faces of people walking past, or in the shadows of my room at night. Adrenalin prickles over my skin like an army of ants and I have to get out, have to walk, skip, do something or I'll go mad.

The fear can be paralysing. Sometimes I don't have the drive to do any of the above. Sometimes all I can bring myself to do is drink. That's proving the hardest habit to break, like saying goodbye to a faithful friend right when you need them most.

I'm lucky. That's what they all keep telling me. Really? Am I? It seems like a pretty ill-fitting word for someone like me. I prefer Doctor Sarah's way of putting it. She says I'm brave (whether she means it or not). But lucky? That implies a lack of choice or control, as though I had no say in what happened to me or how it turned out.

When I left Melbourne, my best friend was willing to pack up her life and move out here with me in a nanosecond. But I'm not 'lucky' to have her – we both put energy into cultivating and sustaining this friendship. It wasn't luck that drove me to leave, although it played a role in those final moments. And it wasn't luck that got us this apartment. It was Cat's tenacity and charm — and the fact that she wouldn't take no for an answer. She wanted me to be somewhere where I could forget the past, she said. Like a change of location has the power to do that. But it's a nice thought anyway.

It is pretty amazing, this place. Not so much the apartment itself — the rooms are small, and there's a disproportionate number of bathrooms to bedrooms (1:4), but it's brand new (still smells of paint), it's high up on the fifth floor with a spacious communal dining/kitchen area, and it has a massive balcony out the front, overlooking the water.

We live right in the heart of the northern beaches of Sydney where I used to come as a child, and I have to say, being this close to the sea is a godsend when it's this stinking hot. We can't really afford to live here, of course, which is why we're looking for a fourth boarder. Ben is studying to be a high-school teacher and works part-time as a support aide for children with disabilities, so you can imagine there's fuck-all money in that. It's noble, though. It suits him, I think. Cat is studying PR and works at the café under our apartment complex.

I don't work — not yet — but I have enough money to pay my share of the rent. I don't worry about money so much; it's the least of my problems. But I know the others do, and it makes me feel guilty.

What I have to focus on, the most important thing, is staying safe. Things could definitely be worse — and they were — but that's in the past. I'm getting better, and I'm letting go. Of course, it'll take time. But it won't take forever. Everything passes, doesn't it?

Sometimes, at dawn, when I've been awake for hours, I get up and tiptoe through the sliding doors that lead from my bedroom to the balcony. There, in the morning mist, amid the salty scent of the ocean and the low roar of the waves, I watch the sun rise over the sea. It's in those moments I feel a sense of calm mingled with a longing, a sadness I can't quite place. Am I nostalgic for a life left behind or for one I never had? I suppose it doesn't matter. Because, for the first time in as long as I can remember, I can almost imagine that everything will be okay.

Chapter Three

The sky is ominous today. Slate-grey clouds hang over the horizon and the sea is the colour of dishwater. Early summer weather is fickle and today it's only sixteen degrees and sheeting with rain.

I tap my foot on the wooden deck, a lukewarm cup of tea in my hands. My eyes flick back and forth to the clock on my phone but time doesn't seem to be passing at all. Why did I agree to this? Cat could have swapped shifts with someone, surely, or Ben could have postponed his 'date'. Isn't this something we should all be doing together?

My foot taps on restlessly, like it's disconnected from the rest of me. *Tap tap tap tap tap tap.* The intercom buzzes and I jump, spilling tea down the front of my T-shirt. '*Shit.*'

Rushing into the kitchen, I drop the mug in the sink and mop at my front with a soggy tea towel, which only serves to spread the moisture. The intrusive buzz sounds again and I jab my finger at the silver button on the intercom.

'Hello?' I say. The word sounds hoarse, as if spoken by a heavy smoker. Silence. I clear my throat, 'Hello?'

'Hi! Yes. Um, is this Mary?' It's a soft, husky female voice, not what I was expecting.

'Yes.'

'Hi! It's Rachel. For the room?'

'Right, yeah. Of course. Come on up.'

'Thanks!'

I press the button for the front door and hear a short, low *brrrrrrpt* on the other end.

She's in.

Swallowing thickly, I pour myself some water, then stop. *Shit, I've forgotten. Today of all days.* Dashing to my room, I yank open the top drawer of my dresser and find the aluminium popper pack. I thrust my thumb into the foil twice and throw back the small, white pills with a slug of water. As I'm wiping my mouth on my sleeve, there's a knock at the door.

'Coming!' That's better. Normal-sounding, friendly. I make myself walk slowly to the door, breathe, then open it.

At first all I see is an oversized grey raincoat with a hood and a shadow for a face. Then the hood slides back and a face appears: pale, angular, with a high, domed forehead and hazel eyes. Dimpled cheeks bracket a wide, even-toothed smile. Two small hands reach up to disengage a bundle of dishevelled, shoulder-length blonde hair from the hood of the raincoat.

All thoughts of greeting are erased by the sudden feeling of recognition. A face like that would be hard to forget, I think. But I can't pinpoint where I may have seen her. I almost ask if I know her, but she's thrusting out her small hand, beaming, and saying in that rough-edged voice, 'It's *so* nice to meet you!'

'Hi. Yes, you too.'

Rachel grasps my hand with fingers that are ice-cold. She's surrounded by the scent of something sharp and sweet. I'm about to pull my hand back when our eyes connect. I feel a jolt; there's something in those wide-set eyes, something that makes me feel exposed.

'Are you okay?' Rachel's peering at me, brow furrowed. I can see the dusting of freckles on her small, upturned nose. She's pretty. Really pretty. And then I wonder if it's okay to think she's pretty when she looks a bit like me. Not a dead ringer, of course, but the basic stats: blonde, slim, around the same age. But I've got nothing on this girl. At my best, I was that balance of plain and pretty that made me approachable, not too intimidating.

'Mary?'

I shake my head to clear it. 'Yeah, yes. Sorry. I just . . . Bit of a headache.'

'You poor thing,' Rachel puts her hand on my upper arm and squeezes gently. The sleeve of her raincoat rides up and I glimpse a black, Celtic-looking pattern on her wrist. A tattoo? 'I get headaches a lot, so I totally sympathise. Do you want some ibuprofen or something?'

I force a smile. 'No, really, I'm fine. Sorry about that. Come in. Would you like a coffee, or a tea maybe?'

'I'd *love* a coffee, thanks.' Rachel kicks off her trainers and walks down the hallway and into the kitchen, placing her handbag on the counter. 'Oh god, *wow*,' she breathes, her gaze settling on the dark, rolling clouds, the grey sea and the misty mountain beyond. The flailing branches of the fir trees by the shore hint at a storm. 'This place is amazing.'

'Yeah. The view is pretty great.' I flick on the kettle and spoon instant coffee into two mugs. 'Did you walk here?'

'Yup. I don't have a car at the moment.' Rachel shrugs out of her raincoat to reveal a baggy jumper emblazoned with the Sydney University logo and a pair of black leggings. Her long legs remind me of a dancer's or a model's, and I wonder if she has that 'thigh gap' everyone has become obsessed with in recent years.

'Sorry, I didn't dress up for you.' She grins and I wonder if she saw me looking. 'I'm more of a "dress for comfort" kind of girl.'

'You're in good company,' I say with a smile, gesturing to my T-shirt and jeans.

'Oh, I love your shirt! Where did you find it? Astro Boy is so retro!'

'It was a gift, ages ago. It's way too big.' I pull at the hem of the shirt, which hangs mid-thigh.

'It really suits you.' Rachel smiles warmly and I feel my cheeks heat up as though a boy I liked just paid attention to me. Rachel is not just gorgeous; she's cool, confident. Like I used to be.

The kettle squeals as it reaches boiling point and, grateful for the distraction, I turn and pour hot water into the mugs. 'Milk? Sugar?'

'Thanks, yes. Milk and two sugars.'

I slop milk into both mugs, some of it splattering onto the counter, and stir in the sugar. 'So,' I say as I hastily wipe up with a grubby cloth and hand Rachel her mug, 'how about you take a look at the room, see what you think?'

Rachel beams. 'Great.'

I lead her down the hall. The room is clean and smells of fresh paint. Cat's family had some furniture in storage so we decided to rent it furnished so we could ask for more money. The space looks neat and inviting. The room is a mirror image of mine, and beyond the glass sliding doors that connect to the balcony, the sea is visible through the mist.

'Jesus,' Rachel murmurs, so softly I can barely hear her. 'I knew it would be nice, but I wasn't expecting this.'

I smile. There's something endearing about her reaction. 'You're available straight away, is that right?' I ask. As soon as the words are out, I cringe inwardly. It sounds like I'm already asking her to move in.

Rachel nods, smiling wide. 'I am, absolutely, yes.' She takes a sip of coffee as she combs her fingers through a strand of fine, blonde hair. 'I'm currently crashing on a friend's couch – *not* ideal – until I find somewhere. I just moved from Melbourne, kind of in a hurry actually, so I'm still finding my feet.'

'Oh! I'm from Melbourne, too.'

Rachel's eyes pop. 'Seriously? Wow!' She beams, hazel eyes twinkling. Again, I have that feeling of exposure, of being really looked at. Being *seen*. I haven't felt that in a long time. 'You know – and please don't think I'm crazy here – but I get this weird feeling like I already know you. You know how sometimes you meet someone and you just *click*?'

A smile touches my lips. 'Yeah. Actually, I do.'

Rachel puts a hand over her mouth. When she pulls it away, she's grinning. 'I was thinking, oh my God, Mary's going to think I'm a complete freak saying that. But you didn't. Thank fuck!'

A laugh escapes and I can't believe it, I actually laughed.

'And now I've gone and said fuck! See how comfortable I am with you already?'

'Oh, don't worry. I swear all the time,' I tell her. 'Fuck is probably the most frequently used word in my vocabulary.'

Rachel giggles, an airy, girlish sound, and I find myself joining in. I feel lighter all of a sudden. Taller.

A sharp trilling intrudes and it's a moment before I realise what it is. I snatch my phone from my pocket.

Aunty Anne calling.

'Sorry,' I say to Rachel. 'I have to take this.'

'No probs.' Rachel waves a hand in the air. 'Take your time.'

I slip out on the balcony, sliding the door shut behind me. 'Hi, Aunty Anne.'

'Mary, darling.' The familiar voice is muffled by the teeming rain. 'How are you?'

'I'm fine, thanks. What's new?'

There's a pause. The storm's moving in, the mountain across the water barely visible through the mist. 'He's been here again.' There's a note of apology in her tone. 'Asking after you. Mentioning something about police this time.'

A cold shiver moves through me. 'Are you okay?' I ask. 'Did he . . .'

'I'm okay, darling. He tried his best to rattle me, but you know your old aunt, I stood my ground. I told him you were still on holiday. He called me a liar and . . . a *fucking bitch* I think it was?'

'God.' I wince. Aunty Anne's not one to mince words. 'That's horrible. I'm so . . .'

'Don't be sorry, darling, I just thought you should know.'

'What else did he say?'

'He said . . .' A meaty cough comes through the phone; she's been recovering from bronchitis. 'Well, just what I told you. He called me a few things and . . .'

I press a finger to my throat, feel my pulse quicken. 'And . . . and what else?'

A heavy sigh. 'I suppose you could say there were threats.'

'Like what? Against who?'

Pause. 'Well, me. He was quite worked up. But that's hardly new! I'm sure he didn't really mean it.'

My throat tightens. I'm sick of it, this feeling. 'I'm calling the police,' I say. 'Doctor Sarah said if he makes any threats . . .'

'Oh, darling, hush. I'm not telling you so you worry about *me*.' Aunty Anne's voice sounds tinny, distant. 'I've got your uncle and you know damn well no one gets past him. Next time, that bastard is going to leave with more than just a warning.'

My shoulders relax. My uncle, Lieutenant General John, is the main reason I felt okay to leave my aunty in Melbourne.

'I just want to remind you to be careful, Mary.'

'I am,' I assure her. 'He can't find me here and if he did, he'd never get into the building.'

Aunty Anne is saying something, but the rain is coming down in sheets and a clap of thunder drowns out her voice. I run a hand over my mouth, turn to go inside.

Rachel is standing in the doorway. With a gasp, I drop the phone.

'Sorry,' Rachel says, looking sheepish. She bends to pick up my phone and hands it to me. 'I didn't mean to scare you. You just looked so upset . . .'

'Aunty Anne? I'll call you back,' I say into the receiver before ending the call.

22

'Are you okay?' Rachel asks. She has a glob of mascara in the corner of her eye; it's all I can focus on. 'You look like you've seen a ghost. Maybe you should sit down.'

I don't want to sit down. I want a glass of wine, and I want to call Cat and tell her what's happened. I want to smash something, but I do not want to sit down. 'No, I'm okay, really. Just some . . . news from back home. Nothing serious.'

'You're sure?' Rachel's standing close, I can see flecks of gold and brown in her irises.

I take a breath, try to smile. 'Everything's fine. I've just got something I need to deal with. Sorry to cut this short, but . . .'

Rachel's face clouds. 'Oh. Okay.'

'I'm definitely interested!' I blurt. 'I mean, this isn't because of you . . . just bad timing. I'll give you a call later, once I've talked things over with the others.'

Rachel's face relaxes and she gives a small smile; for the first time, she seems uncertain. She steps inside, collects her handbag on her way to the door. 'Okay, thanks. That'd be great. I look forward to speaking to you again. I, uh . . .' She ducks her head, tucking a strand of hair behind her ear. 'It was really nice meeting you today.'

'Same here. Thanks, Rachel, I'll be in touch very soon.'

Rachel kneels to put her trainers back on, opens the door and walks out. I'm about to close the door behind her when she looks over her shoulder.

'Mary?'

'Yes?'

A pair of sympathetic hazel eyes stare into mine. 'I think you should go and have a lie-down or something. You really don't look too well.'

Chapter Four

As I approach the entry doors to the apartment block, a pungent, spicy scent invades my nostrils. It's probably coming from the sixth-floor apartment with the balcony directly above ours. The couple who live there are always cooking something exotic, in between screaming at each other and having noisy sex. But there's something not quite right about this smell. It's as though something has started to rot.

Holding a hand to my nose, I reach for the letter box to find it unlocked, the flap hanging from its hinges. Letters are scattered on the slate tiles below, one with a filmy, brown stain on the corner. Slick-skinned and weary from my walk, I'm thinking only of a cold shower, and it isn't until I've gathered the mail, shut and locked the flap and taken the lift to the fifth floor that I stop to think. Why was the letter box unlocked? Cat and I never unlock it; it seems strange anyone bothered to open it in the first place seeing as the envelopes usually protrude from the slot.

A scruffy beige suitcase with a hole in the seam greets me as I enter the apartment. It sags sadly against the white hallway wall like a stain. Rachel arrived at seven-thirty this morning, deposited her belongings, and immediately rushed off to work. She didn't bring much, as the room came furnished. So, all day today, the few items comprising Rachel Cummings' worldly possessions have lain where they fell, awaiting her return.

Flicking on the kettle and glancing at the clock (*five-oh-six!*), I change my mind. *Just a glass or two to end the day*, I tell myself as I open the fridge, take out a bottle and slosh the remains of last night's Pinot Grigio into a wine glass. There's plenty more in the bar fridge in the laundry room, I'm sure. Leftovers from the party.

The wine is cool and crisp as it passes my lips and, after a couple more sips, the familiar warmth curls in my stomach like a cat settling in for the night. Humming a catchy tune I heard on the radio, I flip through the mail. An estate agent advertisement, the electricity bill and a letter, the one with the brown stain on it, addressed to someone named Sophia Gates. It's the second time this person's mail has arrived here; Sophia Gates must have been the previous tenant.

I toss the letter into the recycling, take a long pull of wine and then pause, rubbing a finger along my lips.

I knew someone named Sophia once. Or Sophie, maybe. I think for a moment but my mind's cloudy, and I can't remember anyone specific. It's probably no one important, yet I have that feeling I get at times, like I'm supposed to remember something but there's a brick wall in my mind and my thoughts stop there. A *blank space*, as I've come to call it.

My wine's nearly gone and no one's home yet, so I top up my glass with a bottle from the laundry. I go to my room, sit at my desk and flip open my laptop. I check my email, trawl through my newsfeed. Without planning to, I google the name Sophia Gates. Images, Facebook pages and LinkedIn accounts pop up, but I don't recognise anyone. I'm being stupid, paranoid as usual. It must just be a coincidence.

'Any mail?' Cat's voice calls from the kitchen, startling me. I hadn't heard the door.

'On the coffee table!' I tell her, gulping a mouthful before hiding the glass under the desk.

A moment later, Cat pops her head around the door frame, sleek black ponytail snaking over her shoulder. Her eyes are unusually bright, probably a result of her afternoon Pilates session. 'Is this all?' she asks, holding up the electricity bill.

'Yes. Uh, and there was one for the previous tenant.'

Cat looks at me sharply. 'Oh, where is it? Do you still have it?'

I shrug. Why is she so worried? 'I just tossed it.'

Cat's shoulders relax. 'Okay. Good. I mean, I just couldn't be bothered collecting them all and taking them down to the estate agent's.'

I frown. 'Cat, did we know anyone called Sophie? At school or something?'

She stares at me for a moment. Then, slowly, she shakes her head. 'No. Not that I can remember.'

'Are you sure?'

Cat shrugs. 'I don't remember everyone we went to school with, Mary. Look, I've been meaning to ask. Have you got around to making that appointment yet?'

'Appointment?'

Cat gives me a meaningful look. 'With the psychiatrist. The one Doctor Sarah referred you to. What's his name . . . Doctor Chen? Doctor Chang?'

I worry my lower lip with my teeth, shake my head.

'*Mary.*' Cat clicks her tongue, glancing around the room as if looking for something. I imagine her eyes burning holes in the desk, spotting the wine glass hidden underneath.

'It's on my list, I swear.'

Cat eyeballs me with pursed lips, then releases a sigh that tells me she gives up. 'Pizza for dinner?'

That coaxes a smile from me. 'Obviously.'

As I sit, stealing sips of wine, drumming my fingers on the desk, I do the thing I always promise myself I won't do, but then always do. It's as though some invisible force is steering my hand. I type one letter and, as it does every time, the search engine remembers the sequence of words in an instant.

The articles pop up in the same order they're always in.

Leads in murder investigation go cold.

Investigation meets dead end.

Murderer never found.

The same grainy black and white picture of his smiling, unsuspecting face stares out at me. And I wonder, for the hundredth time, if he ever saw it coming.

A breeze creeps in from the balcony door, fragrant with brine. Goosebumps rise on my arms; I shiver and close the browser window.

Chapter Five

24th November 2016

See? I'm keeping it up. I've promised myself I would. It seems, more often than not, I manage to break my promises to myself. But not this time.

I made it out on my walk today, so that's something. And I'm writing — that's another. But today was warm — too warm, thirty-four degrees — and in this kind of heat, I can't escape that it's officially 'that time of year' again. Decorations are up, songs are playing, adverts are plastered everywhere declaring joyfully that Christmas is coming! *But, for me, they may as well be sounding doomsday signals.*

When the weather starts to warm up, regular people get excited; they smile more, they go outdoors, they picnic on the beach. They dine al fresco — Mark loved that because it meant he could smoke.

And, when it's too hot, they chatter and browse and brunch in shopping malls, escaping the heat in air-conditioned comfort as they prepare for another family Christmas.

Seeing them reminds me of everything I've lost. As soon as I feel that change in the air, the crispness of spring sinking into the muggy heat of summer, the anxiety creeps in. Because Christmas is when it all happened.

So that's where the benchmark has been set. Today I got out of bed, I took a walk, and now I'm writing in my journal. That's my measure of success. I even left my phone on last night. It's been an anxiety trigger lately, so I've kept it off during the night, holding my breath as I switch it on each morning, but there hasn't been any news. No further updates about him from Aunty Anne, which is good. But I can't help but feel it's the calm before the storm.

I suppose I should write it all out here, although I'm not sure I have the strength or the energy to go over it all again. Thinking about those days – still so recent, but a lifetime ago as well – makes me break out in a cold sweat. Melbourne feels haunted; the streets, the apartment, the bars and cafés – I can't picture any of them without remembering him. That's why, when I left him, I had to leave the city, too.

Mark and I lived in Fitzroy North in a bright, spacious two-bedroom apartment a few blocks from busy Brunswick Street. I can still hear the raucous laughter from the streets below, feel the dizzying warmth of the sun slanting through the bedroom skylight in the morning, stirring me from groggy slumber, the pair of us

32

waking to the inevitable hangover. The smell of Mark beside me in bed: tobacco, aftershave and sweat-slicked skin.

In the beginning, I loved it there; the noise, the excitement, the constant feeling that something was happening and that I had to be a part of it. And yet I was never fully part of anything, as I was tethered to my past, and to Mark.

A country girl at heart, I spent many summers on my parents' prosperous vineyard estate, but, after they disappeared, the city became my adopted home. I had to escape somewhere, and those endless city nights, the frenzied crusade for pleasure, drowned out my dark thoughts. As I got caught up in my new world, the memory of those long, hot days in the vineyards picking grapes, my hair in golden braids, Mum and Dad drinking wine in the tasting parlour, grew fuzzy around the edges.

Mark never could have afforded the place we lived in, but I had my inheritance and my government disability payments, so I paid for both of us. I was only sixteen at the time, so everything had to be in Mark's name. Aunty Anne took some convincing, but, bless her, for all her big talk, she could never quite bring herself to say no to her poor orphaned niece.

Mark was twenty-seven back then and, when we first met, he said I was too young for him. But I figured he didn't really mean it; he thought that's what he was supposed to say, because he was always staring at me. I felt like he was trying to see under my clothes. Sometimes there'd be a glint of something — possessiveness, I suspect now — but it didn't occur to me to be frightened back then.

I met him at my group counselling session — the one I forced myself out of my self-made prison to attend. I was there for trauma-related anxiety and depression, following my parents' disappearance, and he was there for drug addiction. That should have rung alarm bells, but, in a strange way, it's like I was looking for exactly that — something new, something dangerous. Something to make me forget.

We weren't in the same group, but I saw him standing alone under a street light during a break one evening, the tips of his eyelashes illuminated by the fluorescent glow, smoke rising above his head in a dirty-white cloud. It made me think of something from an old movie, something sinister yet romantic.

He greeted me with a nod and offered me a cigarette. We smoked in silence, but I could feel his eyes on me, awareness prickling over my skin. It was a stimulus and I craved distraction — any distraction. This became our routine until one night when he asked me if I wanted to hang out with him and his friends later and I said yes. I didn't even hesitate. There was something in Mark. Something I was drawn to, that spoke to a need.

I found out he was moving to the city and needed a flatmate and, as I was desperate to move out from Aunty Anne's, where I'd been since everything happened, and be somewhere new, I figured it was perfect timing. Doctor Sarah had been telling me to try new things, meet new people — and although I was scared, I wanted to try.

One sticky summer evening, just after my seventeenth birthday, we were lounging on beanbags in the new apartment watching fireworks explode over the city. Mark offered me a puff on the joint he was smoking and I was feeling depressed and bored, so I didn't turn it down. We shared the joint and, as it was my first time, I was completely high after only a few puffs. I remember rolling around giggling, then starting to feel weird and tingly and then freaking out that someone was in the apartment.

Mark took me in his arms and spoke in soft, calm tones. His hands were stroking my hair and his breath was hot against my ear and then his lips were on my skin and soon we were kissing, our mouths fusing, hot and wet, his chest pressed against mine, his arms strong and hard under my hands. My mind kept whirring, wondering why it was happening, if it was because I was high, or was it Mark, and did this mean we'd end up together, or was it just because I was there?

I don't remember wanting to sleep with him, but I must have, because he hated men who tricked girls into sex. It was okay, or so I thought. I remember him on top of me and feeling a sharp pain, over and over. Afterwards, he told me I was the most beautiful girl he'd ever met and that he'd been holding back for ages because he thought I was too young. He'd been waiting for me to turn seventeen, because then, as his birthday wasn't until later in the year, it was like it was only ten years between us, which was nothing, really. I was still trying to understand how things with Mark had gone so far so quickly; I couldn't piece together the details. But I had got myself into it, and when he told me about his past – how his older brother had committed suicide when he was a kid, how at five years old he'd found him hanging in the shed — I was struck with all-consuming pity. I could see a deep sadness in him, something that spoke to my own pain. And he seemed to want to be together so intensely, I felt like I was already in too deep. It just seemed like the right thing to do.

We had fun together, for a while. Mark introduced me to vodka and the odd MDMA cap or line of coke, and it felt good. It was just the distraction I'd been looking for. It made me forget myself. I started not showing up for school and then dropping out completely. All I cared about was escaping — quieting my troubled mind with beautiful numbness.

We hadn't been together long when Mark convinced me I didn't need to keep seeing Doctor Sarah. 'If I'm making you so happy,' he'd say, 'what do you need her for? Aren't I enough?'

After I cancelled my last scheduled appointment, I didn't go back to Doctor Sarah for nearly three years.

Looking back, it's so easy to see what was coming. Mark could be anything he needed to be to control me. Attentive or distant. Complimentary or cruel. Cocky or meek. Playing the victim. It was dizzying, addictive. I convinced myself I didn't want 'safe' or 'predictable' — who'd want that when you could have spontaneous and thrilling?

But it was exhausting, too. He was using me up, my energy, my sanity. Day by day, piece by piece.

Sometimes memories of the three years that followed come to me in sensory waves, transporting me back. One cool autumn evening, Mark and I drunkenly weaving our way home from the club, me swaying in heels, the weight of his arm on my shoulder.

Losing my balance, the sound of glass splintering as I drop a bottle of wine. His breath, sour in my face, his voice snarling 'stupid, clumsy bitch!' Later, the crunch of his fist going through the plasterboard wall, the dull thwack of his knuckles on my temple. The bright white spots dancing, the crimson when I shut my eyes.

After a friend's party, when I'd spoken to a guy too long, light shining in my face – a torch, he's shining a torch on me. I'm naked, I'd been undressing when he stormed in, drunk and high. He's waving the torch in my face, 'You think you're so fucking hot, don't you? You think you're better than me. Look at you, you fucking slut. Who'd want you?' And the mirror gleaming, catching the light as he turns it towards me. I see my pale, stricken face, my exposed body, eyes full of fear. I don't recognise myself.

Another night, on my knees in the hallway. 'Look what you've done,' he says as blood and mucus drip from my chin. I've been throwing up again. It's bad this time. Alcohol poisoning, I think. His face is pinched and white, a mask of fury. 'You're as low as a dog. Only a dog would do something like that.' And he points to the floor, where my blood has stained the cream carpet, as though I've deliberately soiled it.

The times like that, when he didn't actually hit me, were the worst. I can see his eyes; hard, yet lit as if by sparks. My shame fuelling his perverse pleasure. It felt like I was being punished for something, but I never understood what. I must have done something to deserve it. That's how I felt, and that's what I ended up believing.

I was easy to blame, being as troubled and lost as I was.

I figured bad things were meant to happen to me. There was something in me that beckoned them. And he helped me to believe it because, apparently, I was the one who started it. I don't remember anything like that, although there was this one night – I can see myself now, ranting hysterically, hitting at his chest, screaming for him to stop. Stop doing drugs, stop lying, stop stealing from me, stop dealing, just STOP. And I was so, so loud, so out of my mind, that it scares me to remember myself that way.

And then there was That Night. The turning point. But I'm not ready to talk about that yet.

You'd think I'd remember where I got the worst of my injuries – a raised scar on my chest that looks like the work of a small blade – but I don't. What I remember is the humiliation, the shame, the fear and isolation.

There are different forms of abuse, you see. Doctor Sarah says that kind of abuse, the psychological kind, can be more damaging than physical violence. It's harder to see coming, can be so insidious, so incremental, that it's easier to tell yourself you're imagining it than it is to see what's really happening.

I never believed it was abuse until the end. Mark got worse just before I left. I'll never know if it was the real him or just his drug abuse getting out of control, fucking with his mind, turning him from a sad, angry person into a psychotic one. He was so paranoid, thinking everyone – including me – was out to get him.

At two a.m. one night in early September, just over three months ago now, I grabbed the overnight bag I'd stashed in the cupboard while Mark was passed out, hailed a taxi and went to Aunty Anne's. She didn't say a word when I arrived. I stepped into her arms with a strangled sob and she just held me, listened as I told her fragments of the story, brought me endless cups of tea. She made up my old room and I knew without her saying it that I was free to stay as long as I wanted.

I spent a week holed up in that room, staring at the peeling paint on the ceiling. The collection of books, posters and stuffed animals seemed then to belong to a different person, a version of myself I no longer recognised. Like a childhood friend I'd outgrown. The rose-petal wallpaper and smiling stuffed toys that I once found so comforting now seemed to be mocking me, not oblivious but apathetic to the fear I felt in my bones. Everything felt unbalanced, wrong. Yet I was too afraid to leave my room, too afraid of what lay in wait beyond those four walls.

My fears weren't unfounded. Mark came a couple of times, making his threats, even after Uncle John threw him out on his back. I knew I couldn't stay there. Not when he knew where I was.

I managed to muster the energy to change my phone number and only gave it to the people I trusted. It was a shock to realise how shallow that pool of people had become: Aunty Anne, Uncle John and Cat. There was no one else. No friendships to show for the years I'd spent with Mark, no one who cared enough to wonder whether I was okay.

Cat came. Of course she did. Aunty Anne called her, told her just enough, and it wasn't long before I heard a familiar knock on my bedroom door. Rap-rap-rap. Rap!

I remember the shame of having to tell her the dirty, rotten

39

truth. Having to admit she was right. But Cat's calm, no-nonsense care was just what I needed. She didn't dwell, didn't say she'd told me so. She let me speak but didn't let me steep in my misery. This is our chance, she said. This is our chance to do what we've always wanted and get out of this dump. Start again. In Sydney, by the beach, the way we used to dream.

So we did it. Or Cat did it, I should say, and I willingly followed. Barely two weeks later, we were piling ourselves and our luggage into a coach, exuberant and terrified, waving goodbye to Aunty Anne as she stood on the porch, a hanky pressed to her mouth. I don't know what she was feeling, whether she was fighting tears or some other emotion. Aunty Anne's thoughts were rarely unknown, but her feelings were always a mystery.

Doctor Sarah dealt out her rules, of course. As did my aunt. But they both trusted Cat. They knew she knew my story, had my back, and would take care of things. Of me.

And so here we are. Starting over. Away from Mark and everything that happened in Melbourne.

Sometimes, still, the guilt slithers in. The seeds he sowed grow inside me. It's all my fault — I'm useless and selfish. I shouldn't have left him. I think of busy Brunswick Street, of the apartment, of those crazy nights and lazy days, the salty tang of fear. I can almost feel the permanent brick in my gut, the waiting and wondering, the rotting from the inside. What will he do next?

I think of those moments when he trusted me enough to let his mask slip, and I saw what no one had ever seen. Something small, startled. Something decaying slowly, eroding what remained of the good in him. Because there's good in everyone. Isn't there?

I suppose it doesn't matter. Mark, and my life with him, is in the past, and there's no going back. Melbourne is haunted now. Every street, every bar, every café. The ghosts of Mark and me are everywhere.

Chapter Six

'Mary.'

My fingers dig into the pillow and a groan escapes.

'Mary, Mary, quite contrary.'

I open my eyes to a room full of shadows, my heart thundering. There's a low whisper somewhere nearby.

Shhhhhh. Shhhhhh.

Is someone whispering? Is it the waves?

A scream pierces the air, followed by a thud.

I lunge for the lamp switch, and yellow light spills into the room. Jaunty shadows paint the walls, but there's no one here.

'*You dumb, fucking bitch! This is the last time!*'

'*Fuck you, you don't even care! You never did!*'

The voices are coming from outside. It's the couple upstairs, fighting again. They must be on the balcony.

I sigh with relief, but my heart is still racing and my mouth is dry. I swing my legs over the side of the bed and tiptoe out the door. The clock on the microwave reads 03:30 as I creep through the fragrant summer darkness into the kitchen. I could wait until my vision adjusts, but I'm dying for water, so I slide my hand along the hallway wall until my fingertips find the switch. Fluorescent lights blink to life and it's a moment before I can see.

Rachel stands in front of me.

With a shout I stumble backwards, the small of my back slamming into the countertop. '*Ow*. Sorry, I . . . I didn't think anyone . . .' I stop. There's something funny about the way Rachel's standing. And her expression. She's hunched over the counter, both hands flat on its surface, staring into what would have been darkness before I turned on the light. 'Rachel?'

She remains silent, staring ahead. A strange chill creeps through me.

'Rachel? It's just me, Mary.'

She cocks her head, those golden-hazel eyes meeting mine, but they're blank. Unseeing.

I take a step backwards. Then something changes. I can't explain it. It's like there was a film over Rachel's eyes, and now it's peeling back and they're clear again. She's looking, not through me, but at me.

'Hey.' She smiles, blinks. She stares down at her hands, still pressed flat to the counter, and pulls them away as though she's been burned. She puts them behind her back,

44

turns to me, smiles wider. 'Just, uh . . . came to get some water.'

'Right, yeah. Me too.' If I knew her better, I'd make some joke, tell her she was out of it like a zombie. I'd ask her if she was sleepwalking, whether that's something she does sometimes. I'd make sure she's okay. But we only met two days ago, this is her first night here, and ingrained social etiquette overrules. I say nothing.

'Did I disturb you?' Her pretty smile is still in place, but there's something in her expression. Worry? I can't help but notice the network of blood vessels in the whites of her eyes, like fine red cobwebs, and the dark circles beneath.

'No! No, you're fine. I'm just thirsty.' I quickly grab a couple of glasses from the washing-up rack and fill them at the sink. I hand one to Rachel.

It's as if the gesture vanquishes Rachel's strange mood. Her eyes shine as she takes the glass. 'Thanks.'

'Sure.' I shrug, looking away, feeling like I should say something more, but *what*?

Muffled shouts sound from outside and Rachel glances towards the balcony doors. She purses her lips. 'Are they always like that?'

I mirror her expression. 'Often, yes, unfortunately.'

Rachel sighs softly. She turns to me, and the way the light hits her eyes makes them gleam. 'Are you okay? After the other day, I mean. I got the feeling something really bad happened.'

'Oh. No . . . well. It's nothing, honestly.'

There's the sound of a door banging, more muffled shouts. Someone crying, pleading.

'Do you want to talk about it?' Rachel looks so sincere. I'm touched that she would remember.

'No.' I shake my head. 'Sorry, um . . . I'd just rather try to forget about it.'

She tilts her head to one side and smiles. 'I know the feeling.' She pauses, not taking her eyes off me. 'Well, night . . . roomie.' Her smile widens, as though she's pleased with the idea, and she steps close to me, her arm brushing mine. Her hair smells flowery, feminine. She pauses – or do I imagine that? – before stepping past.

'Night,' I mumble, shuffling out of her way.

I ignore the weird feeling, the fact that my heart is racing and my senses have gone on alert. I rest my palm over the light switch, watching as Rachel's slim, white figure crosses the living area and disappears into her room. Then I press the switch, plunging the world back into darkness.

Chapter Seven

26th November 2016

I woke up covered in blood.

That is the one thing I'm sure of, the one memory that has survived. But the events leading up to it are fragmented, uncertain. Sometimes it's hard to tell what's real and what I've imagined since. And that's what frightens me. The not knowing.

I said I'd write about the turning point. I'm ready now. It's been on my mind, little things throughout the day triggering memories, beckoning me to dive into those murky pools to see what lies beneath. When it starts to get dark, when the sound of the waves travels faster in the thin night air, it sounds like they're whispering to me. Telling stories from the past. Like what happened That Night.

Mark and I were at a party several months ago. We'd moved

just south of the city — Mark's decision, of course — to an apartment in Black Rock, two streets from the beach. Some rich friend of his, a skinny, drug-addled insurance manager none too ambiguously nicknamed Dealer Dan, was hosting a party in his penthouse apartment overlooking Brighton Beach. To the untrained eye, Mark looked like he had something to celebrate. But I knew better. From the speed at which his stress levels had peaked, I could guess how bad it was — and the deeper the debt, the bigger the blowout.

Mark was on top form that night, high on coke and a cocktail of whatever else, looking for trouble. I'd taken shelter in the bathroom to clear my head after he disappeared without explanation. A line of coke had sent my head spinning in the worst way; that had never happened before, and at one point I was sure I was going to pass out.

That's when my memory gets sketchy. I remember looking at my face in the mirror, seeing irises nearly engulfed by pupils that seemed to pulse as I stared. My face was out of focus, my skin blotchy, unnaturally pale. Someone knocked on the door and, when I turned my head, I saw stars, and then I threw up in the sink until there was red behind my eyelids.

In search of Mark, I followed some people who were making their way down to the beach. But I don't remember how I got there — there's another of those blank spaces. Next thing I knew, I was by the shore. There were houses nearby, and I could hear people in the distance. I think they must have been running into the water; I remember silhouettes against a street light, squeals and laughter, and the rumble of the ocean.

I don't know what happened after that; I must have passed out. Sometimes there are snippets, like the sound of someone yelling, or maybe screaming, a face peering down at me, the ocean whispering its secrets. But mostly, it's blank.

When I came to, Mark was standing over me shouting, hands gesturing wildly, his eyes crazed and gleaming. He was staring at me, at something near my stomach, but I didn't know why, and a coil of panic tightened in my gut. When I looked down, all I could see was blood.

It was a while before my senses returned to me. The white noise in my head cleared and I could hear Mark ranting about something, some eight ball I'd supposedly been carrying for him. I had no idea what he was talking about, but he found the drugs in my purse, wrapped me up in his coat and dragged me to the car. As far as we know, no one saw us.

Later, I stood naked in our laundry, my arms crossed over my chest, shivering with disgust and fear as I watched Mark pile our clothes into the washing machine. As he switched it on and it slowly filled up with water, I knew in my bones that the blood turning the soap suds pink wasn't mine.

Whose it was, and how it got there, I'll never know.

Once I'd washed myself clean, I lay in our bed, awaiting the inevitable. But it never came. Mark paced the hall – I could see his shadow, hear his drunken muttering above the roar and hiss of the sea. But then he went silent and, not long after, I could hear rattling snores in the living room. He didn't come to bed, which was strange. I knew my bag was packed and waiting for me if I needed it. But I started having second thoughts.

49

The next day we heard the news that a guy had been found dead at Dealer Dan's party. An unemployed twenty-eight-year-old man named Tom Forrester, known to police for drug dealing and petty theft. It was shocking to find out someone had died at a party we attended, possibly while we were there, but I didn't know the guy so I wasn't too cut up about it.

It wasn't until Mark started acting strangely that I began to worry. We'd talked about it once we had sobered up, and Mark had convinced me we had nothing to do with whatever had gone on. The guy was found bludgeoned to death. They think it was a brick, even though they never found the murder weapon. Pretty gruesome. If he was a drug dealer, the most likely scenario was that his death was related to money or drugs. Which was what they ended up suspecting anyway, even though the murderer was never caught. The fact I couldn't ignore then, and that haunts me now when I trawl through those old newspaper articles, is that Mark had recently lost a lot of money and − I suspected − was dealing drugs again.

Everyone who was at the party was questioned. We waited for days, for weeks, for the cops to arrive, but they never did. We couldn't guess why, but we considered ourselves lucky.

The blood. Neither of us could account for it. I racked my brain trying to remember details. If I'd seen anything that night, it could have helped with the investigation. I knew I'd headed towards the beach and passed out. I know I woke up with a bump on the back of my head and some bruises on my arms, but nothing more serious than my usual drunken mishaps.

Though Mark had been missing and I couldn't vouch for where he'd been, he told me he was down the road scoring from a mate and, as that was usually the case when he was MIA, I hoped it was the truth.

Mark's story was that he'd come looking for me after meeting his mate, and that he'd asked around but no one knew where I was. Apparently he saw some guy passed out but thought nothing of it because 'it was a drug party, for fuck's sake'. So he went looking down by the beach and found me semi-conscious in a nearby side street. Covered in someone else's blood. Why was I there? What had happened to me?

He convinced me we had nothing to do with the guy's death, that it probably wasn't even the guy he saw. He said I should keep my mouth shut about the blood. It was probably mine, he said, even though there wasn't more than a scratch on my body. It was on him too, I remember that much, but he claimed it came from me, when he'd carried me to the car. He said that maybe I'd thrown it up or something. It would be stupid to say anything about it, he told me.

I knew he wasn't saying these things to protect me, like he claimed. He had enough of a record to get in some serious trouble if it was dredged up, so he was protecting himself from further involvement with the police.

I tried not to think about what it meant that Mark would just leave someone in a state like that. The guy was unconscious. Maybe Mark didn't see the blood – or maybe it wasn't even Tom Forrester he saw, who knows. But he walked away. He didn't *even try to help. I wanted to scream at him, to get him to look at himself, look at what kind of person he'd become. But, by that stage, I'd learned a few things. And I knew what would happen if I questioned him.*

Chapter Eight

The sand is gritty and damp between my toes as I pace the beach. It's late afternoon but the sun is still high and people are swimming, fishing, huddled in groups under beach umbrellas. I've always felt a tidal pull towards the sea. A water baby, Mum used to call me. I feel it now, the pull, as though the ocean is calling to my blood.

I spent many summers on the coast with my parents before they disappeared. It's hard to believe that was five years ago. Something inside me has always known they're not coming back. Not now, after all this time. And yet I watch the families at play, and hope lingers. *Hope dies last*, Doctor Sarah says. But that's not why I'm here, it's really not. I'm here because I have to be. Doctor Sarah says so.

The ocean is a different colour each day. Today it's grey-brown, the colour of a puddle after rain. The storms have stirred things up, clouding the water with seaweed and sand. The humid air is ripe with something, perhaps anticipation, another storm on its way, and I'm edgy, unable to shake the feeling I'm being watched.

I push on, forcing one foot to follow the other, ignoring the prickles on the back of my neck. If I don't do this, I've already failed, and I can't afford that. Doctor Sarah says it's a measure of my control over my anxiety. If I can manage a walk each day, I'm doing okay. I can feel proud of something. An achievement. Because there's not much else I'm proud of at the moment.

Children are shrieking and splashing, their browned, skinny bodies darting in and out of waves. A man stands nearby, motionless, facing the sea. Their father, I suppose.

There's movement in the fir trees lining the surrounding parkland, but when I look, it's only the branches quivering in the breeze. I close my hand around the device in my pocket. It's become a comfort thing, clutching it tight, running my fingers over the small, round buttons. It's a personal alarm, one that cost a small fortune, but it's worth it. I've had it since Aunty Anne started worrying every time I left her sight. Bringing it with me is another of her 'conditions' for me moving out. One press of a button and the nearest law enforcement is notified of my location. Someone will come straight away. You can't put a price on peace of mind, Aunty Anne said. I'm with her on that.

Walking clears my head and most days, after the initial fear, I enjoy it. But today something's off. I check my phone: no messages. I watch people going about their business: surfers bobbing on the waves, teenagers in school uniform eating burgers and fish and chips outside the kiosk, people strolling after a day's work, families squabbling and playing. How do they do it? How do they carry on each day, taking care of business, of their families, of themselves? I used to be able to do the same. I went to school, worked weekends at the local café. I had a family . . .

I plug my mouth with a finger and bite down until I feel the familiar pain. Step after step, breath after breath, I come to the curve in the bay where the water is shallow. This is the spot. A few more metres and I can turn back, my day's quota done.

A heavenly beam of light has burst through the low clouds, illuminating each wave and ripple on the water's surface. There's a houseboat floating a few metres from the shore, a dilapidated-looking thing, mostly wood with peeling white paint, a blue stripe around its perimeter, little round windows in the cabin below its bow. I must have seen it before; those little windows seem familiar. I imagine peering out of them, watching the waves roll past. What would it be like to live on the sea, sailing away whenever you please?

My throat feels dry and I recall the bottle of wine I sneaked into my room last night. It's about time to replenish, so I opt out of walking the last few metres and head back to the apartment.

In the kitchen, Cat's washing up and sipping from a glass of wine. Perfect. I'd forgotten it's Friday – there'll be no hiding tonight.

She smiles at me over her shoulder. 'Hey, you! Nice walk today?'

'Yeah, it was fine.'

Cat nods at her wine glass. 'The rest of the bottle's chilling in the freezer. Mine's warm, I'm afraid. I couldn't wait.' She grimaces as she sips.

'Bad day?' I open the freezer and help myself to the wine.

'You have no idea. Gia's been bawling to me again and I'm like, I already told you! Ben's just not . . .'

'Ben's just not what?' a voice says from behind us.

Cat winces but then breaks into a giggle as Ben stands in the hallway, scratching the hairy, tanned flesh exposed between his shorts and T-shirt.

'Have you been napping this whole time?' she asks.

'Yeah. Have you been talking about me this whole time? What am I "*not*"?'

Cat exhales through her nose. 'Gia thinks you two are dating and I keep telling her you're *not* interested.'

'Who says I'm not?'

'Um, *you* do. You say it all the time!'

'I'm interested in certain *parts* of her . . .'

'Ugh. Ben, you just . . .'

'I was talking about her brain!' Ben laughs. 'I'm just not . . . you know. Into her like *that*.' He turns to me and grins.

'Then you need to fucking tell her, you idiot,' Cat snaps. 'I'm sick of her just showing up here.'

Watching them, I feel suddenly tired. I pick up my glass and go to the couch, start scrolling through my emails. There's a Facebook notification from a name I don't recognise. *Jake Morns.*

Without thinking, I click on it.

I will find you.

My blood turns to ice. The wine glass trembles in my hand as the familiar panic rises. I set the glass down on the coffee table and bite down hard on my lower lip. What was I thinking? I should have known better than to believe blocking Mark's email would work. This is him, it has to be. There's no picture, of course, just the little blue thumbnail with a blank face. Jake Morns. Yup. I rearrange the letters . . . *Mark Jones.*

Saliva sticks in my throat. I close my eyes, and Mark's face appears. And then another image comes, as clear as day.

Mark's mouth, a gaping black hole, open in a scream. Eyes like brimstone under the street lamp, a voice yelling 'Run!' and a name, but I don't catch it. The waves are growling in the background, it's hard to hear. I'm on the ground near a low wall, shivering though it's not cold. Mark's crouched on the ground. He's holding something, something with sharp edges. Something wet and gleaming.

A bloodied brick.

'Mary, Mary, quite contrary. What are we going to do with you?'

The room reappears around me, white curtains, early evening light. Birds are twittering.

'Mary?' Cat's standing by the counter, pale-faced, her brow knitted.

Ben's staring.

My stomach turns over and I stand and run, just making it to the bathroom in time.

Afterwards, I stare into the vomit-specked basin, feeling numb.

'Mary?' Cat's voice calls from behind the door.

I don't answer and she lets herself in.

'Hey, what's wrong?'

'It's Mark,' I say, my voice devoid of emotion.

'What's Mark? What's he done?'

I wipe my mouth on the back of my hand and notice it's trembling.

Mind reeling, I turn to look at Cat. 'He killed someone.'

Chapter Nine

27th November 2016

My mind slips back to that rainy night in late August. This time, there was no doubt that the blood was mine. I watched as the dark red droplets turned into pale streaks and washed away, and once I'd finished purging the contents of my stomach, I stood alone in the shower. The temperature was turned way up, stinging the fresh cut on my head, yet the shivering wouldn't stop. I felt like I was standing at a crossroads, my fate dependent on the path I chose. Danger lay behind and ahead, and though it didn't have a definite form, though I couldn't quite identify it, I knew that somehow I'd choose the right path this time. I had to. My life depended on it.

I coaxed the chunks of vomit down the plughole with my foot and jammed my hand over the body-wash dispenser repeatedly. Amber liquid oozed onto the white tiles and turned to foam beneath the spray, filling the shower with the scent of artificial peach. I aimed the shower head at the foam until the last of the mess bubbled its way down the drain.

When the tiles were clean, I sank to my knees, letting the hot water pound against my back. I splayed my hands on the tiles, noting my grazed knuckles and tattered fingernails. The back of my head hurt. My back hurt. Everything hurt.

Through the drone and whine of the running shower, I could hear rhythmic thudding in the next room. A single crash, then a loud monosyllabic exclamation; I couldn't make out the word.

He appeared through the fogged-up glass like a ghost. He looked different to me somehow, like the structure of him had changed, morphed. Maybe it was the residual chemicals in my system. Or maybe it was because something had changed.

'What are we going to do with you, Mary?' His voice was muffled, but I could hear the familiar sing-song tone in his voice. They were words that would haunt my dreams for months to follow.

After what he'd just done to me, I couldn't bear to speak to him. I was cold under the hot spray, so cold. He stripped off his boxers and opened the shower screen, stepping inside. My body reacted, trembling furiously. And I knew. I knew a line had been crossed this time, that he'd done something that couldn't be undone. Deep and cold in my bones, I knew that if I survived the night that I had to get out. There might not be another chance. If I didn't go soon, I wasn't going to get out of there alive.

I broke, then. I sobbed and sobbed, not from fear, astonishingly, *and not with self-pity. I sobbed for us. For him. And he didn't know what was coming, that we were breaking apart, that we'd already broken. That the end was near and it didn't matter how bad he was, my skin would miss him, my brain and body would crave their fix and my heart would break a thousand times before it would heal. I cried for him, because I knew it would break him too. Because even monsters bleed.*

He didn't know why I cried or why he held me, but still he did it and it made it worse, this small act of kindness, if kindness is what it was. If such a person knows what kindness is. He held me, wet and naked and shivering, and rubbed his hand down my back, pushed my wet hair out of my face and kissed my forehead with finality — or was I imagining that? — and I didn't know what he was thinking. I was too afraid to ask.

So I let him hold me and I cried and cried until my throat was raw, my voice hoarse. Because it didn't matter what he'd done. I had loved him. I had given myself to him and he had squandered that gift, cheapened it, and what was all of it for? Our love, if that's what it was, reduced to nothing. A drop in the ocean. A blip on the radar. A moment in time spent and lost and forgotten. Meaningless. Over.

And it was like I'd known it was coming. Was waiting for the moment when I'd know, for sure. This cold resolve, like steel in its certainty, took over. And the shivering stopped. The crying stopped. And we stood, not speaking, for what felt like eternity, with the white noise of water falling, and I don't know if it was the shower or the rain outside the window, the roar of the ocean in the distance.

We were still for so long, I wondered if we were dead. But he sensed the change in me, felt the shift in my body. And then his hands slid up my back, cupped the base of my skull. Gently, so gently, until his fingers tightened and needles of pain shot down my spine. His thumbs lifted my chin and he whispered, his breath hot in my ear.

'If you leave, I'll kill you.'

Chapter Ten

My head's pounding in time with my pulse as I stare at the peeling paint on the stark, white walls of the waiting room.

'Are you sure you want to do this?' Cat's words, spoken as I left the apartment this morning, reverberate in my mind. She thinks I should be talking to the psychiatrist Doctor Sarah referred me to. She thinks they'll be able to help with my memories, *'if they're real'*. She doesn't believe me, I can tell. And now the doubts have crept in, stealing through the hangover haze, dulling the burn of determination.

My stomach feels like a washing machine. I should have eaten something, but I lacked the appetite. Of course I don't want to do this. No one wants to have to do something like this. But what choice do I have? Knowing what he's done, that he's after me . . .

'Miss Baker?'

I stand abruptly, like an officer called to attention. A twenty-something, slim female cop with fluffy, ash-blonde hair tucked under her cap beckons me from the doorway.

'I'm Officer Dean. Come on through.' She smiles at me, perhaps noticing my unease, and I jerk my lips upwards in a poor imitation.

The hallway is narrow and hot; I wipe the beads of sweat that materialise on my forehead with the back of my sleeve. At the end of the hall, Officer Dean opens a door and, inside, a black-haired man, mid to late thirties, sits behind a desk, a coffee cup pressed to his lips. He sets the cup down and nods in my direction.

'Miss Baker. I'm Sergeant Moore. We spoke on the phone this morning.'

'Yes, of course. Hello.'

He gestures to a seat and I sit as the female officer nods at both of us and leaves the room.

'So, Miss Baker.' The sergeant smiles, a vague, reflexive gesture. He has a chin dimple and a mole on his left cheek the size of a five-cent piece. 'How can I help?'

My mind goes blank. I look from my lap to the sergeant's face and back again, trying to think, trying to rein in the anxiety.

'Take your time,' Sergeant Moore says. 'I have all day.' I can't tell if he's being sarcastic. His expression doesn't change.

My ears burn. I notice his gaze lowering and I wonder

if I've overdressed. I felt a mess this morning, so I put more effort than usual into my make-up and clothing.

Moore taps his fingers on the notepad that lies open on the desk in front of him. 'You wanted to talk to me about the Tom Forrester case, is that correct?'

I sit up straight, try to look him in the eye. 'That's right.'

'What was it you wanted to tell me?'

I swallow thickly. Can I be sure of what I witnessed? Closing my eyes, I see Mark's cold stare, fingers curled around the bloodied brick.

If you leave, I'll kill you.

I glance at the notepad on the sergeant's desk, but he's moved his hand away. I take a breath. 'I want to tell you that I witnessed . . . I . . . I saw my boyfriend kill him. He killed Tom Forrester.'

Sergeant Moore regards me for several silent seconds. 'You saw your . . . *boyfriend* . . . kill Tom Forrester.'

'Ex,' I blurt. 'Ex-boyfriend.'

'Okay. Can you specify exactly what you saw?'

'I didn't . . . I didn't see him *do it*, exactly,' I correct myself, wanting to make sure I tell the whole truth. 'We were at a party . . . He . . . my ex. His name's Mark. Mark went missing for a few hours and I went to look for him. I think I passed out for a while . . . I'm not sure what happened. But when I woke up, or maybe it was before that . . .' My heart pounds in my ears. I'm jumbling it all up, not saying it right.

'Go on.'

'I saw him with the weapon. There was blood . . . There was a brick. A brick with blood.'

Sergeant Moore's lips thin. His eyes remain unreadable. 'So . . . he was holding a brick.'

I grimace. That sounds pathetic, like nothing. But he doesn't know Mark like I know him. He doesn't know the rest.

'Yes. A brick with blood on it. It was the night Tom was murdered . . . We were near where he was found.' I'm not a hundred per cent sure that part's true, but it can't have been far – the body was found somewhere near the beach and I distinctly remember the sound of waves nearby.

'That's all you saw?'

I nod.

'Do you know the whereabouts of this . . . weapon?'

'No. He must have got rid of it. Maybe he threw it in the ocean or something.'

Moore doesn't say anything.

'Look, I know it doesn't sound like much, but if you knew Mark . . . He's dangerous. And it makes sense, it all makes sense. I saw Mark with a brick, the guy – Tom. He was killed with a brick.'

'Yes, I'm familiar with the case.' Again, I can't read the sergeant's tone.

'Look, Mark knows I saw what he did. That's why he's threatening me.'

'He's threatened you?' That seemed to get his attention.

'Yes, I . . . here.' I show Moore the Facebook message.

Moore inspects my phone with a furrowed brow. 'This isn't a direct threat. Unless someone makes a threat of harm against themselves or someone else, we are unable to act.'

'Yes, but he *has*! He's threatened to kill me.'

Moore raises his eyebrows. 'When was this?'

'I . . .' I think back. 'I don't know. Three months ago?'

'And you reported this?'

'I . . . well, no.'

Moore shakes his head. 'Miss Baker . . .'

I blow out a frustrated sigh. 'Look . . . that doesn't matter. I know he did it! It adds up. Tom was a drug dealer . . . my . . . Mark was into drugs. He was dealing at the time, I'm sure of it!'

'Hmm.' Something in Sergeant Moore's face has closed off. He looks almost bored, or annoyed, and this fills me with fear. Why isn't he more concerned?

'Had you been drinking at the time, Miss Baker?'

My cheeks burn. 'I . . . I'd had some wine, yes.'

'And was that all?'

'No.' My voice comes out small. 'I'd had a bit of . . . cocaine.'

'I see. What did you say your first name was again . . .?'

'Mary. Mary Baker.'

'And your boyfriend's name?'

'*Ex*-boyfriend. Mark Jones.'

Sergeant Moore turns to his computer and starts tapping at the keys. His eyes scan the screen and he pauses, frowns. Starts clicking his tongue.

'The thing is, Miss Baker, this case has already been investigated by the Victoria police. Although no one's been charged, it's suspected to be gang-related. Those gangs are hard to infiltrate, but they've got their best people on the job. Your *ex*-boyfriend isn't in a gang, is he?'

'I honestly don't know,' I sigh and reluctantly add, 'but I don't think so.'

'See, the thing puzzling me most,' Sergeant Moore says, rubbing the dimple in his chin, 'is that everyone who was at the party the night Tom Forrester was murdered was interviewed by police. It's all here.' He taps the computer screen, though it's faced away from me. 'And there's no record of any statements from either you or a Mark Jones.'

'Yes. Yes, I know . . . because the police never showed up. We thought it was weird, too.'

Moore purses his lips. All friendliness has vanished from his expression. 'I'll cut to the chase, Miss Baker, so we don't waste any more of each other's time. Maybe you weren't interviewed by the police because you weren't actually at that party. Were you?'

My jaw drops. 'What?'

'It was a private party. There was a guest list. Everyone's name was checked off that list, and neither yours nor your boyfriend's name was on it. As far as the records are concerned, you were never there.'

I shake my head, at a loss. 'I don't . . . I can't explain that. I was at the party. I remember . . .'

But Moore has stopped listening.

'One more thing before you go,' he says, sounding bored. 'I believe you're in possession of a personal alarm linked to the police triple zero emergency line and GPS system? I'd appreciate it if you refrained from using it except in real emergencies. After the next false alarm, our officers might not show up. And the device will be confiscated. Wasting police time is an offence. Do you understand?'

I feel the blood drain from my face.

'Miss Baker?'

I don't trust myself to speak. I don't understand what's going on. I haven't used my alarm — not even once.

'Look. I understand you're afraid,' Moore says, his voice softer than before. 'But these things need to be addressed in the right manner. We're not here to solve petty disputes. If your ex-boyfriend threatens you, feel free to contact me. Otherwise, I'll ask you to refrain from wasting our time.' He picks up a business card and holds it out to me.

I clench my fists to stop myself from snatching the card and storming out.

Sergeant Moore turns to his computer, his focus already elsewhere. 'Officer Dean will show you out.'

I take the card and walk rigidly to the door, down the stuffy hallway and out into the blinding daylight.

Chapter Eleven

28th November 2016

I can't have come this far only to let the bastard win.

But it's impossible to think now. Impossible to do anything when my head's all over the place. I'm running low on meds and have had to ration them. I need my head clear so I can figure out what I need to do, how to make them listen, and that means sticking to the correct dosage. I know I need to book the appointment I keep putting off. I know Cat won't let it go until I do. But therein lies the dilemma; with the way I'm feeling, seeing someone new — someone that's not Doctor Sarah — is unfathomable. But if I don't, I'm going to run out of meds. Soon. And then I'll feel much, much worse.

Even now, despite everything that's going on — or is it because of it? — I'm afraid. I suppose it's natural not to want to have someone peel back your skin and poke around inside with that detached clinical manner some psychs can have. But I can't help thinking there's more to it than that. Can't help thinking, as I sometimes do, that something's missing. That there was something left unfinished with Doctor Sarah, and it's putting me off.

I owe Doctor Sarah my life. Just before I moved to Sydney, when we had our last session, I told her exactly that. She wouldn't accept that, of course. She said I was responsible for my own actions, that it was I who had the courage to leave. But I didn't feel brave. It felt like I'd dodged a bullet, that it came down to luck, more so than any deliberate action on my part.

It took a lot to get me to her office that day. I was ashamed. Because she'd seen the signs, had tried to warn me, and I'd run into the arms of danger anyway. It makes me determined to show her I can do this, that I won't repeat the mistakes of the past. I won't let Mark win this time.

Determination doesn't stop the fear. It doesn't make it easy. But that's what they say, isn't it? Courage is being afraid to do something and doing it anyway.

We hugged at the end of our last session, even though I know she's not really supposed to do that with clients. That's how close we'd become. I know she was proud of my progress, and so was I. She told me that she'd just given me the tools, but I'd saved myself. I know she's right, but it only feels like part of the story.

Ever since, I've had her in my mind. Her voice whispers in my ear when I doubt myself, and I know, I KNOW, what's true and what's right. I know to trust my instincts. I know what Mark has done, even if I can't remember.

There's so much crammed into my brain it hurts. I know what needs to be done and I know the steps to take, but it's like my thoughts are scraps of tissue paper caught in an updraught. Every time I reach out to grasp one, they swirl out of my reach.

I think of Doctor Sarah's last words to me as I left her office, her glasses perched on the end of her aquiline nose, her smooth auburn hair brushing the shoulders of her suit jacket as her eyes held mine.

'Take care of yourself, Mary.'

She didn't say it like a friend would, a throwaway line when saying goodbye, 'take care of yourself!' And of course she'd have meant it quite literally. I was her patient, and my mental health was her concern. But there was something in her tone that alerted my senses. Something that had me replaying the words in my head for weeks afterwards.

I know she feared for my safety. That's why there were so many conditions for me moving up here: the alarm, Cat's protection, seeing the new shrink. Maybe, as an expert, she had a better idea of what Mark was really capable of. Maybe she suspected what he'd done – or at least what he was capable of doing – before I realised it myself. But surely she would have said something if she thought I was in mortal danger . . . wouldn't she?

Doctor Sarah didn't show any emotion in our sessions. She was a true professional and, even though I sensed that she felt for me, 'getting emotionally involved' would have been unprofessional. And, for the most part, she played her role to perfection. I never saw the mask slip. But that last time, I felt like she was transmitting a message, something her eyes were saying that her mouth wouldn't – or couldn't.

And a part of me can't help but wonder. What was Doctor Sarah holding back?

Chapter Twelve

After my visit to the station, I'm down two glasses of wine, drumming my fingers on the kitchen counter while Cat massages my neck. She's making soothing noises, but I'm sure she's thinking *I told you so*. I don't feel soothed. I'm worked up, irrationally angry at Sergeant Moore. The arrogant dick.

I'm angry at myself. I should have planned what I was going to say, should have mentioned Mark's previous offences – the guy has a record! – and what he did to me, what he's probably done to others. I should have shown them photos – I'm sure I took some at the party. I could prove it, prove I was there and that I'm not some crazy ex-girlfriend out for revenge. The anger feels good for the moment; it's better than feeling hopeless and scared.

It's almost eight thirty when the key turns in the front

door and Gia breezes in, bottle of wine in hand. Ben chokes on his beer.

'Well hello to you, too, *bello*,' she says, planting a noisy kiss on his cheek.

Cat turns to me with wide eyes. She bites back a grin.

'Since when do you have keys?' Ben mutters.

'Oh, I ran into Rachel downstairs and she lent me her set. She said she'd bring back some stuff to make mojitos!' Gia laughs, corkscrew curls bobbing.

Cat and I glance at Ben, who shrugs, rolls his eyes and takes a swig of beer.

This is why you can't get rid of her, I think. *You need to grow a pair.*

We wait a while, but Rachel doesn't appear, so we open a bottle of wine.

'Cheers to us!' Gia says, and we clink our glasses.

Tonight's sunset paints the sky with brushstrokes of peach and lilac and the four of us are drawn to the balcony, where we lounge on deckchairs and beanbags. Cat puts on some chill-out music and we chat idly as an hour slips by, along with two bottles of wine.

'So what do you think of the new girl?' Gia's curly head is lolling over the back of the deckchair she's lounged on.

No one speaks for a moment. I clear my throat. 'She's sweet.'

'Ben thinks she's crazy,' Gia giggles.

Ben clears his throat. 'I didn't say that, exactly.'

Cat glances at me, then back at the view.

'Oh, not really of course.' Gia collects herself on her elbows, reaching down to claim her wine glass and throwing back the last mouthful. 'But he's dated crazy before. I think he thinks he's an expert.'

'Ben thinks he's an expert on a lot of things.' Cat rolls her eyes. 'But you don't have the best track record, do ya buddy?'

The two girls dissolve into wine-induced giggles as Ben sulks on his beanbag.

'But seriously,' Gia says in a stage whisper, sculpted eyebrows raised. 'Have you guys noticed that Rachel's *really* thin? And she wears that big, baggy hoodie all the time, which I find weird because girls like that usually like to show off their bodies, you know?' Gia illustrates her point with a shake of her shoulders, which makes her breasts jiggle.

Cat nods as she stares into her wine glass and my hand tightens around mine.

Okay, Rachel wears baggy clothes, I've noticed that too. But it feels too early to be making any kind of judgement. I don't want things to get awkward in the apartment if we start gossiping.

'Maybe she's just got body issues,' Cat says.

'Maybe she's hiding a deformity or something!' Gia exclaims, like she's taking pleasure in the idea.

Ben's pointedly ignoring the conversation.

'Don't say that,' I snap, and Gia's eyes widen. She turns to Cat, but Cat looks away. Just at that moment, I see movement in my peripheral vision and turn to find Rachel standing in the doorway, holding a bottle of rum and a bag full of limes. Her eyes are dark, like the light behind them has been switched off. Without a word, she turns and goes back inside.

Darting a look at the others, who are eyeing each other guiltily, I stand and head inside. The rum is on the living room floor and limes have spilled from the bag and are spiralling over the carpet. I step around them and approach Rachel's bedroom door, which is shut. My fingers touch the handle and that's when I hear it.

Sobbing, raw and guttural, echoes from behind the door. I freeze. Rachel is crying, *really* crying.

Wincing against a stab of guilt, I push open the door a crack and whisper, 'Rach? You okay?'

The sobbing grows louder.

'Rachel, I'm so sorry. Can I come in?' I push the door further open; Rachel is on her knees on the floor at the foot of the bed in near-darkness. Her face is in her hands, her back to me. The only light is a streak of sunset-orange that crosses the length of the room and casts a stripe across Rachel's back. I step forward, crouch behind her and talk over her sobs. 'Please, Rach. We're sorry. I need to know if you're all right.'

Rachel's head snaps around and her eyes, gleaming with tears in the orange light, are like fire.

I stumble back on the balls of my feet and land on my bum.

'I'm not all right,' she hisses, eyes narrowed, body twisted at an angle to face me. 'You want to know why, huh? You want to know why I wear baggy clothes and hide my body? *This* is why!'

She yanks up her jumper and pulls it over her head. The tank top beneath it is ripped off too until she's sitting before me in her bra and leggings.

My eyes travel over her and a gasp constricts my throat. I can't see much in the fading light, but I can see enough.

Dark bruises stain most of Rachel's torso, from the under-wire of her bra, across her stomach and down to the tops of her hips. Some have turned purple and some are tinged with green and yellow around the edges. It looks like she's been beaten with a two-by-four. Or a lead pipe.

I can't help the soft moan that escapes, or the tears that spring to my eyes. And then something unexpected; a hot, pulsing thing in my chest. Anger.

'Fuck. Who did this to you?'

'Does it matter?' Rachel laughs bitterly, still shuddering with the aftershocks of her tears.

'It matters to me,' I say, hesitating before placing a hand on her shoulder, the one place that isn't bruised. 'I mean, I . . . maybe I can help.'

'It's fine now,' Rachel flinches away from me, but when she looks at me there's almost an apology in her eyes. 'It's just my ex. I've left now. The bruises will heal.'

As I watch her, a strange feeling creeps over me. It's like I'm seeing myself from the outside. 'But the emotional ones take longer,' I say softly.

Rachel nods, her head down, her hair hanging limp around her tiny face, and I'm overcome with such empathy that I want to wrap my arms around her, cradle her against me and tell her it's all going to be okay. But I don't know her very well and I'm afraid to touch her bruises, so I hold back.

'Look,' I whisper. 'I . . . have some idea . . . what you're going through. So, um . . . I'm here if you need me.' It's all I can think of to say. It feels so inadequate.

'Thanks.' Rachel sniffs and looks up at me with those killer eyes, made luminous with tears and amber light. 'Please don't tell the others.'

I pull a strand of hair into my mouth. I've never kept anything from Cat before. But I also know what it's like to have a secret like this, and I know I have to make Rachel feel safe. If that means making her this promise, I'll do it.

'Mary, please.' Rachel's small, cold hand slips into mine. 'Gia's not the nicest person if she's about to just judge me like that. And I know you're friends with Cat and everything, but I just don't feel . . . I don't trust her. The way she looks at me sometimes . . . and the way she looks at you. It's like you're her *property*. I think you should be careful. I've met people like her before.'

My mouth opens and closes and I have to look away. Cat's my best friend; I trust her implicitly. I'm not sure how Rachel got the wrong idea, but I'm sensing now's not the time to discuss it.

'Girls like us have to stick together,' she says softly. 'Not everyone gets it. Not everyone *knows*. Men are scum, they're motherfucking *scum*, and . . .' Rachel stops, seems to battle with something internally. She buries her face in her hands. 'I'm sorry, Mary. I'm sorry, I'm so sorry.'

She's crying again, and I ignore my misgivings and pull her gently by the shoulders and into my arms. She smells sweet, her face is pressed to my neck and I can feel her tears on my skin, her body shuddering with broken, silent sobs.

'I promise I won't tell anyone,' I say, stroking her hair. 'This is just between us.'

'I knew I could trust you.' Rachel raises her head, gives a quivery smile. Something flickers in my chest. 'I can, can't I?'

'Of course,' I say with a conviction I vow to myself to keep.

Chapter Thirteen

29th November 2016

Anger is good. It's the heat spreading from my chest, prickling up my spine, giving me strength. I won't let fear win, and I won't let him win. Seeing what happened to Rachel has fuelled the fire . . . If I don't stop him, there will be more of us. More Rachels, more Marys. And I'm sure as hell not going to end up another fucking statistic.

Just now I was about to call the Victoria police, ask to be connected to someone involved in the Forrester case, but I stopped myself. There's no point talking to them without any proof. They'll just dismiss me like Sergeant Moore did. They're not going to reopen a case because some girl calls and says she might have seen her ex-boyfriend holding a brick in the dark.

And according to their records, Mark and I were never even there. As far as they know, I could be some crazy girl with a grudge, desperate for attention. Or revenge.

I could lie. I could say I saw Mark do it, and then they'd have to investigate him. Wouldn't they?

Maybe that's too risky. I need evidence. I need to be prepared this time. There has to be something that can prove what happened. Something the police missed that only someone who was there — who saw — would know.

If only I knew what happened during that blackout. If only I could remember.

I've been poring over my memory files, but it's the same old data. Darkness. Mark leering over me, shouting. Mark holding the brick. Waking up covered in blood. Blackness, stretching for hours. I don't know the order of events, but I've done my best to make a list of the facts. When I speak to the police again — and I will — I'll be ready.

Things I know about the night of the murder:

1. Mark was missing for a few hours. It would have been some time between midnight and 3.30 a.m., as Mark and I returned home at 4 a.m. and I went looking for him at around 1.30 a.m. after he'd already been missing for over an hour.

2. According to the papers, Tom Forrester was bludgeoned to death with a brick at around 2 a.m. He was found the next morning by a jogger at 6.20 a.m.

3. *I saw Mark holding a bloodied brick. Unsure of exact time, but must have been around 3–3.30 a.m.?*

    ★Can't prove this and the weapon was never found – no DNA evidence.

    ★Also, I didn't actually see Mark do it. Or I did (would explain the blood) and can't remember?

4. *The victim was a drug user/dealer.*

5. *Mark was a drug user/dealer, suspect he was dealing at the time. Mark told me he was scoring drugs and was missing within the time Forrester was killed.*

    ★Evidence of this?

6. *I woke up with blood on my torso. Mark was shouting at me, but can't remember what he said. Sometimes I think I can remember someone else's voice shouting too, but it's unclear, and that might have happened earlier. Mark had blood on his clothes.*

    ★We did not have any major injuries, no more than bumps and scratches. Therefore, the blood was someone else's.

7. *There is a gap in my memory, the time lost between leaving the party and waking up to Mark shouting. No accounting for what happened between the hours of 1.30 and 3.30 a.m. Pretty sure I was passed out for some of it.*

8. *Somehow I ended up with bruises and a sore bump on the back of my head, suggesting I did pass out.*

9. *Mark has a history of violence and drug addiction. He physically and psychologically abused me. He is capable of anything.*

*Never reported him

*He has other convictions – could be used against him?

10. *Mark behaved strangely, out of character, after the night of the murder.*

*Just my opinion, no proof.

It's a lot easier seeing it written down. It's also painfully clear how little I have to go on. Mark kept me separate from his friends, so I don't have any contact details, but I'm friends with some of them on Facebook. I could get in touch and try to find out if he was affiliated with the victim in terms of drug dealing or whatever. Although that's risky, because they might tell Mark I'm trying to get evidence on him. I don't want to give him a heads-up.

Doctor Sarah. Maybe talking to her could help. She knows what Mark's capable of, knows the history. But I haven't told her about the blood. She'll wonder why I didn't mention it before. Another mistake.

Now I know what Mark did, I suspect the blood on me came from him. It's a relief to have that explained. But if it did in fact come from him, that means I must have been nearby when it happened – that he held or touched me and the blood transferred to me. Which means it's possible I saw more than I'm remembering.

Of course, the blood also implicates me. And yet I wish I'd held on to those clothes, because that's evidence – the police would have to listen to me if I had bloodstained clothes to show them.

And they could suspect me if they wanted, and of course they would. But it wouldn't matter. Because that would be enough to get them to listen to me, to investigate Mark, and then they'd find out the truth.

I found some photos from That Night on my phone – I thought I'd taken some but had never had the urge or the need to look at them before. I've been over and over them for the last few hours, seeing if there's anything I've missed. There's one of me and the girlfriend of one of Mark's friends, posed with standard toothy smiles, our eyes red from the flash. You can just make out Tom Forrester in the background – I recognise him from the news articles, but the photo gives nothing away. He's standing by himself, drinking from a bottle, not even in focus. He's probably unrecognisable to most people. But I know it's him – I've studied it for long enough. And this proves that Sergeant Moore was wrong – Mark and I were there.

Facebook was no help. Most of the pictures from That Night have been deleted out of respect and those that remain are fairly innocuous.

I want to scream with the frustration of it all. To think I didn't do anything before, that I continued to turn a blind eye. If only I'd said something, done something, maybe none of this would have happened.

I hate him, for the first time. Even at his worst, my anger always gave way to pity. I could never hate him. But I can now. It zings through me and I feel more alive than I have in years. I'd be able to pin him for this, I'm certain, if I could just remember the details. It's my fault for being so weak, getting so messed up. For letting him sway my thoughts and emotions, convincing me he'd done nothing wrong. But part of me always knew. He won't get away with it.

Yes, the anger is good. It's a ball of fire in my stomach. When I close my eyes, I can see his. Glazed, hatred glinting. I can feel the fear, taste the blood. I simmer with the certainty of it. Mark is a cold-blooded murderer.

It's later and I'm shivering now. The haze of booze and rage has faded, so I'm drinking from a whisky bottle I keep hidden in my closet. And I'm glad I looked there, because I found something. My red dress, the one I wore on one of our first nights out as a couple. It hung like the shadow of a memory between my grey blazer and the woollen beige cardigan that my grandmother knitted before she died. I could see my pale arms in those crimson sleeves, see me painting my lips the same bright colour, smiling at my flushed reflection in that white, bright bathroom. Seventeen-year-old me, thinking how grown-up I was.

Transported back, I can sense him behind me, watching. Even then, in those early days, his presence was like a weight over my body; I felt encompassed by him. Looking down, I'm wearing my red suede shoes with the ankle strap. I feel constricted in these shoes, with their tight straps like shackles.

I wasn't wearing that red dress the night of Dealer Dan's party. I was in some flimsy silk thing – short, with a plunging neckline. Before he went missing, Mark was yelling about something, calling me a whore. I'd forgotten that until I remembered the dress; one that Mark specifically asked me to wear. He was strange like that. He wanted me to show off my body, but then he would blame me when men looked at me or tried to talk to me. Fucking hypocrite.

No, I wasn't in my red dress that night. And the silk number is long gone; shoved down the garbage chute along with Mark's shirt after the bloodstains refused to be washed out. But I was wearing the shoes. The red shoes that very easily could have absorbed and concealed drops of blood.

And I know exactly where they are.

Chapter Fourteen

I knock lightly on Rachel's door and a few seconds later it opens. Her face appears through the crack, sleep-mussed hair in a halo around her pale face, and she breaks into a smile.

'It's you. Hey.'

'Good morning,' I reply. A funny feeling flutters in my chest as she opens the door wider. I step into the room, handing her the cup of coffee I've brought.

'You're so kind.' Rachel's voice wavers, and the smile she gives me makes me feel like I just handed her a life jacket rather than a cup of coffee.

'No problem. I thought you might need it.'

It's warm in her room with the morning sunshine streaming through the open window. There's the faint odour of perfume in the air. Piles of clothes and shoes are strewn about, a pair of hot-pink knickers hang from a floor fan. Most of the drawers in her dresser are half open and her vanity is cluttered with make-up and jewellery, coffee mugs and an empty wine bottle.

'Sorry about the mess,' she says, gesturing towards the bed.

I sit, clasping my hands in my lap. 'How are you feeling?'

Rachel shrugs. She's in a pale blue nightie with thin straps, a slip of material that barely reaches her thighs. I can see the edge of a yellow bruise above the neckline, and her breasts are visible through the thin material. I quickly look away.

'Better,' she says as she perches next to me on the bed, takes a sip of coffee. Her eyes avoid mine.

I'm unsure what to say. This is a different girl to the one I first met, the person I saw as beautiful, confident, carefree. I've been told that's how others see me, too. Or at least, that's how they used to see me. Perhaps Rachel and I are more similar than I first thought.

'I meant what I said. You can talk to me any time.'

She looks up at me through her lashes and her eyes are red-rimmed, luminous. 'Thanks, Mary.'

Doctor Sarah's voice pops into my head, as it sometimes does, and I wonder if it might be a good time to 'share'. I've kept everything hidden for so long. But Rachel, with that ex of hers, may understand what I'm going through. And telling her might make her feel less alone.

But as I open my mouth, the words stick in my throat.

I don't know Rachel well enough. There's too much at stake right now. I can't.

Rachel seems expectant, as though she's aware I'm on the brink of something. Is it my imagination, or does she seem disappointed? Her posture is stiff, her shoulders hunched.

'You're not going to tell anyone, are you?' she asks.

'No, of course not.'

'What about Cat?' There's an edge to Rachel's voice.

'I won't say anything if you don't want me to.'

Rachel stares at the faded chequered bedspread, her expression unreadable. 'It's just that I don't trust her. I know you guys are close. But there's just something about her . . .'

I don't know what to say. How has she got Cat so wrong?

'You won't tell her, will you?'

'I promised I wouldn't.'

'People judge you for that kind of thing. They . . . it's too raw. It's just not worth it. Besides, Cat said . . .'

'Cat said something to you?' I say, surprised.

Rachel's eyes widen. 'Uh, no. Not exactly. Just don't say anything, okay?'

'I won't. I always keep my promises.' As I speak the words, I wonder whether they're strictly true.

Rachel's shoulders relax. Her eyes find mine. 'I know. I trust you.'

It's the second time she's said this, and I wonder how

she can be so sure. She barely knows me. And, while I can understand she might be desperate to latch on to someone, to feel secure after everything she's been through, there's something intoxicating about being needed. I want to help her. I want to make her feel safe.

Her free hand slides along the bed towards me. I watch as she lifts it and places it over both of mine, which are still in my lap. 'You can talk to me any time too, you know.'

Our eyes lock and hold, and there it is again, that feeling of exposure, as if she knows something. Knows *me*.

'Do you want to go somewhere and talk properly some time?' she asks, tracing my fingers with hers.

I clear my throat. 'I'm going away tomorrow. To visit my aunty.'

'Oh,' she looks down. 'For how long?'

'Only a couple of days.'

'How about tonight, then?'

I answer before I can think. 'Okay.'

She breaks into this bright, goofy smile, and she looks so pretty. It's a bit unsettling. 'I know a place. I found it when I went walking the other night. We can bring a rug and some wine and stuff . . . It'll be fun!'

'Great. Can't wait.'

Before Mark, I used to head to this lookout a few kilometres from my aunty's place where I sat and relished the feeling of being alone. There's something freeing about being disconnected from the human world, with no one knowing where you are. Something exhilarating – like for a moment, it's possible you might not exist at all.

But things are different now. And tonight, at the lookout Rachel's taken us to, I'm feeling nervous rather than exhilarated, my fingers grasping the alarm in my pocket so hard I fear I'll crush it.

We cycled along the perimeter of the beach to a camping area at the tip of a crest at the northernmost end of the beach. There are campers nearby, so we're not completely alone, but I can't help it. We shouldn't be here. Not with Mark out there, looking for me, even though logically I'm sure he can't know where I am. I should be more worried about tomorrow, when I'll be at Aunty Anne's house. A place he knows.

We're spread out on a picnic rug under a Moreton Bay fig, looking out at the sea. There are boats out there, cruisers and houseboats, holidaying families and rich kids with a party agenda. It's humid as the orange sun crawls towards the skyline, the tang of brine in the air. It feels weirdly romantic.

'He was a friend of my foster father's,' Rachel says suddenly, her voice nearly swallowed by a sudden gust of wind. Her comment comes out of the blue, making me jolt. 'The guy I was seeing, I mean.' She's picking lint off the skull-emblazoned, sleeveless T-shirt she's wearing, and I notice she's left some bruises visible.

'You were in foster care?' I ask.

A flock of seagulls flies over us, their cries piercing the quiet.

'Yeah. My parents died when I was little.'

'God. I'm so sorry.'

Rachel laughs. 'Yeah. Me too. I know some people have good experiences in foster care, but not me. My foster father . . . *Steve*. He was such a bastard. Disgusting old perv. You have no idea.' Her face darkens. Then she looks at me in a way that makes me feel like I'm being examined. 'Or maybe you do.'

I ignore the rush of heat to my cheeks, look away. 'He sounds horrible.'

'He was,' she nods. 'I started seeing Dean to piss Steve off, to start with. Dean was always hanging around. I know he wanted me. Lots of guys do, you know.'

I don't say anything. I get that she's not looking for validation. She's not saying it in a conceited way. If anything, she sounds sad.

'He was thirty-seven and I was fourteen. I know, right? I actually thought *I* was using *him* at first. What a joke. I just wanted to get away from Steve and Marnie – she was my foster mum, but she was useless, a total drunk. And Dean offered me a place to stay. I packed up my stuff and got out of there.' She looks at me, almost defiant, as if she expects me to be shocked.

'Go on.'

'I thought I was so smart, Mary. But I was just a dumb kid. I thought I'd found my saviour, you know? He was a douche, but he was a million times better than *Steve*.

I never called him dad. I refused to. What he did . . . it's not something a father should do.'

Rachel's eyes beg me for understanding and, though I'm shocked – horrified – I use one of Doctor Sarah's tactics, staying silent, waiting for her to continue.

'Dean got me into drugs. I wasn't keen, at first. Even *I* wasn't that stupid. But he was persuasive. He made it sound like it would be the answer to all my problems. And you know what? For a while, it was. It felt good. I'd forgotten what it was like to feel that way.' Rachel's chin is high but her lower lip quivers. I reach out, place my hand over hers and she looks at me gratefully. 'I was there for nearly five years. Can you believe that?'

'Yes.' Of course I believe it. I've lived it myself.

Rachel releases a puff of air that might be a laugh. 'I knew you'd understand.'

The sun has set, yet ribbons of purple, pink and grey dominate the darkening sky. I feel warm from the wine, the humidity, the intensity of the conversation.

'So this was the dickhead who hit you? Your ex?'

Rachel flicks me a glance; for a second I could swear she looks guilty. 'Dean was the first,' she said slowly. She sighs. 'But it was my most recent ex that gave me these.' She gestures to her torso. 'He was worse.'

'God. I'm so sorry.'

Rachel shakes her head. Her expression has darkened. 'Don't worry about me. He wasn't the first, but he'll be the last. Believe me.'

I watch her, unsure what to say. After Mark, I swore I'd never be fooled again. But maybe it's not that easy. Rachel's been through so much more than I suspected, and something tells me it's not the full story. I'm unsure my pain can even compare.

She lifts her head and luminous hazel eyes gaze into mine. 'Thanks for listening, Mary. I'm really glad we're friends.'

I smile hesitantly. 'Me too.' Refilling our glasses, I choose my words carefully. 'Can I ask . . . why do you hate him so much?'

'Who?'

'Your foster father. Did he . . .' It's as far as I get, but it's enough.

Rachel's shoulders shake, and though it's almost dark now, I know she's crying.

'Oh, Rachel.' I put my arm around her, pull her close, and she lets me. It's a basic human need, physical intimacy, and I wonder if she's ever been held without someone wanting more from her. It's a dark, lonely thought. 'I know. It's okay. I know.'

Rachel clings to me, her hands fisting my T-shirt, her face at my throat. I rock her back and forth as her tears fall, hot and wet, against my skin. Her body shudders in my arms.

'Sorry.' She pulls back, hiccoughs. 'Sorry.'

'Shhh, hey. What are you sorry for? That your foster father's a sick bastard?'

Rachel makes a funny sound in between sobs, and it takes a moment to realise she's laughing. She hiccoughs again. Then laughs harder.

I find a crumpled napkin in my handbag and hand it to her.

Rachel blows her nose and wipes her eyes on the back of her hands. Mascara smears her cheeks. 'It started when I was six.'

Something hot and ugly throbs inside me.

'No one believed me.' She gives a bitter laugh. 'That's fucked up, isn't it? Why would a little kid make up something like that?'

I want to pummel something, but I rein it in, breathing slow.

'I believe you,' I say, surprising myself with the ferocity in my voice. 'And I'm so glad you left. That was so brave, Rachel. And even if you did end up with some arsehole for a while, you're safe now.'

Rachel's eyes glimmer in the moonlight. 'Thank you,' she whispers. She catches my hand and holds it to her heart, as if making a vow. 'You're safe, too.'

I manage a half-smile, thinking that's a strange remark. But, of course, Rachel doesn't know how wrong she is.

Chapter Fifteen

30th November 2016

It feels unnatural keeping something from Cat. Especially when it's about someone we're living with, someone with the potential to impact on our lives. But there are some things I just can't share with Cat, and Rachel's secret is one of them.

Cat's been there for most of my life. Literally. Sometimes I think my parents had more faith in her than they did in me. She was always a go-getter, trustworthy and hard-working. Loyal to a fault. With the exception of when I was with Mark, but that was my doing. I withdrew, shutting out the world. It doesn't matter that she doesn't fully understand what I've been through. No one can. But she's there. Always. And that's enough.

Cat's the kind of person who wouldn't hesitate to give you the shirt off her back if you needed it, but may hold a grudge if you forget to give it back. Aside from my aunt, she's the person I trust most in the world; the one person I know will always stand by me. That's why Aunty Anne trusted her to take care of me. That makes me sound like a shut-in or an invalid or something, but it's not as serious as all that. It's more like someone to check in, make sure I'm taking care of myself. Someone to report back to Aunty Anne to make her feel better about her poor messed-up niece living far away in another city. Since I'm shit with numbers, Cat manages the bills, my disability payments, all the things Aunty Anne took care of before. It's not that I'm incapable – it just makes life easier not having to think about all that. I can focus on recovery and it gives my aunty peace of mind.

The arrangement with Cat was part of the 'conditions' of me moving out alone. After what happened with Mum and Dad, my interrupted therapy and recovery – and then the trouble I got into with Mark – I suppose I was considered a bit of a liability. Doctor Sarah and Aunty Anne weren't keen on the moving out idea at all. They thought I needed more time. But then Cat came to my rescue, offered to step in. She wanted me to be able to have a normal life, to enjoy my youth and my freedom instead of continuing to pay penance for the things that have happened to me.

I'll never be able to repay her for that. I couldn't ask for a better ally, someone who understands my needs better than I do at times. It hasn't always been the most stable relationship, but it's been the longest lasting.

I can still recall with clarity the day I met Cat. It was on the first day of Year Two, and I was crying behind the library building because a boy – this fat, freckly Year Four bully called Simon – had taken my lunch, eaten half of it and flushed the other half down the toilet. Cat found me, listened when I told her what happened, called Simon stupid names until I laughed, then shared her lunch with me.

By then Cat had had her fair share of run-ins with bullies. For some reason, she was a target. I could never quite pinpoint why; maybe because she was so much cleverer than everybody else. I always believed she'd taken me under her wing, but Cat swears it's the other way around. She swears she'd have suffered severe and swift social death if I hadn't come along. That she only learned to fit in by association.

I'm not sure whose version of events is true. I do know that after that incident, we ate lunch together every day for the rest of the year, and every year after that. We went to the same high school, made the same friends, took the same classes. And it's been her and me ever since.

I found out later that on that first day she'd found the boy who'd been mean to me and thrown his backpack over the fence and into two lanes of traffic. His sandwich was splattered like roadkill.

We had our ups and downs in high school. All girls do, I guess. Especially when they're as close as we were. She never had any luck with boys, and for some reason, I did – which in itself is a recipe for disaster. But we never had any epic fall-outs like some girls do. And these days, if anything, she gets more attention than I do. Even though it's usually from the wrong kind of men.

Not Mark-status wrong, of course. But every guy she dates ends up having some spectacularly unexpected quirk, like a funny but unfortunate twist in a rom-com. And it's always a deal-breaker, like the bartender who was 'between jobs' and still flat-sharing with his ex, or the incredibly charming restaurant owner who turned out to be polygamous and already married to two other women. Or the hot bearded guy with the rats. (Seriously. Thirty-two pet rats. All named Charlie.) Cat makes light of her romance fails, but it has to wear her down. Just hearing about it is exhausting. But I have to say, it does make me feel better about not being on the dating scene for the moment. I don't know when I'll be ready for that.

Back at school, it always felt like she looked up to me. I can't think why — if anything, it should have been the other way around. Cat with her logic and practicality, her sensible mind, her no-nonsense attitude. She's the one who deserves admiration. She's a real doer, as my aunty would say. And I'm someone who fucks around. I can be lazy. Self-absorbed. But Cat seems to have missed the memo on this. For some unfathomable reason, she's put me on this pedestal and, no matter what I do, I can't seem to fall off it.

So, when I think about it, of course she'd jump at the chance for us to move away together. We've been planning it since we were kids. Cat, particularly. Fantasising about running away, leaving everything behind and starting a new life somewhere by the sea. And to think I nearly blew it all. To think I moved out with Mark and left Cat behind.

I owe that girl so much. But I can imagine why Rachel might

not see it that way. Straight-talking and with zero tolerance for bullshit, Cat does have a history of rubbing some people up the wrong way. She can come across as arrogant, inflexible. And, though Rachel doesn't know it, Cat doesn't believe me about the worst of Mark's crimes. That's okay – I get it. It's not that she doesn't trust me. She's just concerned. I know my memory of things hasn't proven to be the most reliable source in the past – or of late. But I haven't lost faith that Cat will come around. Soon she'll see. Because I'll have proof. Proof even the cops won't be able to question.

Chapter Sixteen

The lizards will be happy now Rufus has gone. This is the clearest thought in my head as I sit on the back steps of my aunt's farm house, listening to the rustle of leaves in the bushes that can only mean the skinks are on the move.

Rufus, our old retriever, had to be put down a month ago when his kidneys failed. It was awful; I'd known him for sixteen of my twenty years and even though I hadn't been there at the time, I felt the loss like a kick in the spleen. I can't count the number of times I'd sobbed into his fur, how often I'd told him the secrets I couldn't share with anyone else.

But our faithful friend had a tendency to murder unsuspecting lizards, and so as I watch a family of skinks skitter out from behind a shrub, I wonder if they know they're safer than they were four weeks ago.

Despite the heatwave, Aunty Anne's garden is thriving and the country air is fragrant with life. There's a sense of renewal in coming back here, even though it's just for a couple of days. It almost makes me forget why I've come.

'Here you are,' Aunty Anne hands me a cup of tea before lowering herself onto the step beside me with a grunt. A gnarled hand shades her face from the intense glare. 'Sorry, no milk. Not after, well . . . you know.'

'It's okay,' I say, smiling at my aunt's warm, deeply lined face. It's a face I know better than any other, a face that reflects decades of toiling on sweltering farm-land. So unlike Mum's, who cared more for image than work. 'How's the calf surviving?'

My aunt winces.

'Sorry.' I cringe. Often, when a pregnant cow dies, the calf can be saved. But I've never forgotten the year I found an orphan at the bottom of the paddock, its body stiff with rigor mortis, its eyes lifeless and milky.

'You didn't have to visit so soon. Tickets are expensive.'

'Not really,' I counter. 'There are some pretty cheap return flights to Melbourne, and the coach out here costs nothing. Besides, I wanted to come.' My tongue burns as I sip my tea. I want to add, 'Because I owe you my life,' but it's too raw, too real. I don't want to cry in front of her again.

Besides, it's not the main reason I've come.

My aunty's brown hand covers mine and I look at the contrast in our skin. It's sobering, beautiful, the way her weathered hand encases my soft one, and I think how old she's becoming and that I can't live without her.

'You're doing it again,' Aunty Anne tuts, shaking her head, but her lips twitch upwards at the corners. 'That mind of yours is always working. You're just like Sylvia that way.'

I try to smile as I sip my tea, but the mention of my mother always leaves me hollow. 'How's Uncle John? He's been around, hasn't he? Not stationed off anywhere?'

'Oh, my, yes, I can't get rid of him.' Aunty Anne grins and winks.

Some of the tension leaves my body. 'Good. I'm glad. And . . . And Mark . . .?'

Aunty Anne meets my gaze. She knows something, I can tell. 'He wouldn't dare.'

I'm always fascinated by the way my body responds when I think of Mark. Now, for example, it's as though my skin is twitching and my heartbeat speeds up and stutters.

'Don't open the door to him,' I say, wiping my clammy palms on my jeans. 'He's more dangerous than you think.'

Aunty Anne pats her crisp silver curls, tilts her head to one side. 'Well, darling, I won't if I can help it. We know what he is, don't we? We've both seen it before. We . . .' She sucks in a breath through her teeth, slants me a guilty look.

I turn away, watching a pair of skinks dart in and out of the wild lavender. A clap of thunder sounds in the distance and I look up to see clouds gathering. 'Really? Now?'

Aunty Anne groans just as a drop of rain lands on my nose.

'It's been a tropical spring,' she tells me, getting to her feet and beckoning me down the front path. 'Utterly unpredictable.'

We scurry indoors just as the sky opens and raindrops begin to plummet. It's darker inside, almost like night, and Aunty Anne lights a few candles and places them around the kitchen and adjoining dining room. 'Power's gone out three times this week,' she explains. 'Might as well be prepared.'

The wall clock tells me it's after five and my eyes wander to the fridge; I wonder if Aunty Anne still keeps it stocked with wine from the family vineyard. I look around at the familiar spaces and objects, bathed in candlelight. Somehow it feels like I've been gone longer than a few months.

A picture frame stands on the bench in the corner of the kitchen, coated in a film of dust. It's a picture of my parents holding me as a baby. I'm startled to realise they must be around my age, maybe a couple of years older. How strange to think I could have a child of my own, that I could have that kind of inescapable duty, to be responsible for another life. It seems unfathomable.

There's a large stone pestle and mortar on the counter; it must be new. I trace its rough surface with my index finger. 'I'll make dinner then?' I offer.

Aunty Anne's eyes twinkle in the low light. 'I'll confess I'd hoped you'd offer. I fear I didn't inherit that gene. Not like you and Sylvia.'

'It's like Mum's old one,' I say, turning the cool weight of the pestle over in my hand.

Aunty Anne chuckles. 'Yes. That's why I got it. Can't you just picture her, banging away on it like a madwoman? No wonder she became a chef. She was always obsessed with cooking. You're very like her in that way, too.'

'I do love to cook,' I murmur, staring at the glowing, proud face of my mother holding her child. Then suddenly, without intending to, I pound the pestle into the hard stone with a loud *crack*. It's oddly satisfying.

Aunty Anne gazes at me warily.

I smile, flexing my hand. 'Would you excuse me for a minute?' Without waiting for an answer, I head to the staircase that leads to the second floor.

I hear the television come on and an up-tempo version of 'White Christmas' drifts up the stairs. I shudder. I don't think about my parents much – if I do, I'll go mad. But this time of year never fails to dredge up those old feelings. Though I might not remember exactly what happened that summer, my body does. It's a part of me. Muscle memory.

I shake it off and focus on the task at hand. There are only two rooms upstairs: the second bathroom and my old bedroom. I climb the stairs two at a time, the sound of 'White Christmas' slowly fading, and push open the bedroom door. I make a beeline for the old wardrobe with its peeling sage-green paint. It's lighter up here with the curtains open and the windows facing west. I find the cupboard mostly empty, as expected, but there's a bag of old clothes I never got around to giving to charity. Fortunately, Aunty Anne hasn't got around to it either.

Releasing a breath I didn't know I was holding, I turn the bag upside down and its contents tumble onto the floorboards. *Thunk, thunk.* That's them, those clunky heels. Those little straps, constraining my ankles, making me feel shackled – that's why I threw them out. Or at least that's what I told myself.

I dig through the clothing heaped on the floor, picking up items and flicking them aside until I see a flash of tell-tale crimson. I reach my hands into the pile and pull out one red suede shoe, then the other. I know it must be my imagination, but I could swear they feel warm. I turn them over in my hands, lift them to my face, inhale deeply. Cow hide, musky and earthy. Like flesh and bone, like a living thing.

I shudder and place them neatly on the floor, the toes pointing away from me, tuck my legs under my body and lean over them. There's a darker patch of suede on the right one, just to one side of the open toe. I run my finger over the dark spot, pressing firmly. When I draw my finger back, the tip is coloured by a rusty-brown smear.

Blood.

Chapter Seventeen

1st December 2016

When I was a child, I used to lie in bed and imagine I was inside a coffin. Or not a coffin exactly, more of a glass box that I could see out of but no one could get in. Kind of like the one in Snow White, I suppose. I imagined tiny holes all over the surface of the coffin, big enough so I could breathe, of course, but they couldn't be so big that something could be poked through them, like a sharp pencil. Or a knife.

The imaginings continued into my early teens. It got to the point where I couldn't sleep unless I could picture my imaginary shield around me. But by then I had realised that a glass box was too fragile to protect me. What if it shattered and the shards sank deep into my flesh? No. It had to be thick Perspex or bulletproof glass — transparent, so I could still see out — and heat-resistant so I couldn't burn alive in there. It had to lock from the inside but not the outside and it had to have an escape button, just in case there was any risk of me getting trapped. I remember wishing it could be invisible, but I didn't believe in magic, even then. It had to be realistic. Practical, sturdy. Something I could build if I had to.

Every evening I'd lie in my bed, listening to the dull blare of the television and my parents' murmured conversations downstairs, and I'd imagine my bulletproof coffin. Then, and only then, when the white-hot summer sun had disappeared at last and the warbling magpies in the eucalypts fell silent, could I permit my eyes to close, my body to relax. And, if I was lucky, I might just sleep until morning.

Doctor Sarah thinks these memories are significant. That it means something that I was afraid to go to sleep. But I can't think what I could have been afraid of. I had a happy childhood. Sure, I had my share of scraped knees, friendship dramas, blow-outs with my mum – we were both strong-willed and she was fond of her wine. But nothing out of the ordinary. Nothing that would qualify as something to fear.

I was privileged, and I know that now, although of course as a child I had no understanding of anything beyond my own reality, could make no comparison. As an only child, I had my parents' undivided attention, and that was the way I liked it. I had a loyal ally in Cat and plenty of friends at school. I remember weekends skiing at Thredbo and holidays in Europe and endless summers in that hot, wet heat by the sea.

It never occurred to me that anyone could be jealous of me.

But, looking back, looking at everything we had, who wouldn't have been?

But it wasn't perfect, was it? Even before my parents went missing, there was always this sense of . . . unease. Like we were all waiting for something to happen. Like we all knew something we weren't saying.

Or am I imagining that? God knows my memories are rusty from disuse. Most of the time, I prefer to leave my parents in the past. Whether it's healthy or not, it's easier. I don't even let myself google them anymore. And every time I'm tempted, all I need to do is let the mouse hover over the search window and a surge of nausea has me running for the bathroom. Though I know there can't be any information out there that I don't already know, I get the feeling sometimes there's more to the story than I'm remembering.

I keep thinking: it was only a few years ago. It's not like this is a fifty-year-old cold case. Surely someone out there knows something. Surely I know something. But I also know some people really do go missing and are never found. It happens more often than you'd think. Someone is reported missing 38,000 times a year, in fact. Australia's a big country. Lots of bushland, ocean and desert. Lots of places to get lost, or hidden, and never found. Lots of families left behind, forever trapped in limbo.

When I let the memories come, it's always of the vineyards, at least at first. I can feel the warmth of the sun as I pick grapes with my father, his hand firm on my back as if he's trying to keep me close. I can hear the bleating of the lambs in the fields beyond, the twitter of finches as they dart and hop.

We were always going places; my parents never seemed to be able to sit still. We were happy, I'm certain of it. Sure, I always sensed a bit of tension between Mum and Aunty Anne. I used to think it was jealousy – Mum 'had everything' and Aunty Anne was a 'spinster', as Mum called her. She never married or had children (not that that's the be-all and end-all), although now she's got Uncle John. I can see now that they were just different. My aunty didn't go for any of the superficial stuff Mum was into. She never wanted kids and never wavered under the pressure to give in and have them. She was a straight-talker, practical. Sharp and outspoken, yet laid-back in ways that Mum wasn't. Mum was always a little overly concerned with what other people thought of her. She liked her wine a little too much, but that was easy to excuse, working in the food industry and running the vineyard with Dad.

I never saw Mum and Aunty Anne in the same place at the same time for too long. They always found excuses to be elsewhere. But they loved each other, and I'm sure of that. I was always close to Aunty Anne. I loved staying with her over the Easter break every autumn. She let me eat as many chocolate eggs as I wanted. She let me walk around with bare feet and make a mess in the kitchen and stay up until midnight. She didn't care about keeping the cream-coloured sofa spotless or grubby finger-prints on the screen door. Staying with Aunty Anne felt like freedom.

Now my parents are gone, it's easy to romanticise the past. But I know we weren't without our problems. Mum came from a poor family and she never let me forget that, or how lucky

I was to have grown up in a household of means. I know part of her was proud that she was self-made — she was more well-known than Dad when they first met — but another part of her was ashamed of her past. She spent money outrageously at times, but the girl inside her who came from humble beginnings couldn't quite be banished. Sometimes I'd find her washing used aluminium foil and saving it in a drawer, eating out-of-date food and keeping vegetables in the fridge drawer long after they were withered or rotten. She taught me to scrimp and save, to be grateful for what I had. In a disposable society, she taught me to hang on to things. Even things we didn't need. Even things that had long ago lost their value.

Sometimes I wonder if that's why I chose not to throw Mark away. Even though he was rotten from the start.

Though no one ever explicitly said it, I know Mum and Aunty Anne had it tough growing up. Their parents — my grandparents — died when I was a baby, so I never knew them. Mum rarely spoke of them, and Aunty Anne only grunts or changes the subject when I broach it. Once or twice, often if she'd had a bit too much, Mum would say something throwaway like 'at least your daddy doesn't hit you' — and I'd be so confused and hurt, because it sounded like she was angry with me. And maybe she was, partly. Because she was right: my daddy wasn't always a nice man, but he never hit me. Maybe she was envious that life was so much easier for me than it had been for her. And I can't really blame her for that. Although at times it made me feel lonely. Misunderstood. As though my problems were invalid because I hadn't suffered the same way she had.

It's hard for me to write this. I tend not to think about my parents. It's so much easier not to, despite what Doctor Sarah says. But sometimes, when I close my eyes, I can see her face. She's looking down at me, eyes soft, golden curls backlit by the afternoon sun. And it doesn't matter if there was ever any bad blood between us, real or imagined; I can feel her love as warm as that sunlight. But then, just the same way it always happens, as if I'm finding out she's gone for the very first time, my chest squeezes with a pain so sharp I lose my breath.

That's what I miss most. That safe place, that knowing that someone who loved me was there to take care of me. Unconditionally.

I suppose that's why I leant on Cat so much, was so willing to relinquish control to her. It made me feel safe, cared for. I suppose I let her mother me, in a way. But it's different with Rachel. There's less of an imbalance, more of a feeling of being on equal ground. Only it's worse for Rachel, in many ways. While my safe place was taken away, she never had one. Because of that, I think she might be able to understand me in a way no one else can.

I'd forgotten about my imaginary coffin until the imaginings returned one day as if they'd never left . . . around the time my parents went missing, I guess it was. The glass box that kept me safe from danger. Was it just my imagination running away with me all those years? A child's groundless fears? Or is there some connection . . . was Doctor Sarah on to something? What was I afraid of? And what did I want to keep out?

Because sometimes I wonder. Did I know something bad was going to happen . . . ?

Chapter Eighteen

Four days without a drink and my first wine slips down quickly, smoothing away the edges of panic. My appointment with Sergeant Moore is less than a week away, but it feels like a lifetime to wait. After everything, I'm surprised he agreed to see me. But I have evidence now. The shoes are concealed in a plastic bag in my wardrobe, waiting. I can almost hear them breathing. I could have taken them to the Victoria police, who originally dealt with the case, but I want to make a point to Sergeant Moore. Prove that I can be trusted about this.

Shouts and heavy footsteps sound from outside. The couple upstairs are at it again. Behind the wall, the shower gurgles to life and I wonder if Cat's home. I sigh at the thought. Yesterday, when I got back from Aunty Anne's, I showed her the shoes. She looked at them sceptically, asked if I was sure I wanted to go ahead. She told me to be careful, said to make sure I had my facts straight before I talked to the police again. *'You don't want a repeat of last time, Mary.'* Well, of course I don't. But what choice do I have? It's that or let Mark walk free.

Inhaling deeply, I rub my knuckles over my eyes, take a long pull from my wine glass. I have to get a hold on this anxiety, it's getting out of control. I haven't heard anything more from Mark, and he didn't make an appearance at the farm, but I feel sick every time I check my emails. I jump whenever my phone beeps. Without doing anything, he's still controlling me.

There's a shriek from outside, a smash, like glass breaking. Then a distant *thunk, thunk, thunk.* I jump up, run out onto the balcony and peer over the railing.

A man in a crumpled business shirt with tousled hair stands in the middle of the side street. It's a moment before I recognise him as the man who lives upstairs; one half of the noisy couple. Clothing and various other items lie strewn at his feet. Head bowed, shoulders slumped, he kicks a solitary shoe across the pavement. It lands in an oily puddle with a splash.

A door slams somewhere and the man flinches. He looks up, catching my eye. He's younger than I thought, with a slight build and fair skin. One of his eyes looks larger and darker than the other. I hold my breath. A black eye.

Something brushes my shoulder and I shriek and whirl

around. Ben stands by the railing, looking embarrassed. 'Wow, sorry. I didn't mean to scare you.' His embarrassment turns to concern. 'You okay there?'

I'm sure I'm blushing. 'Yes, fine. I . . . sorry. Didn't meant to scream.'

'It was kind of cute, actually.' Ben's eyes crinkle as he smiles. He has warm eyes, a funny mix of brown and green. His hair is damp; it must have been him in the shower. 'Cat's out tonight. She said to check on you, see if you needed anything.'

'Oh.' I search his face but his expression gives nothing away. 'I'm good. Thanks.'

'Listen,' he says, looking uncomfortable. 'If you ever need anything . . . I'm just in the next room. Feel free to call out, yeah?'

'That's nice of you, Ben. Thanks.'

There's a crash from outside.

'Those two again.' Ben shakes his head. 'Poor guy.'

'Poor *guy*?'

'You didn't spot the shiner?'

'Ah. I did, yeah.' I don't mention the fact that my instinct was to wonder whether it was deserved.

'I had a mate once, who was beat up by his girl. We told him to get rid of her, but he wouldn't listen, of course. Fortunately she ended up leaving him anyway. Still a shit thing to happen.'

Our neighbour is scrabbling to collect his clothes from the wet ground.

'It's not just guys who can get violent, I guess. Should we help him?'

'I'll go see if he needs a hand. I'm just on my way out.' I smile. 'Okay.'

'Well then.' Ben looks right in my eyes. He takes a breath, opens his mouth as if to add something.

I wait, strangely eager to hear what he's going to say. But then he closes his lips, gives an embarrassed smile.

'See you, Mary.'

I watch from the balcony as Ben approaches the guy on the street. He puts a hand on his shoulder, says something I can't hear. Then he bends down, collects the last of the clothes, wrings out the water and mud. He helps the guy to his car. I smile to myself.

My phone vibrates, shaking me from my trance. A new Facebook notification.

YOU CAN'T HIDE FROM ME FOREVER. WATCH YOUR BACK.

Another message from the same account, *Jake Morns*. Written all in capitals. There's no question who it's from.

'Mary?'

I step back from the railing with a gasp.

'Sorry,' Rachel's husky voice says from behind me. I turn to find her smiling, her fair hair almost translucent, backlit by the afternoon sun. She frowns when she sees my face. 'Are you okay?'

'Yeah, fine. Just . . .' I close my eyes, willing my pulse to slow down.

Rachel fixes me with a serious look. 'Mary? You've gone pale.'

I open my eyes, force a smile. 'I'm okay. Really.'

Rachel's gaze lingers on my face. 'Look. I don't know what's bothering you, but I do know what will help.'

I offer her a weak smile. 'Oh?'

'You need a drink,' Rachel says with authority. 'Come on. Let's go out.'

By quarter to six, two empty wine bottles sit alongside another half-full one and we're giggling like truants. The chink of glass on glass and the rumble of talk and laughter surrounds us. It's the sound of people enjoying themselves and, right now, I feel like one of them.

'When's your birthday?' Rachel asks, draining the last of her glass of house white and pouring another. We've been playing this 'get to know you' game she invented and it's serving as an excellent distraction. Mark's message is a distant memory.

'October twelfth,' I say between mouthfuls of pizza.

'Ninety-six?'

'Yup.'

Rachel's jaw drops. 'No way! I'm the seventeenth. We're practically the same age!'

I giggle into my wine glass. 'How random.'

'Okay, okay. Let me try another one. Where in Melbourne did you grow up?'

'Well, I moved to the country with my aunty when I was fifteen, but Wallarma, originally.'

'Now you seriously have to be kidding. I don't believe you.'

'It's true! I was born in the old hospital on North Street.'

'Fuck off! I grew up in Wallarma too. Only I just made it into the postcode. We lived at the dodgy end. It was practically a caravan park,' she laughs, rolling her eyes. 'What area did you live in?'

I look away, feeling the familiar twinge of guilt. 'Uh, near Briscott House. You know that old manor place they turned into a function centre?'

'Whoa,' Rachel's eyes widen. She sighs, looks wistful. 'You must be *rich*.'

I smile tightly. 'My family was.'

Rachel gives me a funny look. 'Right, yeah. God, these have gone straight to my head.' She gestures to the empty bottles.

'Well, you've barely eaten anything.'

Rachel has been pushing a limp piece of cucumber around on her plate for twenty minutes. There were only a few measly slices to begin with and the salad is all she ordered.

'Don't you want to eat more than that?' I ask. Rachel's wearing an oversized T-shirt and leggings but it's obvious how thin she is underneath.

She looks at my plate, devouring the food with her eyes.

'Go on, have some. I know you said you weren't hungry, but I feel like a pig here. Pizza's for sharing, anyway.'

Rachel looks at me uncertainly. 'If you're sure . . .'

'Of course. These pizzas are amazing, even though they're cheap. That's why Cat and I come here all the time.'

'Right. You go out together quite a lot, don't you?' Rachel smiles, but it doesn't reach her eyes. I don't know how to interpret her tone.

'Go on, eat!' I say to break the awkward silence that follows, gesturing to my plate.

Rachel snatches up a slice and takes a bite so fast I'd have missed it if I blinked. She closes her eyes and gets this blissful look on her face as she chews and swallows, before repeating the process.

'It's kind of embarrassing, what I'm about to tell you,' she says when she's done. She takes a long gulp of wine and smiles, seeming more relaxed. 'I actually don't have a lot of money at the moment. Since leaving my ex, I haven't really had any support.'

An image comes to me – Rachel's pale body covered in bruises – and I feel that hot, ugly thing throb inside me. 'I'm sorry to hear that.'

Rachel smiles, but it's more of a wince. 'It's cool. I don't want you to feel sorry for me or anything. I mean, I'm living with you guys in that *amazing* place, so things are way better than they were. I needed to get as far away from my ex as possible, as fast as possible. So I hitch-hiked up here and, well . . . Here I am!'

'I don't feel sorry for you,' I say gently. 'I think it's incredible you had the courage to leave, after everything you've been through.'

'Thanks,' Rachel's eyes glisten and her lips turn upwards in a tiny smile. 'It's so nice to talk to someone who understands. I think I've done okay, considering.'

'You got out. That's the most important thing.'

Rachel's eyes catch mine. 'Absolutely.'

I'm feeling buzzed from the wine, the warmth of Rachel's gaze, and I open my mouth before I can think. 'If you need anything, I can help. I have money from . . .' I stop. This is exactly the thing I don't ever say to people. It changes things, when they know. But Rachel's been through so much and she's still suffering. It doesn't seem fair to keep quiet, when there's something I can do to help.

Rachel looks at me expectantly. And I say it, because her honesty gave me permission. That's what normal people do, isn't it? They talk, they share. It's been so long since I've met anyone I *wanted* to share with.

'My parents disappeared.' My voice comes out surprisingly calm, like it's a regular thing that happens to everyone. 'When I was fifteen. They're presumed dead. That's . . . that's why I have money. Inheritance.'

Rachel's mouth opens in a tiny 'o'. 'Mary . . .' she whispers.

'It's okay,' I say, avoiding her eyes. 'So anyway. I'm happy to help, if you need it.'

'Wow. Thank you, Mary. You're so kind. But I couldn't. I wouldn't dream of taking your money.'

'I know you wouldn't. But if you ever need to borrow . . .'

Rachel throws back the last of her wine then smiles, her eyes moist. 'You're so generous. It must have been hard for you to tell me that. I get the feeling you don't tell many people. I'm grateful. Grateful that you trust me enough.'

I stare at the pearls of condensation on my wine glass, catching one with my finger.

'What happened to them?' Rachel's voice is almost a whisper.

The sounds in the crowded pub grow distant and all I can hear is the echo of 'White Christmas' ringing in my ears. I don't know if I'm imagining it.

'Mary?'

'I don't actually know. One minute, we were getting ready for Christmas. The next . . .' I shrug. 'They just . . . disappeared.'

'That's so strange. And they never found them? They just . . . vanished into thin air?'

I catch Rachel's eye and she holds my gaze. Again, I feel like I'm being examined. I can't bring myself to answer and Rachel's focus shifts to something in the middle distance.

'It must be nice not to have to worry about money, though, right?' Rachel says, playing with a strand of her hair. 'I mean, I've never had any. And it just makes things a lot harder, you know? You can't just pay for your problems to disappear.' Suddenly she gasps, claps a hand over her mouth. 'God, that was such a dumb thing to say. I'm sure you'd much rather have your parents back.'

I try to ignore the stab of pain in my chest.

'I'm sorry, Mary. That was so heartless of me. You must think I'm such a bitch, and after you've been so nice to me. I'm *so* sorry.'

A horrible feeling comes over me, one I shouldn't be having, but I can't help it. It feels like she *wanted* to hurt me.

'Don't worry about it,' I say.

'No, I mean it, Mary. I would never want to upset you. *Ever*.' Rachel's eyes are wide with worry. She reaches across the table and clasps both my hands. 'It's just . . . I just feel comfortable with you. I forget myself, sometimes. Since we met, it's like I already know you, we have so much in common . . . Our birthdays, the Melbourne thing, our parents . . . I knew we'd be friends. I said that when we met, didn't I?'

I shake off the bad feeling. Rachel's been through a lot and she's had a bit to drink. She said something thoughtless; it didn't mean anything. 'It's fine, Rachel. I understand. Don't worry about it, honestly.'

'Really?' She squeezes my hands. Her fingers are cold but the look she is giving me is warm.

'Really,' I tell her, squeezing back.

She looks so relieved that I smile.

'I know we don't know each other that well, but I'm no stranger to drama.' She gives a husky chuckle. 'You've done so much for me already and . . . well. You'd say if you were in any kind of trouble. Wouldn't you . . .?'

Despite my previous misgivings, I'm struck by the sudden urge to tell her everything. I can taste the words, feel the salve of sympathy. It would be such a relief to share the load . . .

Without warning, Mark's face flashes in my mind.

'Mary?' Rachel's voice suddenly sounds like she's speaking underwater.

You can't hide from me forever.

The fear creeps in and I shut my eyes, seal my lips.

Watch your back.

Chapter Nineteen

5th December 2016

I dreamed that I was standing on the edge of a cliff at dawn, the grey sea rolling below, the cool morning breeze swirling around my bare ankles. There was someone standing close behind me and I had nowhere to run. They were going to push me. I don't know who they were or how I knew, but death was imminent. They'd push me unless I could tell them what really happened That Night. If I didn't remember, I'd die.

I woke in a cold sweat to find my bedroom door open and the air in my room as cold as a refrigerator. It took a while before I could adjust to reality, to accept that I was safe in bed and not about to jump to my death.

But the fear stayed. Because the fear is founded.

This isn't the first time I've struggled with my memory. I tell myself it's the booze, and it is – I'm not trying to kid myself it has nothing to do with my little habit. But I'm sure there are things I used to know – not just recent events, but memories from a long time ago – that are missing. Things I know are in there but I can't quite reach them anymore.

Today, I saw a family playing by the water. A blonde mother in a sixties-style polka-dot one-piece with a red ribbon in her hair. The father was hoisting his daughter up in the air as she squealed with delight, then throwing her into the water. He did this over and over until somewhere along the line she wasn't squealing with delight anymore. She was screaming in fear.

Her screams and the sound of the crashing waves triggered a sudden reaction inside me – the feeling of nostalgia, of this having happened before, was so strong it hit me like a wave, so hard I stopped in my tracks. I watched them with my heart pumping, as if anticipating something. But the girl calmed down and they played on happily and I was left wondering why I felt like something was missing.

Even as a child I was known for being forgetful. I was intimately familiar with the unsettling feeling of déjà vu: that tingle of awareness, the feeling of having been somewhere, done something before, as if there's another version of you walking around and you've somehow crossed paths. The sense of things happening just outside of your reach, beyond your control.

When I remember my parents, it's in brief flashes, often in vivid colour, always accompanied by a kick in the guts. There's this one memory I keep having of Mum where our eyes meet and we say a word – 'nonsense' – at the same time, then exclaim

'Jinx!' and fall about laughing. I remember this with perfect clarity. Or what passes for clarity as far as memories go. God only knows why this particular moment remains a fixture in the grey matter taking up space in my skull. Why do certain moments stick with us while others fade? Is it just nerves, neurons and synapses doing their thing, or is there more to it than that?

Humans are so unreliable, so flawed. Even our memories can't be trusted. Because everything we see is through a lens of our own bias. Two people could look at the same thing and see it in two completely different ways. Like the way Mark saw himself as the victim, me as the abuser. The way we remember things is already twisted by our biased brains. No wonder Sergeant Moore thinks I'm full of it. He's probably an expert on dodgy testimony.

I used to believe that there's more to us than just a mash-up of flesh, organs and chemicals, that we're more than just bio-robots programmed by our genes and experiences. But I just don't buy it anymore. And if our brains are just computers storing and sorting input, making and severing connections, there must be a way to recover lost files.

I wake from dreams sometimes and I know something terrible happened, but I can't remember a thing. Only the last image lingers in my mind: my father's face, with his mouth open and eyes wide. I can't tell if he's frightened or angry.

There are gaps in my memories of the weeks surrounding my parents' disappearance. I don't remember finding out about it, or how I reacted. Apparently, I just didn't speak for weeks. Doctor Sarah thinks that's significant. That maybe there's something from that time I'd rather forget and have blocked out.

Well, of course I'd rather forget such a traumatic event in my life. Who wouldn't?

But there are places in my mind I don't dare to tread for fear of what I might find there. Sometimes I think of my mind as a forest. It is full of dark places. Memories like fireflies dancing, teasing. If I'm feeling reckless, I chase them. Once or twice I've been close to catching them and I almost, almost *remember. But they disappear, back to a place I know, but has faded. It's like I've forgotten the path there. Like I've trained myself not to remember, have crept into my mind with a pair of scissors and snipped the connections. And all I'm left with is blank spaces and a deep fear in my bones.*

But seeing that family today . . . it makes me wonder. Makes me feel like I'm supposed to remember something.

I just don't know what.

Chapter Twenty

I wake in fright. My mind grasps at fragments of a nightmare, but they slip from memory, irretrievable. There's a square patch of sunlight on the duvet cover next to where I'm lying, still fully clothed. The quality of light tells me it's afternoon and the quilted material is warm when I run my hand over it.

I don't remember falling asleep, but the crick in my neck and the phone clutched tight in my hand tell me I haven't moved all night. There's an unread text from Rachel.

Thanks for last night. It meant a lot to me. :) R x

Layers of sound filter into my awareness; the gentle roar of the sea, the murmur of voices. The voices are coming from behind my bedroom door.

I sit up with a groan, lifting a hand to my throbbing head. I feel dehydrated. Raw. I swing my legs over the side of the bed and head out to the living room. As I lift my hand to the door, I hear Cat's voice.

'*Seriously*. I'm warning you.'

Silence follows. Who's she talking to? I know that tone. She doesn't sound angry, not exactly. It's as she phrased it; a warning.

I push the door open to see Cat and Rachel standing by the couch, facing each other. The television is on mute in the background, an overly enthusiastic woman with coiffed hair and bright lipstick talks animatedly as she cradles a hot-pink bottle of laundry detergent. Cat's back is to me, but Rachel looks visibly upset. Her eyes meet mine and widen a fraction.

'What's going on?' I say.

Cat's head whips around. She does an odd little sidestep when she sees me.

'I thought you were out.' She looks at her watch and frowns. 'It's nearly three. Were you sleeping?'

'Yeah, I just . . . had a nap. Are you guys okay?'

Rachel holds my gaze, as though she's trying to communicate something.

'Don't worry about it, it's all good,' Cat says. She smiles. 'We were just talking about what we should order for dinner. Tonight's takeaway night, right Rach?'

'I have errands to run. I'll be back soon,' Rachel mutters, her eyes downcast as she crosses the living room. She looks at me as she passes but I can't read her expression.

'Seriously, what's going on?' I say once Rachel's gone.

Cat releases a puff of air. 'Oh God, it's nothing. Just rent stuff. Not something for you to worry about.' She goes to the fridge and takes out a bottle of wine, pours two glasses and gulps from one.

I pick up a glass. 'Hey, I live here too. If it's about rent . . .'

Cat swallows and blinks a few times as if trying to clear her mind. I notice she has dark rings under her eyes. The roots of her hair have grown out longer than usual.

'Are you okay?' I use a softer tone. 'Is Alex giving you shit?' Alex is the latest contestant in the disastrous dating show that is Cat's life.

Cat leans against the counter. 'No, but I think I'm pretty much through with him this time.'

'I'm sorry.'

Cat rolls her eyes. 'Don't be. It was a long time coming and we all know it.'

I don't know what to say. I didn't really 'know it', as she says, and it makes me realise how long it's been since we've had a proper chat, or commiserated over a long, boozy lunch like we used to.

'I'm sorry,' I repeat. 'Do you want to talk about it?'

She gives me a weak smile and I'm reminded that Cat rarely shows her true feelings. Could she be hiding more than she's letting on?

'I'm fine, really. It's not that. Look, Rachel's already behind with rent, okay? I'm pretty pissed off about it.

We got someone in because we needed it covered. She's working, right? Shouldn't she be good for it?'

'She's only just started this new job. She's . . .' I lower my voice, even though Rachel's gone, '. . . a little short on money at the moment.'

'Yeah, well, I figured that.' Cat rubs her eyes, then looks at me, hard. 'Look, just be careful, M. I'm not saying she's a bad person or anything. It's just . . . maybe we were a little hasty having a stranger move in. Maybe we should have waited until someone we know, a friend of a friend or something, was looking. With what you've been through, we should've been more careful. You don't need any more crazy in your life.'

My mind flashes to Rachel on her knees in the bedroom. The look on her face. The dark marks on her body.

'She's going through some stuff,' I say, surprised by how defensive I sound. 'She confided in me, after Gia said those nasty things about her. Maybe it'll take her some time to get back on her feet, but I think we should give her a chance. I can cover her rent if . . .'

Cat looks at me sharply. 'You're kidding.'

'No. You know I . . . I mean, I *could* if I wanted to. I have the means.'

Cat closes her eyes briefly. 'Mary. That's not your job. You barely know her.'

'I know, but . . .'

'You've done this before . . .' Cat mutters.

'What?'

138

'Look. Don't you think maybe it's time you booked in with Doctor Chang?'

I gape at my friend. Where did that come from?

'Sorry,' Cat mumbles. 'I didn't mean to say it like that. It's just, you know the arrangement. And you know your aunt. She'll be giving me hell if I don't look after you.'

I take a long swallow of wine. 'I've been getting better,' I say and Cat's expression softens.

'I know, M. And I'm proud of you. But . . .'

'I know, I know. It's on my list. I'll do it soon,' I tell her, wondering if I'm telling the truth. The thought of hour-long sessions in those airless rooms makes me feel bone-weary and anxious at the same time. 'I still think we should give Rachel a chance. Come on. You've given me plenty of chances, haven't you?'

Cat sighs. She almost looks sad. 'That's different.'

'Well, Rachel's been through some things too.'

'What things?'

'I . . . I promised I wouldn't say.'

Cat's eyes narrow. She looks primed to argue, then shakes her head and sighs. 'Okay. Fine. Let's give it another month, see how we go.'

Cat finishes her wine and heads off for a shower, leaving me to mull things over. I think of the words I overheard, '*I'm warning you*'. That's going a bit far, isn't it? When Rachel's only a bit behind on rent? She hasn't been with us long; she can only have missed one or two weekly payments.

I think of the dark rings shadowing Cat's eyes. Her untidy hair. Her latest failed relationship. I see Rachel's battered body in my mind again, hear her begging me not to tell the others, *especially Cat*. I think of Mark and Aunty Anne and the shoes in the closet in my room.

I stare at the gathering clouds on the horizon, the swell of the grey sea as it rumbles across the shore. My hand finds the wine bottle, lifts it and pours the remains to the rim of my glass.

Chapter Twenty-One

'Mary, Mary, quite contrary.' His voice is soft, taunting. I'm turning in all directions, searching for the source of the sound, but it's no use. He's everywhere.

'You can't hide from me forever.'

The back of my neck tingles. Invisible fingers trail down my spine.

'Watch your back.'

I wake to blackness. For a second I panic, the remnants of a dream lingering. Where am I? Why is it so dark? Then I remember the blackout blinds; Cat had them installed yesterday. I fumble for my phone and check the time: 10 a.m. The blinds are doing their job.

I'm about to plug my phone in when it vibrates, giving me a start. I eye it warily, but it's just a text from Cat, warning me the shower's broken and I'll have to use the public ones in the common area by the pool.

Great. I don't want to go out, let alone shower in public, but I'm in dire need of a wash. My head aches, I'm clammy and my body is sore in strange places. What was I doing last night? I try to think back but it's blank.

I reach for the lamp and wince in the sudden glare. My mouth is dry, my tongue thick. There's a wine bottle on the floor, a sour stench in the air. Snack-sized packets of crisps are littered around the room. I don't even like crisps. I swing my legs over the edge of the bed and find the carpet wet under my feet.

After tidying the mess, I grab some clean clothes and a towel and creep out of the room. It's eerily quiet, the smell of coffee and perfume lingering in the air as if someone has only just left. I'm glad I'm alone. God only knows what I must look like.

The hot water is heaven on my hyper-sensitive skin. I moan as the water lashes my aching back, my sore limbs. *Three more days*, I tell myself. Three days until I meet with Moore and then . . . well. I can only hope for the best.

When I'm done, I dry myself and head back. As I'm rounding the corner, I walk right into someone.

'*Watch your back.*'

I gasp, looking up into a pair of fierce eyes that, after just a second, soften and crinkle at the corners.

'Oh, it's you.'

'Ben!'

He laughs and I'm filled with relief.

'What did you say? When I . . . bumped into you?'

'What? Oh, uh . . . I said *watch yourself*. Crazy girl,' Ben laughs, but his amusement quickly vanishes. 'You okay there?' He steps closer, I can feel the heat from his body, the warmth of his breath on my face.

'Seems that's all anyone ever asks me,' I say with a nervous laugh. 'I'm fine.'

'Don't look it.' Ben reaches out, his fingers brushing my throat. I feel a sting and he pulls his hand back. 'Sorry.'

I look down and see a graze above my collarbone. Another unexplained injury. Did I fall or something last night? Is that why I ache in strange places?

'How'd that happen?' he asks.

'I don't know.'

Ben gives me a strange look. 'Looks painful.'

I shrug. 'Didn't know it was there 'til now.'

'You should put something on that.'

I tighten my towel around my chest and turn away, embarrassed. 'It'll be fine.'

I feel Ben's eyes on me as I cross the courtyard, the back of my neck tingling. I close my eyes, see the words as if they're scrawled on the back of my eyelids.

Watch your back.

Chapter Twenty-Two

6th December 2016

I can't bear it anymore. I need to take action. He's out there, somewhere. Plotting his next move. Thinking he can still pull my strings and I'll dance for him. All those years spent with my mind and body invaded by him; it feels like a violation, makes me feel dirty. It's like looking back at a different version of myself, as though for a time I was possessed, someone else inhabiting a Mary-shaped lump of flesh. He thinks his threats can frighten me.

Well, I'm done being scared. I'm done being weak.

7th December 2016

This morning my head feels like a bag of rocks and every time I move they clunk around. Last night's bravado has vanished, along with all the water in my body. I feel nauseous, dehydrated. But today I woke with something more than a hangover. I had that sinking feeling I'd done something terrible. A Stupid Thing, as I used to call it. A Mary Thing, as Mark used to say. I have, in a way, but I'm not sure I should regret it.

You see, I looked through my phone again and saw something in that photo of Tom at the party. I've started calling him Tom now, like he's a friend. I'm not sure why. Maybe because this is about him, too. Justice for both of us. And maybe I feel guilty. Because if I'd been brave enough to do something back then, things might not have ended up like this.

Anyway, in that blurry photo of Tom at the party, something caught my eye. There was a symbol on the T-shirt he was wearing. A logo. I couldn't make out the words, but I recognised the shape and colour from the ads on TV: Zak's Mechaniks. There's a store in almost every suburb in Melbourne.

There was a Zak's ten minutes' drive from our Fitzroy apartment. I know because Mark used to frequent it. Not for car stuff, even though he was always writing off one vehicle or another. It was where he did 'business'.

We went there the one and only night Mark consented to meet up with one of my friends. Cat, in fact. He was so worked up by the prospect that I'm pretty sure he was high before we even went out. We sat at that table in the overcrowded pub, Mark and me on one side, Cat facing us on the other. I clung to his arm tightly, as if I could communicate how important this was to me, as if I could somehow stop him from being . . . him.

I couldn't, of course. And it was awful. Cat kept this fake smile plastered on her face, but her eyes kept darting to me. She was worried; I can see that now, but at the time I was angry at her. For being concerned, for not playing along like she was supposed to. For not buying my act, for thinking I could be anything other than happy, like she was. But I kept it up – smiled brightly, laughed at Mark's sexist jokes, bore it when he drank too much and made a pathetic attempt at being charming. It didn't work on Cat, she could see straight through him. I hated her more for that, somehow.

We left early, as we always did – Mark making his excuses, slamming the car door closed on my metal prison. He drove, though he'd had too much. He blew up at me in the car as he swerved in and out of traffic, swearing at other drivers and at me. He wasn't even making sense. He was so angry. I didn't understand why, though I think now that he was stressed. It stressed him, having to be nice to people. Having to talk. Having to pretend to be a good person, I suppose. Pretending to be normal took it out of him.

We pulled up at Zak's Mechaniks at about 10 p.m. I didn't know about his 'business' then – not in the way I do now – and I remember asking why he was bothering when they were obviously closed. He didn't answer, just got out of the car. I asked him what he was doing and he said 'nothing, back in a bit' like always. I don't know why I kept asking, because he was never going to tell me. But later that night, after he stumbled to the toilet to take a long, dribbly piss, I went into the bathroom and found a sachet of white powder on the floor. It must have fallen out of the idiot's pocket while he was peeing. And then I knew what went on at Zak's Mechanics after dark.

But back to last night and the Stupid Thing I did . . . It started out okay; I wasn't too tipsy, just buzzed, feeling confident. So I decided I'd contact Zak's and ask some questions. It was five-thirty-ish, nearly closing time, but I got the manager on the phone and asked about Tom. I didn't think I was drunk, but I must have been further gone than I thought because I can't remember much of what I said except for the Stupid Thing. I pretended to be a cop. Detective Helen White, specifically – who, Google tells me, was one of the detectives on Tom's case. The manager must have bought it because he answered my questions and said he'd already spoken to the cops and didn't know anything else. He knew the victim, he said. Tom was one of his best mechanics. But he'd already told us that, so he didn't understand why we were asking again.

I told him we had a new lead and asked if he knew Mark Jones. He said no, but then I remembered something . . . Mark's 'code name' for when he was doing business. He used an anagram of Mark Jones, one of those generic names that could be anyone. Jon Markes. And when I asked if he knew that name, the manager paused then admitted, yes, he did know him. I panicked and hung up. Stupid, stupid. I should have kept him on the phone while I had him, should have got him to tell me whether Tom was affiliated with 'Jon Markes', but I freaked out.

This morning I realised something terrible. I'd called from my own mobile. And that means the phone call, with my mobile number, will be recorded on Zak's manager's call log. If anyone finds out what I did, I could get arrested. Couldn't I? Isn't it an arrestable offence to impersonate an officer?

★　★　★

I don't know what's happening to me. I'm not thinking clearly or planning things right. I'm imagining things, losing chunks of time, confusing dreams and reality. Sometimes it's like he's still in there, inside my brain, working the controls even from a distance. How did I get here? How did I ever get involved with someone like Mark?

But I know the answer. Oh yes, Doctor Sarah would tell me that it all happened organically. That it's understandable. That it's all cause and effect; I am the product of my past, I was vulnerable, and he took advantage of that.

But sometimes I wonder if I had a certain power in it all. If I am responsible for the way things turned out. We choose our abusers, in many ways. They fill a dark place inside us, finding what already dwells. We feed each other's perverse needs; the prey throws off a scent, the predator sniffs it out. It's basic biology, really. And, in the grand scheme of things, I wonder whether it's only natural.

Oh, our big, complex human brains can explain so many things, but we've never effectively evolved beyond our baser instincts, have we? And there's something seductive about the predator. Humans are seduced by danger, by the thrill, the uncertainty. And I am clearly no different.

Because, let's be honest. While I couldn't predict exactly what would follow, I knew all along what Mark was. Someone divorced from his emotions. Someone full of fear and anger. A narcissist, unable to empathise with others. And I was drawn to him. I ignored every red flag, strode past every warning sign that screamed 'DANGER! TURN BACK!'

So what does that say about me?

Chapter Twenty-Three

The heat is suffocating. Steam rises from the sun-scorched streets, the rain from this afternoon's sun-shower evaporating as quickly as it fell. Summer is in full swing and there's no one less enthusiastic about it than me. Aside from the obvious association with my past, this time of year makes for hellish hangovers.

Sweat clings to my body and I'm itching for a shower, so I jog the last block home, take the stairs and thrust myself through the front door and into the cool air. I moan as it hits my skin.

'Hot out?'

I startle before spotting Ben slouched over the bench in the corner of the kitchen, beer bottle paused halfway to his mouth. His smile is hesitant.

'Oh yeah. Scorcher.' I wipe my brow with the back of

my hand, suddenly conscious of my wet, matted hair and sweat-soaked T-shirt.

'Cat was looking for you.' Ben nods towards Cat's room. His eyes drop to my chest, then quickly dart away.

I fight the urge to smile. 'Thanks.'

'The, uh. The shower . . .' Ben swallows visibly. 'It's playing up again.'

'Great. And with me like this. I thought they fixed it the other day. That shower's *meant* to be brand new.'

'Yeah, it's bullshit. Cat's getting on to the landlord about it.'

There's an awkward silence as Ben pulls on his beer, his eyes on the misty ocean view beyond the balcony doors. I watch his Adam's apple bob in his throat as he swallows. For some reason, I can't look away.

When our eyes meet, the air in the room feels thicker.

'You want one?' Ben holds up his beer, gives it a little shake so the remnants swish around the bottom of the bottle.

'Sure.'

As Ben pops the caps on two fresh beers, relief floods my system. It makes me conscious of the tension in my body, so familiar I scarcely notice it's there. I take the bottle and press it to my lips. I'd have preferred wine, but the ale is cold and refreshing as it slides down my throat.

'I like that,' Ben says, his unusual green-hazel eyes twinkling.

'What?'

Ben inclines his head, his eyes lowering again to my chest.

I look down at my wet T-shirt, my hot-pink sports bra visible through the clinging material. 'Oh. Uh . . .'

Ben makes a choked sound. 'Oh, no. *Shit.* Your necklace . . . What I mean is . . .' There are two pink spots on Ben's cheeks and laughter bubbles up in my chest. It feels good and I find myself grinning.

'It's okay,' I tell him, fingering the silver trinket at my throat. 'I like it, too. It was a gift from my mother.'

Ben looks relieved. 'Does it mean something?'

'It's the symbol for eternity.'

Ben steps forward, his eyes on mine. They seem to hold a question, and his hesitance, the kindness I sense in him, makes me bold.

I trace my finger over the tiny figure of eight and smile up at him.

Ben takes the charm between his thumb and forefinger. 'So it is. Pretty,' he says, holding my gaze.

'Mum was into symbols and stuff. It's meant to represent how long she'll love me,' I say. Embarrassed by this inadvertent confession, I clear my throat. 'Um, it's . . . that's what she said, anyway.'

Ben smiles. He lets the charm fall back against my skin. 'Your mum must be a special lady.'

I nod. 'She was.'

The brief bewilderment that crosses Ben's face is replaced by understanding. I know this expression well.

'I'm so sorry.' Ben's voice is soft.

'Don't be.'

I see pity mingled with something else, curiosity perhaps. Even attraction. I'm like that to some people; an enigma, something to be figured out. The allure of mystery is a dangerous drug, one with which I'm all too familiar. I don't want to encourage him.

'I should go see what Cat wants,' I say.

Ben's eyes clear and he shakes his head. 'Sure. Of course.'

Cat's room is the farthest from the kitchen, the last room at the end of the hall. The air con doesn't make it quite this far down and it's claustrophobically stuffy when I reach her door.

I can hear murmurs from inside, laughter and then silence. The door is ajar, so I push it open to see Cat with her back to me. She stands hunched over her desk, her phone pressed to her ear. Her free hand is splayed across a low stack of papers on the desk.

'Don't worry, she doesn't know. No, I swear. No idea.' Cat laughs. 'Okay, I'll do my best. Yes, I'll be in touch again soon. Okay. Okay. Bye.'

'Who doesn't know what?'

Cat whirls around at the sound of my voice. 'Mary!' Her face is white, like she's had a fright.

I laugh at her expression. 'Yes, only me. What's the matter? You were expecting someone else?'

'God, no. I wasn't expecting anyone. But weren't you

154

ever taught to knock?' Cat laughs, but there's exasperation in her voice.

'Sorry.' I frown. 'Private call?'

When Cat looks at me, her face is pinched in the way it gets when she's stressed.

'What are you doing? Have you been talking to Alex again?'

Cat closes her eyes, shakes her head. 'Oh, no. No, it's nothing like that.' She glances behind her and my eyes follow hers to the papers on her desk.

I get a flash of panic. 'The, uh . . . the benefit payments are still coming in, aren't they?'

Cat wrinkles her brow. 'What? Oh. Yes, of course. No need to worry, M. You know I'd tell you if anything was amiss. But that reminds me . . .'

'What?' Her tone doesn't fill me with confidence.

'Well, they won't be coming in for much longer, unless . . . I'm afraid to ask. Have you made that appointment? I mean, it's been *ages* now, Mary.'

I wince. I know I've been putting off seeing Doctor Chang. I've been rationing my meds, telling myself I can wean myself off and be fine. But it's not just the meds that are a problem now. If I don't keep seeing a shrink, I won't get my benefit money.

'Not yet.' I admit.

Cat clicks her tongue. 'Anne's been getting on to me about it, M. Come on. We had a deal.'

'I know. I'm sorry, and I will make an appointment. Is that who you were talking to?'

'Talking to?'

'Before, when I came in. Were you talking to Aunty Anne?'

Cat's eyes seem to want to look anywhere but at me. 'Aunty Anne. Yes. Yup, I was talking to her. She says to say hi.'

I stare at my friend. Her kohl-lined eyes blink at me as she shows her teeth in a smile. Her long, dark locks, usually styled to perfection, hang over her shoulder in a thick tangle. Something's changed. She's on edge, stressed, and it's not like her.

We've been tight since primary school, Cat and I. And as far as I know, we've always been honest with each other. But if I didn't know better, I'd say she was hiding something from me.

156

Chapter Twenty-Four

I emerge from another groggy sleep, glance at the clock, and groan. 4.06 a.m. The sheets are damp and tangled around my ankles and my hair is stuck to the side of my face. I really don't want to be awake. It feels like I haven't slept at all; I can't remember getting into bed. This is happening a lot. I'm not sleeping well, and when I do manage to drift off – or pass out, as is the case more often than not – I dream. Nightmares. Some I remember, others evaporate when I wake.

I try telling myself it's nearly over and that I just have to hold on until tomorrow's appointment, but it doesn't stop the reel of bad thoughts as they crank along their well-worn tracks.

I'm wide awake now, my fingers twitching in awareness as if I've been woken by something. Or someone.

As I bring my phone to life with the pad of my thumb, the screen glows neon white in the darkness. There's a text from an unknown number.

YOU THOUGHT YOU COULD ESCAPE ME? THINK AGAIN.

Adrenalin prickles over my skin. How did he get my number? It's then that I hear it. A familiar sound, coming from inside the room. The sound of someone breathing.

I use the light from my phone to illuminate what's in front of me, and then scramble for the bedside lamp, blinding myself for a second as it immediately blinks on.

A figure stands in the corner of the room.

I give an involuntary shout, my pulse in my throat. But then I realise who it is. Hovering there, perfectly still, is girl in a white dress. Rachel.

She's not moving. Her eyes are blank, her lips are stretched in a peculiar smile.

'Rachel?'

She seems to glide until she is standing at the end of the bed. My brain catalogues the features of the face before me. It's Rachel, yet she wears a stranger's face.

A different kind of panic edges its way in, at odds with logic. *It's just Rachel*, I tell myself. Yet my brain is transmitting dark memories, and I'm breathing hard and fast.

'Are you . . . okay?'

Rachel raises her arms, places both hands on the bed. She moves as if to mount it, her expression trance-like.

'Rachel,' I'm unconsciously scooting backwards. 'Rachel. Are you . . . awake?'

She cocks her head to the side.

'Come on, Rach. This is . . .'

And then the glass splinters. She's *sleepwalking*. My shoulders sag in relief. That's probably what she was doing when I found her in the kitchen that night. Do I wake her? No. You're not supposed to do that. I should play along, lead her back to bed.

'Can you tuck me in?' Rachel's voice startles me. She's looking at me – through me – with that distant gaze, her head still on one side like a curious dog. My eyes have adjusted now, and I see she's not wearing white at all; she's in a light blue nightgown. Delicate and pale, there's hardly anything of her.

'Of course,' I keep my voice soft. Moving slowly, I crawl forward and slide off the bed. Rachel turns to face me and a waft of sour breath tells me she's been drinking. I don't blame her. Breathing deeply, I take her hand. 'Come with me.'

A stained-glass lamp sits on Rachel's bedside table and the room is bathed in soft light; a mosaic of purple, pink and blue. On one side of the bed is a stuffed rabbit with tattered ears. Empty wine bottles line the perimeter of the dressing table.

'Tuck me in,' she says, her voice soft, child-like.

'Okay.' I hesitate, but Rachel slips between the sheets and curls into the foetal position, her back to me. Her hair, golden in the low light, spills across the pillow. My fingers hover over the sheet before pinching it and drawing it up to her chin. I smooth a hand down her arm. 'Okay?'

She nods without turning her head. 'I won't tell anyone,' she whispers.

I freeze. The silence closes in, thick like smoke, and all I can hear is my throbbing pulse, a faint ringing in my ears.

'Do you love me?' Rachel's voice is small.

Something painful and cruel squeezes inside me. My teeth clench and I hear them grind.

'Yes,' I tell her. 'I love you.'

Rachel sighs, her shoulders relax. She pulls the tattered rabbit to her chest and soon the room is filled with the sound of her rhythmic breaths.

I watch her for a moment. What was going on in her mind just now? Shaking my head, I shut the door and turn to find Ben standing in the hall, his features in shadow apart from his eyes. Cat's behind him, looking sleep-rumbled and concerned.

'Don't panic, only us,' Ben whispers. He has such kind eyes. Fatherly, almost. It makes me want to tell him things.

'Rachel's upset,' I admit, then wonder if it's okay to share that. 'Sleepwalking, I think.'

'We heard,' Cat says in a loud whisper. 'So strange, I've never seen anyone do that before. Is she okay?'

'I . . . I don't know.'

'You're shivering,' Cat says. I can't see her face clearly, but I can tell she's frowning. 'What did she do? Did she upset you?'

'No. A little. But it's not her fault.'

Cat sighs. 'I feel bad for the girl, but you don't need this right now. This is getting too much. You need your rest.'

'I'm okay.'

'Whatever, M. Come here.' She opens her arms, moves toward me, but Ben gets to me first. He tugs me to his chest and I resist for a second, then give in. He's warm and solid and it's nice to be held. He has that smell that every guy has, the thing that makes them smell like men, different to us.

Suddenly, I want to cry. Everything is all wrong, it's too hard. I want someone else to do it for me. I'm tired of carrying this all on my own. Ben seems to sense this, or feels me shaking, I don't know which. His grip tightens and he presses his chin to the top of my head. That does it. A sob escapes and hot tears spill down my cheeks. I allow myself to cry for a moment, enjoying the release.

'It's okay, let it out,' Ben whispers.

I catch Cat's eye over his shoulder, but she turns away. 'I'll leave you two to it,' she mutters before walking away, leaving Ben to hold me in the semi-darkness.

'Night,' Ben murmurs into my hair and I think he's talking to me until I realise he means Cat. He pulls back, runs a thumb over my cheek. 'Okay?'

I don't trust myself to speak, so I nod. We stare at each other for a long, pregnant moment. Ben's thumb hovers near my lips.

'Mary,' he whispers, but doesn't say anything else.

My fingers creep up the back of his neck until they're playing with the soft hairs at the nape. I hadn't meant to touch him, but it feels nice. I trust him.

It's me who makes the first move. I stand on tiptoe to kiss him and I know he won't resist. He makes a sound in the back of his throat; it makes me think he's thought about this before. He's shy at first, nervous to touch me. It's sweet, makes me feel special. Soon his kisses grow urgent and so I lead him into my room and pull back the covers. I'm as surprised as he is.

He grins and it makes me grin back. He climbs in with me, holds my face in his hands. He touches me slowly, reverently, like it means something. His hands are shaking. And when I feel him inside me for the first time, it's like we're erasing something.

Chapter Twenty-Five

Ben is snoring softly when I wake, so I creep from the bed and slip on some clothes before heading out for my walk. My pace is fast; this is no stroll in the park. I've got somewhere to go. Somewhere important.

I take the beach, intending to walk its length before heading across town, a recycled grocery bag slung over my shoulder.

The sea is green today, a lush teal with darker patches where the clouds cast their shadows. The sea breeze makes me shiver, and then I smile to myself, because I'm remembering what happened last night, and I'm getting tingles – down my arms, between my legs. I liked it, feeling special, having control. Perhaps it was another Stupid Thing I'll regret. But I've got too much on my mind to think about that just now.

The seagulls are circling overhead, squawking above a young family eating fish and chips. A cluster of rowdy, soft-drink-swilling teens are in their usual spot by the kiosk. One elbows another and they look at me and grin. I look away, pick up my pace.

The houseboat is still there, its windows like blankly staring eyes. It's a sad little thing, squatting there on the water, rust eating away at it like cancer. I squint, trying to see through the windows, but they're coated with grime. I wonder what's happened to the owners, why their little boat remains bobbing, alone and neglected.

In my peripheral vision, I see a jogger approaching me from the left. I stare ahead, but they seem to be hovering. When I turn, it's a young man, smiling at me. 'Hey,' he says.

I slip a hand in my pocket, closing my fingers around my personal alarm. I don't reply.

'Hey, it's you, isn't it? From the other night?'

I shake my head. 'I don't think so.'

The guy slows down to a walking pace and falls in step beside me. 'Oh. Sorry. I don't mean to bother you, but I thought . . . Weren't you at the beach party down here last week?'

I turn to look at him. He has a square jaw and white teeth. Light eyes – green, I think. A tanned face. A nice face, really. But I know I've never seen him before in my life.

'Sorry,' I say as I pick up speed. 'I think you've got the wrong person.'

There's a pause. 'Right, okay. Sorry, then. Well, have a nice day.' The jogger sprints ahead and disappears into the trees lining the foreshore. It's not until he's out of sight that the sharp pain in my palm registers. I pull my hand from my pocket and it's mottled red and white from gripping the alarm.

Officer Dean gives me a tight smile that doesn't reach her eyes as she presses a button on her desk, leans down and speaks in a low voice. 'Someone here for you, sir.' She waits for the muffled response, then gestures to the hallway leading to Sergeant Moore's office.

'Miss Baker.' Sergeant Moore nods without smiling.

I don't bother taking a seat. 'Mark's threatened me.'

Moore raises his eyebrows.

'He has my phone number. I don't know how he got it, I changed it when I left and he doesn't know any of my friends. He said I couldn't escape him, that he was coming after me.' I show him the text and notice my hand trembling.

'I see,' is all the sergeant says.

'It's him,' I tell him. 'I know it is.'

Moore lifts his gaze to meet mine. 'Has he ever hurt you before?'

I nod.

'Did you report it?'

'No.'

He sighs. 'I want to help you, Miss Baker. But you see,

165

it's hard to prove you're in any danger without a history. No direct threat of harm in this message, either.'

'But he's dangerous!' I say, the volume of my voice surprising me.

Moore places his hands flat on the table. 'Okay, here's what I can do. How about I take down that number and if you receive more threats, I can run a check on the person connected with it. That's the best I can do for you right now, Miss Baker.'

I bite my lip, weigh my options. 'Here.' Without asking, I grab his notepad and a pen and scribble down the number. 'You could run the check now. He has a criminal record.'

'We have no cause to at this stage.'

'But, the murder . . .'

Moore frowns and leans forward in his chair. 'As I've *told* you, Miss Baker, our records show that the Victoria police have already investigated this matter. It's their case, not ours. Now if you receive a direct threat, I'm happy to—'

'I spoke to the mechanics' company Tom worked for,' I interrupt.

'Tom . . .?'

I blush. 'Tom Forrester, the . . . the victim. The manager said he knew Mark, admitted he came there. I bet if we call him again we can get him to tell us that Mark was affiliated with T—'

Moore holds up his hands. 'I'm stopping you there, Miss

Baker. There is nothing in our files or in the statements you have given us to indicate that your ex-partner had anything to do with Tom Forrester's murder.'

'I have evidence,' I blurt. 'I'll show you, then you'll have to believe me.' I reach into my bag and feel for the familiar shape. My heart stops. I open the bag and look inside. My running trainers stare back at me. *No.* I feel the colour drain from my face. 'I swear . . . I swear they were here.'

Moore sighs. 'This isn't some kind of game, Miss Baker. I'd like to ask you to please stop wasting police time.'

Heat rises in my cheeks. I slam my hand on the table and one of the framed photos on the desk falls face down. 'I know it's not a game. Don't you get it? He's killed Tom and now he's after me!'

Sergeant Moore remains perfectly still, but his eyes darken. He presses a button on the desk phone and barks 'Dean? Miss Baker's ready to leave.'

Chapter Twenty-Six

The warmth of the sun on my face and the sound of the ocean lull me into a trance. My limbs feel loose, like they're flesh without bone, and when I close my eyes, I see clouds drifting in a sapphire sky. I'm not sure where I am, and it doesn't seem to matter.

He's singing to me, my favourite nursery rhyme.

'Mary, Mary, quite contrary, how does your garden grow?

With silver bells

and cockle shells

and pretty maids all in a row.'

'Again, Daddy!'

But he doesn't sing again and soon there's another voice, calling my name. It grows more urgent until I can't ignore it any longer. When I sit up, I realise I'm on a boat. A houseboat, the one I pass every day with its grimy windows and battered hull. The warmth of the sun fades and the sky grows dark. Then darker still until it's pitch-black.

I don't know where he comes from, but suddenly he's there. 'Don't fight me,' he commands, forcing me against the wall. My head connects with something hard.

Stars dance behind my eyelids and for a second I'm out of my body. The relief is tidal; I'm dreaming, thank God. Then my nerves register pain, I taste blood and smell sweat. There's another voice; it sounds far away, like someone's yelling under water. 'Sophie! Sophie!' I look around. Darkness. There's no one else here. 'Run, Sophie!'

'Shut up,' he mutters as he forces me backwards and my head slams against the hard thing again. Was it me yelling? Where am I? What's happening?

Pain, sharp and deep. My brain fumbles to accommodate this unknown sensory input, and when it makes room, there is inner silence. As though someone has walked into my mind and systematically switched off each one of my senses.

Now all I can do is wait until he's finished.

I jerk upright, lungs slamming against my ribcage. I heave, cough, press my hands to my chest and will myself to breathe. My room comes into focus and the dream vanishes. I try to remember it, but it's gone.

My phone tells me it's four thirty in the afternoon; I must have fallen asleep when I came back from the station. Ben left a note saying he was going to work for a few hours; I was kind of relieved to be alone. I'm not ready to face the repercussions of another Stupid Thing.

My head's all over the place. How could I have taken the wrong bag? I could have sworn I put my red shoes in the recycled grocery bag and my trainers in the plastic one, not the other way around. But now the plastic bag is empty, and my red shoes are missing.

They weren't in the cupboard or any other of my hiding places. They can't just have vanished and I can't imagine Cat or Rachel would have taken them without asking. And why on earth would anyone have swapped them? It doesn't make sense. I feel like I'm losing my mind. What am I supposed to do without evidence? No one will ever listen to me now!

I throw my legs over the edge of the bed and cradle my face in my hands. I'm breathing too fast, too shallow. My eyes drift to the top drawer of my desk. It's tempting. Way too tempting. I could pop a Diazepam, lie in bed and stare at the ceiling. I could let the bad thoughts shuttle through their neural pathways, clinking and clanking over those well-worn tracks. Until the drug kicks in, and that beautiful numbness takes over. Silencing my thoughts, smoothing away the jagged edges.

But I know I shouldn't. I've already thrown back my daily meds, a low-dose benzo and an antidepressant, with a swig of whisky. I can't keep taking the easy route. It's not just that I need to keep my wits about me – my supply is getting dangerously low, and there's only one refill left. If I don't man up and make an appointment with the psych Doctor Sarah referred me to, I'm going to run out.

Hands shaking, I rummage through the top drawer of my dresser and pull out my tangled skipping rope. Finding my iPod and sticking in the earbuds, I close my eyes, let the music blast through my thoughts. I do a quick hundred rotations, stop, gulp back some water, and do another hundred. My heart is pumping but I've barely broken a sweat. I know this feeling. The flight or fight response; adrenalin with nowhere to go, tightening my muscles, constricting my chest. I could skip forever, run forever, and still feel edgy.

Tossing the rope aside, I find my swimming costume and beach towel and change quickly, focusing on breathing. Throwing a light dress over the top, I tiptoe through the empty apartment, not bothering with shoes, and head out to the common area where the pool is situated.

I hate this part of our building. It's a huge rectangular slab of sandstone tiles in the centre of the apartment complex with twelve startled-looking palm trees jutting up from square, manicured garden beds around its perimeter. I'm guessing the aim was to create a beach atmosphere. It didn't work. The palm trees do nothing to obstruct the view of the surrounding eight-storey apartments, all with windows and balconies inwardly facing the turquoise-tiled pool, which glints and sparkles in the middle of the common area. I feel exposed, as though a thousand eyes are watching me.

I step onto the wooden deck at one end of the pool and glance around before sliding my dress over my hips and stepping out of it. The sun is hot on my back, the deck warm and smooth beneath my feet. There are some guys in a group standing on their balcony and I can hear them murmuring to each other.

Closing my eyes, I breathe deep. *Get over yourself, Mary. If they look, they look. No big deal. This is just an oversized back yard. There's plenty of security. You're safe.*

I shut off my brain and dive into the pool, gliding through the water. Cool water and bubbles zing along my body, awakening my nerve endings. My head breaks the surface and I take a breath, start swimming laps. My hands scoop through the water, legs kick, arms stretch and bend over and over. It's rhythmic, soothing.

By four laps I'm feeling it in my muscles. When did I get so out of practice? I pause at one end, panting. That's good. I'm responding to the exercise; heart pumping, muscles twitching. I'm starting to feel the endorphins. Just a few more laps . . .

A wolf whistle pierces the air. 'Hey sexy!' a male voice shouts, with the hint of a sneer. Or am I imagining that? Another laughs. 'Hey, you. Blondie.'

I start swimming again, shutting them out.

'Hey!' The shout comes again as my head breaks the surface of the water. 'You look lonely down there. Wanna come up here and join us?'

Just ignore them, just ignore them. Swim. Breathe.

'Aw, come on pretty girl. You know you want to. Don't fight it.'

Don't fight it.

A sudden image comes to me – Mark's eyes like flint, and someone else, another face. Tom, eyes closed, covered in blood. I clutch the edge of the pool, chest heaving.

'Come on, Blondie. We're just after a little fun.'

Don't fight it.

Don't fight me.

Who said that?

Whose voice am I hearing?

I squeeze my eyes shut, reach into the deepest corners of my mind, but come back empty-handed. The memory is gone.

Another wolf whistle. Something said about my arse, but I can't quite catch it.

I have to get out of here. I haul myself out of the pool, painfully aware of my exposed body, and scrabble with my towel before wrapping it around my chest. I grab my dress and my keys.

'What are you, deaf?' A different voice this time. Taunting. Superior within the safety of the pack.

Do I respond? Just wave, be nice, move along?

Ignore them. Walk. You can do this.

I force myself to walk across the deck and through the common area, towards the entrance to our apartment wing.

'I think she's ignoring you, man.'

'Piss off. She's not. Come on, Blondie, come join us!'

Reaching the entrance, I wave the swipe over the sensor, yank open the door. It slams against the sound of boos and protests on the other side. I lean against the wall, gasping air into my constricted lungs, tears burning down my cheeks. Why am I crying? What's wrong with me?

Someone enters the corridor and I pull the towel up to my chin, hurry down the hallway. The lift is there for once, so it's only a minute before I'm back in the safety of the apartment.

'G'day, whoever that is!' It's Ben's cheerful voice, coming from the kitchen. He sounds so normal, so *everything's-awesome*, and for a moment I'm paralysed with exquisite envy.

Wiping at my face, I close my eyes and will myself to breathe. *It's okay to feel this way*, I tell myself in Doctor Sarah's words. *Let the feeling be there. Don't fight it. Just let it be there.*

I manage a smile as I reach the kitchen. Ben is leaning against the counter, not even trying to hide the fact that he's drinking milk from the carton. His hand pauses on its way to his mouth. 'Hey.'

'Hey.'

Ben tilts his head to one side. He's unshaven, scruffy-looking, but his eyes are bright and smiling. 'You okay?'

I nod, shrug.

Ben places the milk on the counter and shoves his hands in his jeans pockets. His eyes meet mine and the look he's giving me feels private, like we share a secret. And I suppose we do. 'Been for a swim?'

'Yup.'

'Nice. I, uh . . . I was really late for work today.'

175

He shifts his weight from one foot to the other. 'You must've left pretty early.'

'I had somewhere to be. Sorry.'

'That's fine.' Ben straightens his shoulders. 'So, everything's okay, then? You're, um . . . you're okay?'

I bite back a smile. He has a way of making me feel better, somehow. 'I'm okay.'

Ben nods. 'Good. Good, I'm glad.'

I glance at the clock. After five. There's plenty of wine in the fridge; my attempt at making up for all the bottles I've stolen. Watching Ben's face, his slight, uncertain smile, a thrill moves through me and I have the urge to feel that way again, like I did last night. I could reach out, take his hand. Smile coyly, wait for him to take the hint. I could escape for a while.

But something stops me. Ben deserves better than that. With a feigned grimace, I say, 'Actually, I think I might be getting a headache. Too much booze lately.' It's a weak excuse, pathetic.

Ben looks at me, then turns away as he nods. 'Okay. Probably best to sleep it off, then.'

I shake off the pang of guilt and head to my room.

Later, in the silence, I look at Tom's photo. Tears roll down my cheeks. I undulate my hand so the small, white pills roll back and forth along my palm. Then I throw them back with a swig from the whisky bottle.

Chapter Twenty-Seven

It's a bright and breezy Saturday, and although weekends are meaningless to the unemployed, I can still feel it in the air, the energy of thousands of school kids and nine-to-fivers revelling in their freedom. I envy them. Freedom is a luxury I must fight for.

I'm going to the police again. And I won't be leaving until they agree to track Mark down. It's been a slow start, what would have been a regular hangover amplified by too many downers, and I've thought of putting it off more than once.

But I'm not giving up. I've made progress. I spoke to Officer Dean, the nicer of the two cops I've had contact with, and she promised to look up the number for me, see if it's connected to Mark. I think she felt sorry for me. Which is nice, and I appreciate her trying, but it hasn't helped much. She rang today to tell me the number is connected to a Raj Menkos (another anagram of Mark Jones – he thinks he's *so* clever). It's definitely him. But I have no way to prove it. I'm not sure I even know his real name, the more I think about it.

I've almost mustered the courage to leave the apartment when my phone rings. I freeze, hesitate before picking it up. It's not Mark's – *Raj's* – number, but I recognise it from somewhere. I hesitate before answering. 'Hello?'

'Hi, yeah. It's Bruce Larson here. Is this the detective who rang me the other day?'

I hold my breath. 'Yes, this is she.'

A wheezy laugh comes through the receiver. 'Listen, darlin', I know you're no detective. See, after you hung up on me the other day I got to thinking.' He laughs again. 'The detective that came about the case back then was a bloke. I don't remember any Helen White. I bet I know who you are. You're one of Jonny's girls, aren't ya?'

For a second, I have no idea what he's talking about. And then all I can hear is my pulse in my ears. *Jonny. Jon Markes. Mark's 'business' name.* I clear my throat, but Bruce keeps talking.

'Which one are you, then? You're not Sophie, are ya?'

'Who? No, my name's . . .' I stop. I don't want to tell him my name. 'My name isn't Sophie.'

'Sorry, darl. He's got a few. Don't blame you for chasing him up, he's a dodgy bastard that one.'

I'm stunned into silence.

'Look, kid, I didn't want to say when I thought it was a cop calling, but I should probably warn you . . . your Jon's in hot water more than he's out of it.'

Finding my voice, I mutter, 'That, I do know.'

That earns me a chuckle. 'Listen, you asked if he knew Tom. Well, I can tell you he did. Good bloke, our Tom. Such a rotten thing that happened, all the guys here were pretty cut up. And if Jon had anything to do with it . . .'

'Hang on, you think Mar— er, Jon might have had something to do with Tom's murder?'

The silence that follows feels thick, like cotton wool in my ears.

'Bruce?'

'Now, look,' Bruce has lowered his voice, 'I don't want you repeating this, 'cause if anyone asks, I'll just deny it.'

I breathe in.

'But Jonny, you might already know, did a lot of business around here. You know what I'm talking about?'

'Yes, I do.'

Bruce grunts and I think I hear him spit. 'Well, our Tom was in a bit of trouble himself. He was just a kid. His family was a bit messed up; he grew up dirt poor and all that. So he goes and gets involved with the wrong kind of people, you know how it goes. He owed old Jonny money; that was one thing. And right before it happened, in fact, I reckon it was the night before he was killed . . . I saw 'em fighting.'

I release the breath I'm holding. 'So, do you think . . .'

'I don't know. It doesn't prove much, does it?'

'It gives Jon a motive!'

Bruce exhales loudly. 'Yeah. I didn't really think about it 'til now . . . guess I'd forgotten. But when you called and asked whether Tom knew Jonny, I put two and two together.'

'We have to do something about it!'

'You can try, kid, but I'm not getting involved. Got enough of my own business going on to want the cops sniffing around again. What good will it do, anyhow? Not gonna bring Tom back.'

'Are you serious? Jon's dangerous! What if he does it again?'

Bruce sighs. 'Yeah, that's the thing, isn't it? Problem is, those fancy detectives don't give a shit about kids like Tom. They're after your serial killers, your kiddy fiddlers, that kinda thing. But some kid messed up with drugs who gets himself killed? No one cares. Why d'ya think no one's been caught yet? Seems to me they let the case go cold pretty quickly. Chasing after something juicier now, I reckon.'

Maybe Bruce has a point. The cops were dismissive of my testimony and if Tom was involved in drugs you'd think that would be the first – and most obvious – lead to follow.

'You wouldn't even consider speaking to the police? It might help . . .'

'Nah, love. Like I told you, this conversation never happened.'

'But, I—'

'Sorry, love.'

'There must be something more you can give me! A name, anything!'

A long pause, then Bruce clears his throat and says in a low voice, 'Sophie.'

'I'm sorry?'

'Some girl Jon was seeing at the time.'

My pulse accelerates. 'Are you sure?'

'Pretty sure. The night it happened, well, I delivered some goods to Jonny down the road from the party. There was a girl with him – Sophie, I heard him call her. Don't know her last name. I remember 'cause that's my niece's name. My bet is you find her and she might have some idea what went on that night. If Jonny was involved, that is.'

'She might not have been with him later that night. She could have just been a friend,' I say, but the suggestion feels weak even to me. 'Someone wanting to score drugs . . .?'

Bruce gives a meaty laugh. 'Nah, love. They were a lot more than friends, that's for sure. Sorry.'

I take a long, slow breath. 'Do you know anything else? What time was it? What did she look like?'

I can almost hear him shrug. 'It was about one in the morning, maybe two, I guess.'

So around the time Mark was missing.

'Not sure what she looked like. Didn't get a good look. Small, blonde. Young.'

'How young?'

'She looked like a kid. Fifteen, sixteen? But I'm an old man, so you all look like kids to me.'

My stomach twists. He could almost be describing me a few years ago.

'Thanks,' I say. 'I'll see what I can do.'

'No worries, darl. I hope you catch the bastard.'

Ending the call, I sit down on the bed and stare at the wall with unseeing eyes. There was someone else. And she was with him when he went missing at the party. *Sophie*. Why is the name familiar? Had Mark mentioned her before? Was she a victim, like me? Did she see something that night?

I know now why Mark wasn't on the guest list. He was going by Jon. I should have suspected; he always knew how to cover himself. There was no Mary Baker either, but with Mark's status in that group he could've shown up with anyone and be let in. He could have met up with *Sophie*, sneaked her in later.

All at once it's hard to breathe. My eyes burn with tears. It's a stupid reaction; I know what Mark is, and he's done far worse, and yet . . . a part of me somehow still believed it was different with me. That he chose me because I was special, because I mattered to him. But that was just another lie he told me. He chose me because I was vulnerable. *Weak*, as he always said. I was an easy target.

All the control, the power I thought I had, melts away and is replaced by something else. A surge of anger brings me to my feet. That fucking, *fucking* arsehole. Storming to the closet, I yank open the door and shove my coats and dresses to one side. The overnight bag I brought from my aunty's sits in one corner; I plunge my hands into its depths and rip things out one by one. An old cardigan, books, cards and letters, a creased photograph. I hold up the photo and stare at Mark's leering smile, his cold eyes, his perfectly straight teeth. A hot, fierce thing burns in my chest. I spit on the photo, right on Mark's stupid, smug face.

Then I tear the room apart, searching for the one thing I have that will prove what I saw that night. I have to find those shoes if it's the last thing I do.

I don't know how long I've been at it when there's a knock at the door. I stop, panting, certain I look as wild as I feel.

'Hey, Mary. Can I come in for a sec?'

I drop the armful of crumpled clothes I'm holding as Rachel enters the room wearing a smile that quickly vanishes. 'What's going on?'

I can't answer. Blood is roaring in my ears.

'Oh, Mary, what's happened?' Rachel crosses the room and kneels down on the floor beside me. She looks around. 'Did you lose something?'

I nod dumbly.

Rachel puts a hand on my back and rubs it in small circles. 'Don't worry, you'll find it. I'm always losing things; my friends used to call it "pulling a Rachel"!'

That draws a weak smile from me.

'Probably caused by too much wine, most of the time,' Rachel's lips twist in a self-deprecating smile. 'Do you want me to help you look?'

I find my voice. 'It's okay, thanks. But listen . . . you didn't happen to see a pair of red suede shoes around or maybe . . . borrow them . . .?'

Rachel frowns. 'I wouldn't borrow anything of yours without asking.'

'I know, I didn't mean . . .'

'It's okay.' Rachel's smile is back. 'I didn't take your shoes, Mary. But I'm sure they'll show up. Unless you've moved them, they have to be around somewhere. Are they special or something?'

'Yeah.' That's an understatement.

Rachel holds my gaze and I have that feeling she gives me, like she sees something deeper than I want to show. Up this close, her eyes are an unsettling shade of gold.

'I've been worried about you,' she says in a soft voice as she leans closer. Her hair brushes my cheek and it's like silk. 'You must be going through a lot, and you're always holed up in your room. We need to get you out.'

I shrug and bite my lip.

'I'm serious. That's actually what I wanted to talk to you about. It was so much fun when we hung out before. It meant a lot to me that you opened up . . . you know,' she lowers her voice, 'about your family.'

I nod and Rachel places a hand over mine. When I look up, her expression is deadly serious.

'I'm not going to lie to you, Mary. I know something's going on.'

My heart gives a little kick.

'It's all right.' She strokes my hand. 'But let's not bullshit each other, okay? I mean, what's the point? Life's too short. I believe in honesty, and I want you to know . . . you don't have to hide from me.'

I blink beneath her scrutiny. And, despite the fear, I burn to tell her. Rachel, above everyone else, might understand best.

'I want to be important to you, Mary.' Rachel's still touching my hand. 'I want you to open up. You shouldn't carry it all alone. So whenever you're ready to talk . . .'

My heart's pounding for some inexplicable reason and I'm struck with the urge to throw myself at her feet and sob, let the whole story come spilling out.

'I'd like that,' I say, a tremor in my voice. 'I really would. Thanks, Rachel.'

A flash of something crosses Rachel's face. She looks almost triumphant. 'Well.' She smiles and lets go of my hand. 'I have to head to work, but let's talk soon, okay? You should go for a run or something. That always makes me feel better.'

My gaze slides towards the empty closet, as if I can will the missing shoes to reappear.

'Sure.' I smile. 'That might be a good idea.'

'And don't worry,' Rachel stands and heads for the door. She winks. 'Whatever you've lost will turn up. Things have a habit of showing up when you least expect them.'

Chapter Twenty-Eight

The restless grey sea mirrors the sky as if this morning's brightness has leaked away. My feet slap in time with my heartbeat as I jog the beach; I've been at a brisk pace for ten minutes but I'm still edgy, jumping at every shadow.

My thoughts scratch at the inside of my skull. Who is Sophie? And what has happened to my shoes? Cat wouldn't have borrowed them – her feet are too big. No one else has any reason to. No one knows of their significance but me.

Could Rachel have been lying? Could she have borrowed them and was too embarrassed to admit it? I should go back to the house, take a quick look in her room. I won't go through her things or anything – just a peek won't hurt. After all, this is a matter of life and death.

Something catches my eye, a fluttering in my peripheral vision. I look over my shoulder, but there's nothing but the empty beach, sprawling behind me for miles. I'm seeing things; every change in the light, every ripple on the water is distracting me, making me nervous.

The withdrawal doesn't help – I really overdid it last night. My nerves are scrambled, screaming for me to replace what's been lost. I'll top up the last refill of meds (I swear some are missing, even though I've been so careful to ration them over the past few weeks), stop at the bottle shop on the way home. God knows I have reason enough today.

A group of runners pass and I feel exposed, as if they can read my thoughts, see my panic. *Help*, I think. *Someone help me. Someone fix this.* As I close my hand around my personal alarm, I wonder, will they come, now? If they know it's me, will the cops respond?

I near the houseboat and its sightless eyes stare out at me. There's something different about it, but I can't place what, and suddenly I'm desperate to inspect it. It's low tide, so I kick off my shoes and wade into the shallows until the boat is only a metre away, then half a metre. A pinpoint of light glints off one of the front windows. Only it's not sunlight. It's coming from inside. Stepping closer, I strain to see through the layer of filth. There's movement, a shadow passing. Then a face appears.

'Hey, Mary!'

I shriek and fall backwards, landing on my bum with a splash. Someone's standing above me; I squint up at them as I get to my feet. 'Ben!'

'Steady on!' Ben laughs, taking my hand to help me up. 'We have to stop meeting like this. Still in one piece?'

'Just,' I pant, wrapping my arms around my chest to conceal my clinging, wet T-shirt.

Ben's grin is wide and genuine. He's shirtless and holding a beach towel and I find myself remembering him that night. I hadn't noticed the scar sitting just above the line of his board shorts, like he's had his appendix removed. It all felt so different in the dark, almost like a dream. 'What were you looking at just now?'

'Oh. I thought I saw someone . . .' I look back at the boat's grimy window. There's no light, save for the sunlight glinting off the glass. The only thing looking out at me is my murky reflection. 'But I guess I was imagining things.'

'It's dangerous, isn't it?' Ben says.

I look at him sharply. 'Dangerous?'

'Having an imagination.' He winks.

'Oh.' I laugh, relieved. 'Totally.'

'How've you been doing? I, uh, haven't seen much of you lately.'

I look down at the water. 'I've just had a lot on my mind. There's a lot going on for me at the moment.'

Ben nods. 'Yeah, I kind of got that feeling. Look, I know I'm a guy and everything, and therefore grossly under-qualified to give good advice when it comes to, you know . . . emotional stuff . . .'

I give a weak smile and Ben clears his throat.

'But I'm a good listener. So if there's anything you want to talk about . . .'

Standing there in the water, looking into Ben's warm, open face, I consider telling him the truth. I want it with an intensity I could never have anticipated. *Take this from me*, I want to say. *Make it go away.*

'Ben . . .'

'It's okay,' Ben whispers with a grin. 'I won't judge.'

Looking in his eyes, the words are there; I can hear myself speak them. I tear my gaze from his. 'I'm sorry. I just . . . I can't. Not yet.'

Disappointment flashes in Ben's eyes. 'I understand.'

'Ben, I . . .' Without thinking, I take his hand. I want to bring back the warmth in his eyes, that look that feels like it's just for me. 'It's not that I don't want to . . . It's complicated. I don't want . . . I don't want you to get hurt.' Goosebumps rise on my flesh as I speak those words. What if Mark were to find out about us? What would he do to Ben?

'Mary?'

'Yeah?'

Ben takes a breath and smiles. 'I get that things are complicated. I do. Hey, life's complicated. But I really like you, you know. A lot, actually.'

Warmth stirs in my chest and spreads. 'I like you, too.'

We stare at each other until a breeze picks up and I shiver in my wet clothes.

'I guess you'll want to head back and change, then.'

'I'd better, I guess.'

'I'll walk you. Here.' Ben moves towards me and at first I think he's going to hug me. Instead, he drapes his towel around my shoulders. It's a bit damp yet warm from the sun and I feel warm inside, too.

'Thanks,' I smile, tugging the material around me.

As we walk back the way I came, the warmth inside me fades and I get a little shiver – unpleasant, like adrenalin. I look over my shoulder at the boat and think of ghosts and ghouls, then shake my head at my stupidity. Because it's not someone dead I should be afraid of.

We walk in silence, and as Ben slips his hand in mine, the back of my neck prickles. I can't shake the feeling we're being watched.

Chapter Twenty-Nine

I wake with the sense I'm not alone. Floating in between sleep and consciousness, I hear a rhythmic sound, like a drumbeat. Or footsteps.

I jerk upright and fumble for the lamp. Light sears my corneas and I blink back spots until I can see. The room is empty. No one here but me. And then I hear a creak from outside and a shadow moves beyond the balcony doors.

I suck in a breath. A silhouette is backlit by the balcony light. Someone's out there. Heart thudding, I reach for the baseball bat I keep stashed under my bed. As my fingers close around it, the sliding door judders and creaks open.

I hold my breath. The curtains move to one side and a figure steps through.

'Jesus!' My breath rushes out and the bat slips from my fingers. 'You scared the shit out of me.'

Rachel stands in the doorway, her shoulders slumped, face slack. Her dead eyes are engulfed by pupils. I can hear her ragged breaths, synchronised with mine, like an amplified pulse.

'I hate you.' Her voice is soft, deadly calm.

'W . . . what?' I try to breathe, to calm down, but the look on Rachel's face is chilling.

'I. Hate. You.'

I get to my feet. 'Rach, you're asleep. We need to get you back to bed. I'll—'

'Fuck you!' The shrill exclamation pierces the air and Rachel lunges. Her eyes are like black holes, her hair a lion's mane. She runs forward and grabs me by the throat. She squeezes. Hard.

Arms flying out, my hands scrabble for grip. Her fingers press deeper and my ears fill with the sound of roaring blood. Finding her shoulders, I shove at her, and she's so slight she jerks backwards, her head snapping back.

There's a moment when her grip loosens and I scrabble backwards, arms jutting forward as she recovers and lunges again.

'Rachel, stop! STOP!' I grab her before her hands can reach me and throw her onto her back. There's a tangle of arms and legs and then I have hold of her wrists, and I pin them above her head.

'I'll kill you,' she's sobbing. 'You bastard. I hate you, I *hate* you.'

Understanding comes like a shower of ice water.

194

'Oh, God. Shh, shh. It's me. Mary. Shhh.'

The sobbing rises in pitch and her breathing stutters.

'Shh. It's okay, you're okay.'

Her face is to one side, her eyes squeezed shut, and she's trembling. Her limbs have loosened and I lower her arms to her sides. All of a sudden she's limp, as if she's left her body.

My throat tightens. I recognise that response. It's a victim thing; once you realise there's nothing left you can do, your psyche steps in to spare you the worst of the pain. You switch off, try to leave your body. Until it's over.

'I'm not going to hurt you,' I'm saying. 'It's okay, Rachel. It's okay.'

Rachel's breathing evens out, her chest rising and falling. I push her hair back from her clammy forehead, stroke her head until I'm certain she's asleep.

As the first rays of sun creep through the curtains, I prop myself on one elbow and look down at Rachel's small, still body. My eyes feel like they're full of dirt; they ache to close, but I know that if sleep wouldn't come last night, it isn't coming now.

As Rachel wakes, she turns her head to face me, a hesitant smile on her lips. Morning light makes her skin gleam gold. She's so pretty that I get a pang of jealousy in my stomach.

'I came in here last night, didn't I?'

I nod. Her hand twitches at her side and I reach over to clasp it. It's cold, as always.

'I didn't mean . . . I don't know how . . .'

'I know.' Something burns inside me, a fierce, protective thing.

'I do that sometimes,' she says vaguely, staring into the middle distance. Sunlight illuminates the tips of her eyelashes. 'Did I say anything? Like, anything weird?'

I squeeze her hand, feel her fine-boned fingers pressing against my palm. 'No, nothing that bad.'

Our eyes lock and hold and there it is again, that feeling of exposure. Even though it's her who's been exposed.

Rachel's face darkens. 'I'm really sorry, Mary.'

'It's okay,' I tell her, meaning it. 'I understand.'

Rachel sits up suddenly. 'What's the time?'

'Er . . . six-ish?'

'Shit! I have to be at work by seven.' Rachel scrambles from the floor. 'Sorry. I'll see you later?'

'I'll be here.'

Rachel crosses the room and reaches for the door handle. She hesitates before looking back over her shoulder. 'Mary?'

'Yeah?'

Rachel's weary smile makes her looks older, somehow. 'Thanks.'

Chapter Thirty

It's pitch-black outside. The sea is barely visible beneath the cloud-covered moon, its dark, slick surface pinpricked only here and there with starlight. Even the handful of dim, amber lights that mark the few houses across the water have blinked out, one by one.

Sleep wouldn't come, so I'm sitting on the balcony at 2.36 a.m., listening to the silence. My tongue and head are thick from too much wine; the beginning of a headache blooms behind my eyes.

I rest my head against the wall, my ear pressed to the narrow space between the sliding glass doors that lead to my room and the ones that open into the living area. A safe space, where no one can sneak up behind me.

My mind keeps flitting to the shoes. I can see them so

clearly, I could reach out and grab them. But I can't, because they're gone, and I don't understand it.

I'm tired. I can't think tonight, don't have the energy. I just want to drink. Be drunk. Forget.

I glug the remains of the wine from my glass, shake my head. Even my thoughts have stopped making sense now. Time for bed, Mary.

I stand on wobbly legs and make for the door. Steadying myself on the back of the chair, I wince as the chair legs scrape along the deck. But the sound I hear isn't the sound of the chair scraping. It's a floorboard creaking. Inside.

I freeze, waiting for the sound to come again. It's hard to hear over the roar of my pulse, but then I hear it: the distinct sound of footsteps.

It's just one of the guys, I tell myself, but my stomach flip-flops. I suck in a breath, step towards the living room door. The movement triggers the sensor light. For a second I'm blinded, then all I can see is my own startled reflection staring back at me.

Footsteps again, closer now. Whoever's in there must be able to see me. Panic fires through me. I blink away the spots behind my eyes as the light disappears. It's too dark to see; there are no lights on inside. Who's in there walking around in the dark?

I'm stone-cold sober now. I peer through the glass. Nothing. I sidestep and look through the glass door connecting my room to the balcony. The curtains are drawn so I can't see in. I try the handle but it's locked.

Wait. Locked? I stop and think. I came outside through this door. It can't be locked.

From behind the door, a floorboard creaks. My blood runs cold. The squeaky floorboard, between the bedroom door and the vanity dresser. Someone's in my room.

My mind flashes to a pair of ice-cold eyes and my throat tightens.

Run. Now.

I go back to the living room entry, inch the heavy sliding door open with my breath held. My eyes adjust to the dark and I can make out my bedroom door – *closed* – to the right, the front door at the end of the hallway ahead, light shining around its edges. I mentally calculate how long it will take to run there.

When the gap is wide enough, I slip through the doorway and into the apartment. Just as my feet hit the carpet, my bedroom door creaks open.

I freeze, staring at the slowly opening door. It seems to take an age. *There's still time to run!* – but I can't move. It's like everything has been leading to this moment, and there's some relief in the finality of meeting my fate.

As if in a dream, I watch as a figure steps out and, in slow motion, turns to face me. It's him.

Wait.

No.

The hair is wrong – too long. The outline broader, shorter.

Air gushes from my lungs and I almost laugh.

'Ben.'

'Mary? What are you doing here?'

'What am *I* doing here?'

'Sorry?' Ben looks confused.

'You were in my room.' The wind picks up, causing a faint howl to pass through the nearby trees. I slide the door shut, wrap my arms around my chest.

Ben shakes his head. I can't see his face clearly, but I see him clench and unclench his hands. 'I'm sorry, I thought you were out.'

'Oh, and *that* makes it okay.'

There's a pause. 'You're angry.'

'Yes!'

Ben laughs. I can tell from the slight slur in his words that he's drunk. 'Oh shit. It's not what you think! I'm so sorry, Mary. I came home from the pub and I couldn't see you anywhere. I thought you were out, so I went in to make sure your door was locked.'

'You scared me.'

'Oh fuck. I'm so sorry. I know it's stupid to be paranoid, but I can't help it, after . . .' I wait, but he doesn't finish his sentence. I'd never thought of Ben as the paranoid type before. How much has he had to drink?

'I don't think there's much to worry about from out there.' *Believe me, I've thought about it.* 'We're on the fifth floor.'

'Yeah.'

'Are you really worried about someone getting in?'

Ben shrugs. 'It's dumb, I know.'

There's silence for several beats.

'It's not dumb.'

Ben takes my hand and the sudden heat spreads down my arm. His hands are surprisingly rough. 'Listen, can we talk for a minute?'

The adrenalin from earlier is gone, and in its place is the comfort I find myself feeling in Ben's presence.

'Okay.'

I let him lead me into my own room, and just as I'm about to close the door, I see Rachel's bedroom door click shut.

Ben stumbles along in the dark. There's a bump and he swears, then the bedside lamp comes on with a *plink*. The room is bathed in a soft, warm glow. Mum's old brass lamp with pastel-pink-coloured panels liked stained glass; a perpetual reminder of my childhood.

Ben's rubbing his shin. 'That's better. It's bloody dark tonight. Almost got lost on the way home.'

I smile. Then I see where he's looking – the empty wine glass on the vanity, the collection of bottles in the waste-paper bin. His gaze travels to the half empty Pinot Grigio by the bed.

There's a pregnant silence, which Ben breaks in a cheerful voice. 'Mind if I have some?'

My cheeks feel hot. 'Sure. Uh, I'll get a clean glass.'

'No need.' Ben picks up the wine glass and an empty mug and sloshes wine into both. He hands the glass to me and grins, but his eyes are serious. 'Cheers.'

201

'Cheers.'

We sit awkwardly on the bed, elbows bumping. I feel an intense surge of gratitude towards him for his silence, his lack of judgement.

'I might understand better than you think,' he says in a soft voice. He's lost the slur. 'And I want to explain . . . about being in here before. I don't want you to think I'm some creep. The door locking, it's . . . it's become a bit of a compulsive thing.'

'Okay . . .'

Ben cradles the mug in his hands. 'We had a break-in, at my old place. I was sharing with a mate just outside the city – not the best area. It was pretty dodgy really. But it was close to uni and it was all we could afford. Some crackhead broke in one night and robbed us while we were sleeping. I woke up and caught him. My instinct was to try to stop him, wrestle him to the ground. It didn't work out so well. The guy wasn't right in the head. He had a knife.'

He takes a gulp from the mug and places it on the bedside table. Then he lifts his T-shirt up to the ribs, revealing a deeply tanned torso. His skin is peeling where he's been sunburned. There's a darker patch of skin, maybe a couple of inches long, just above his boxers. The scar I'd noticed at the beach. It's a moment before I realise what I'm looking at.

My breath quickens. 'Oh Ben.'

He pulls his shirt back down. 'That's why I'm here. I was looking for somewhere . . . safe.'

'Yeah. I get that.' The words rush out of me and Ben nods. 'And uh, the security system. That's a plus.'

'Sure is. And look . . . I haven't . . . I mean, I joke about it when I've had enough to drink, but it wasn't . . . I didn't cope that well. After, I mean. PTSD, I guess. It's normal.'

'It's totally normal. It would be weird if you . . . *didn't* react. To something like that, I mean. It's pretty . . . intense.'

His eyes meet mine at last. They crinkle at the corners. 'Yeah. Thanks.' His hand covers mine. 'I get it, Mary. I recognise the signs. I don't know what's gone on, exactly. I can guess. But if you ever want to talk . . .'

A lump forms in my throat and I fight the sudden urge to burst into tears. 'Thanks. You're quite nice, you know.'

Ben's teeth gleam in the low light as he smiles. I like his smile. 'You're quite nice, too.'

We look at each other in silence for a minute. Then his expression turns sheepish. 'We share a wall,' he says.

'Huh?'

He ducks his head. 'Sometimes you, uh . . . talk in your sleep.'

My spine stiffens.

'Don't worry . . .' He squeezes my hand. 'I'm not eaves-dropping or anything. But sometimes . . . Look. Whoever he was. Or *is*. You deserve better.'

For second I forget to breathe.

'Was,' I clarify. 'Definitely *was*.'

It's embarrassing to imagine what he might have heard. And I can't help but wonder if he's doing that guy thing, swooping in when I'm vulnerable. Playing the hero. He doesn't seem the type, but I've been wrong about that kind of thing before. And isn't he technically seeing someone else? We've slept together. Not exactly a hero move.

I don't say anything else and he doesn't prod further. After a moment, he says gently, 'You haven't touched your wine.'

I blink, shake my head, and take a long pull from my glass. I wait for a moment before I speak. 'And what about you?'

Ben cocks an eyebrow.

'Gia,' I say, before I can lose my nerve. 'Is she . . .?'

'What? Oh! No. No, like I said, we're just friends.'

It's my turn to raise an eyebrow.

Ben laughs. 'Honest! I know Cat loves to give me shit, but I haven't led Gia on. Really. I've told her I don't think about her that way. She just doesn't seem to believe it. Either that, or she's actually happy being just friends.'

I nod, realising I've believed that all along. 'Yeah. Someone's got to set her straight though – tell her that being "just friends" isn't going to lead to anything more.'

'Don't I know it.' He shakes his head. His next words are softer. 'Was he bad to you?'

The lump in my throat returns. But I owe him this, at least. 'The worst.'

'You deserve better,' he repeats. It's all he says, but it's enough. Our eyes hold. He seems to be waiting for something. Then he surprises me by kissing me on the forehead. 'Goodnight, Mary.'

A rush of disappointment fills me. 'Couldn't you . . . stay?'

Ben's looking at me like he wants an explanation. And I know I owe it to him, but I'm too unsure of everything. I can't make promises and so I don't.

The moment passes and Ben looks away, clears his throat. He shakes the bottle and pours the remains into our cups. 'Something, uh, something strange happened earlier.'

'Oh?' I take a sip, grateful for the change of topic, and the fact that he hasn't left yet.

'Cat and Rachel were fighting.'

'What?'

'Well, that's what I thought. I've seen them fighting before.'

I sit up straight. 'You have?'

'Sure, yeah. Not *fighting* exactly. Just Cat getting up her about the rent and stuff. Rachel was pretty angry though, so I wonder if something else was going on. I heard your name . . .' Ben stops and looks sheepish, like he's said too much. 'But I wouldn't worry. It's kind of flattering, really. Like they're in competition as to who can be a better friend to you or something.'

'Pfft. I doubt that's what it is,' I say, but suddenly I'm not so sure.

'Anyway, that wasn't the weird thing,' Ben continues. 'Earlier, I could have sworn I heard Cat and Rachel in

Rachel's room – Cat's got a distinctive voice, right? – and there was this conversation going on . . . someone was shouting, saying *stay away from her* . . .' He pauses, rubs a finger along his upper lip. 'Well, I think that's what they said, anyway.'

'What else did you hear?'

Ben shrugs. 'I couldn't make out what they were saying and I didn't want to eavesdrop. But then I heard a glass breaking, so I went to see what the trouble was. I knocked on the door but there was no answer, and when I opened it, Rachel was just sitting on her bed, staring at . . . I don't know. Nothing. She had this really weird look on her face. Like she wasn't really . . . there.'

A shiver moves through me. I've seen that look before.

'What did Cat say?'

Ben turns to me, his eyes reflecting the lamp light. 'That's the thing. There was no one else there. Rachel was alone.'

CRASH!

I sit upright in bed with my heart in my throat.

BANG! *Screeeeech*. THUNK!

It's pitch-black, so I make a manic grab for my phone, stabbing at it until it emits its pale white glow.

'Please!' a voice wails, shrill and desperate. 'Please don't go. No, please!'

A thud.

'. . . Shouldn't have come back here . . .'

The sound of something being dragged across the floor.

'. . . Not after last time . . .'

Thunk!

I swallow the fear that's risen, try to slow my breathing. It's just the couple upstairs.

'. . . Didn't mean to . . .' It's the woman's voice, muffled now. They must be inside. '. . . Never happen again . . . Please. *Please!*'

The sobbing starts; it's so pitiful, I can't help but feel sorry for her.

Ben snores on in the bed beside me, oblivious. Once I've calmed down, I reach for the bottle of water I keep by the bed and realise I've knocked it off. Fuck. The floor will be wet now. And I'm dying of thirst. I step gingerly onto the floor – a dry patch, mercifully – and tiptoe across the room by the light of my phone.

The cool air in the living room is refreshing after the stuffiness of my room and Ben's clammy skin on mine. I'm almost to the kitchen when I realise some-one's there.

'Cat?'

Silence. Even the noise from upstairs has stopped.

Then the sobbing starts up again and I unconsciously step backwards.

I reach for the hall light. It flickers on and I blink, wondering if I'm seeing right. Cat and Rachel stand in the kitchen, both heads turned in my direction. Both sets of eyes on me.

My relief morphs to confusion. Something isn't right. 'What are you two doing here in the dark?'

Cat looks down, but Rachel's eyes remain on me.

There's another thud and a wail from above.

'Those guys upstairs,' Rachel says. There's a strange cadence to her voice. She sounds almost formal. 'We both got woken up.' She runs a hand through her fine hair and I watch as the feather-light tendrils fall against her cheek.

Cat drags a palm across her mouth, shakes her head. She looks rattled.

'Are you okay?' I ask. I'm not used to seeing Cat flustered.

Her eyes dart towards me. She flashes an unconvincing smile, snatches a glass from the countertop and fills it at the sink. 'Of course.'

There's the sound of a door slamming from above, then silence. He's left.

'Finally,' I say with a nervous laugh.

Nobody says anything.

The moment for asking questions seems to have passed, and in its place is an awkward silence. To break it, I say, 'It's her, did you know? Not him.' I grab a new bottle of water from the fridge and drink greedily.

'I know,' Rachel says, looking skywards. The shadow of the ceiling fan falls across her face. 'Fucked-up bitch.'

A string of tension pulls inside me. I glance at Cat, but she's looking past me. I turn and follow her line of vision.

Ben is standing in the doorway of my bedroom, bleary-eyed and rubbing the back of his neck.

'What's going on out here?' he asks.

I'm hot with embarrassment when I turn back to the others.

'Nothing,' Rachel says. 'Just came for some water.'

'All of you?' Ben rubs his eyes, looking from me to Rachel to Cat. I don't know if he's forgotten it's my room he's just come out of, or whether he doesn't care.

Rachel watches Ben, her face giving nothing away. Then a strange smile creeps along her lips.

When I look at Cat, her face is naked in a way I've never seen before and she's not quick enough to cover it. For a second, she looks like she just lost her best friend.

Chapter Thirty-One

It's eight in the morning and though my head pounds and my body aches, it's too hot to sleep. Ben's gone — he's left me a cute little note on a scrap of paper next to the bed saying 'Morning, Sunshine!' with a smiley face and two kisses — but I don't know where. Work, presumably.

I peel the sheets from my body and spend twenty minutes in the shower, alternating the temperature between hot and cold to try and wake myself up. When I'm done, I dry myself and pull on my running gear. I'm awake and it's too early to drink — I have to stay sane somehow.

It's hot already. The smell of freshly brewed coffee from the beachside vendor fills the air and the morning sunlight glints off the sunglasses of morning joggers as they pass me. The air is muggy and the sun has that vicious glare to it that promises a scorcher ahead.

I close my hand around the alarm in my pocket, my heartbeat in my ears as my feet pound deep prints into the wet sand. The tide is headed out, leaving an expanse of shiny-slick sand in its wake, and I avoid looking at the houseboat as it nears, instead following the tracks of a family of three and a large dog. My mind snares on an image of Mum laughing with Rufus in the water one summer. My chest tightens and when I open my eyes I see a cabin, far across the water. And I'm struck with a sudden feeling of familiarity.

After two laps, the heat is too much and I head home. As I round the corner of our building, I spot two familiar figures at the table outside the trendy brunch bar that recently opened on our street. I slow my pace, watching as Cat shakes her head, lifts her hands as if in supplication. Or exasperation. She's seated with her back to me, but I see Ben's face over her shoulder and he looks like a scolded child. He speaks and I'm sure I can lip-read the word 'sorry'. Then he sees me and his eyes widen. He taps Cat on the arm and she turns. I don't miss the pause before she smiles.

'Hey,' she says as I near their table. I'm dripping sweat and must look a sight.

'Hi.'

Ben smiles at me, but I can tell he's uncomfortable. What were they talking about? Why are they having breakfast together and I didn't get an invite?

Cat glances at Ben, then back at me. 'We thought we'd try out this new place.'

'I've actually got to head to work,' Ben says. His smile is more of a grimace. 'Sorry.'

'Okay. Uh, have a good day.'

'You too.' As Ben passes me his eyes catch mine with that private look and suddenly I'm biting back a smile.

'Have a seat.' Cat gestures to the chair Ben vacated.

'I'm all sweaty, I might just—'

'*Sit*,' Cat insists, and I know better than to ignore that tone.

I do as I'm told, and when I look up, Cat's eyes are narrowed, her nose wrinkled like something smells bad. I glance down; the hands cradling her coffee cup are trembling. How many has she had?

'So, you and Ben, huh?' she starts.

A small, startled sound escapes my throat. I'm unable to think of anything to say. But the fact that she's upset about the two of us – I get that old feeling of guilt, and I wonder if it's because Cat likes Ben. But that doesn't make sense. She knew him before I did. And she gives him shit about Gia all the time. Surely, she'd have done something, said something to me earlier if she liked him that way?

Cat laughs, but it's more of a snort. She gulps back a mouthful of coffee, sets down her cup. 'Do you really think that's a good idea?'

'Nothing's . . . happened.'

'Bullshit.'

Her sharp tone takes me by surprise. What's it to her anyway? 'We were talking and I . . . I asked him to stay.'

Cat shovels a forkful of scrambled egg into her mouth and doesn't say anything.

'Nothing happened,' I repeat. 'We just slept in the same bed.' Okay, so something more than that *did* happen the other night. Why am I lying by omission? And to Cat of all people?

Cat stabs a piece of bacon with her fork. She lifts it halfway to her mouth and then sighs. 'Don't you think it's too soon?'

My head's pounding again. I pick up Ben's empty glass, pour some iced water from the jug and slug it back.

'Besides, I didn't think he'd be your type,' she mutters as she rips open two packets of sugar and stirs them aggressively into her coffee.

My glass hits the table with an audible *chink*. 'Excuse me?'

Cat points her fork at me and grease drips from the strip of bacon. The sight makes my stomach turn. 'Well, what would Doctor Sarah say?'

That throws me, but only for a second. My chest swells with indignation. 'She'd say it's a good thing I'm moving on with my life,' I say, and it's the truth. Okay, it mightn't be the smartest move getting involved with someone right now. If you can call whatever's between me and Ben 'involved'. Maybe it's just a rebound thing. Maybe it won't last. But at least I'm moving forward instead of standing still. And maybe I'm a little sick of being lectured, even if it's 'for my own good'.

214

'Well,' Cat sniffs. She seems suddenly more interested in her breakfast than in me. When she speaks again, her voice is unusually high. 'You know I'm just concerned about your well-being, Mary. You know you haven't always – and don't hate me for being harsh here – but you haven't always made the best choices. And speaking of, did you hear Rachel last night?'

'*No*,' I snap. Then I remember what Ben said about the 'fight' he overheard. And the weird moment I interrupted in the kitchen last night. 'Is *that* what you two were talking about last night?'

Cat shakes her head, seems not to hear me. 'We've got to find someone else for the room. I like her and all, but with the rent and all this weird shit . . . and you two getting close . . .'

My indignation swells, feels righteous. 'So, hang on. You're concerned about my well-being but you don't want me making new friends? Or seeing anyone?'

Cat looks hurt. 'I honestly feel like I can't win here. I'm playing the role of your aunt because she's not here to protect you, and I'm the only person that knows the real you. Your past. Yet it's costing me our friendship. After everything we've been through . . . Please can you just trust me about Rachel, M?'

'What is it about her exactly? What is it with you two? I like her. She's been through a lot, and yeah, she's got some problems. But is that a reason to just chuck someone out?'

'Mary—'

'Ben said he heard you two fighting. And you looked . . . I don't know. You looked weird when I found you in the kitchen last night. What was that about?'

Cat gets this look like she's been caught out and I feel a stab of something in my gut. Something that feels suspiciously like betrayal.

'Are you warning her against being friends with me?'

Cat's eyes widen. 'No! I . . .'

Something Rachel said echoes in my memory. *She acts like she owns you.* Has Rachel been on to something all along? 'Is it really because you're worried about me? Or are you just jealous?' The harsh word echoes in my ears and I can't believe I've just said it.

'Mary.' Cat shakes her head slowly. 'You've got it wrong.'

'Then tell me what you've been fighting about.'

Cat's eyes plead with me, but she doesn't say anything.

I have this horrible feeling that I'm at a crossroads and I can only go one way. One way I choose Cat, the other I choose Rachel.

'And what were you talking to Ben about?'

More silence.

'Cat?'

When Cat's eyes raise to meet mine, she looks defeated. I notice once more the dark circles under her eyes, the strip of blonde regrowth down the parting in her hair. 'I told him you'd just come out of something and weren't ready for this. I told him he should stay away from you.'

I feel like I've been punched. 'You had no right to do that,' I say. My voice is soft, but inside I'm seething. I stand up suddenly, knocking over the glass of water. It spills and dribbles over the edge of the table as I walk off.

'Mary!' Cat calls after me.

I don't stop walking, but when I look over my shoulder, Cat wears a haunted expression.

'For what it's worth – he didn't listen.'

Chapter Thirty-Two

11th December 2016

I spent another restless night tossing and turning, sleep evading me until the early hours. I couldn't stop replaying the conversation I had with Cat earlier in the day, growing more angry at her and then more frustrated with myself as that anger whirred through my mind and body, stopping me from sleeping. I even started to work myself up and question whether she was right about it all. But then I focused on Ben, on the fact that he obviously stuck up for me. It calmed me, knowing that he's on my side.

When I eventually dropped off to sleep, it felt like just minutes before I was awoken by footsteps — Rachel was sleepwalking again . . .

It was bad this time. She really scared me. It was like she was possessed or something, though I know it wasn't really her. I could see by the way she looked through me, rather than at me. Like she was seeing something that wasn't actually there.

I've heard about that kind of thing. Doctor Sarah talked about disassociation, once or twice. People who've been through serious trauma of some kind or another – usually some kind of abuse over a long period of time – disassociate themselves from the person it happened to, taking on a different personality.

I don't know, though. With Rachel it's like the other way around. In everyday life she's this carefree, confident girl – or at least, that's what I thought when I first met her – but when she's asleep, unprotected by her conscious mind . . . it's like she's still the little girl all those bad things happened to. In her head, something is happening and she's reacting to it. Reliving the pain over and over.

Mark used to tell me I talked in my sleep. I'd shout things, but they never made any sense, it was all just gibberish. I don't know if he was telling the truth because I could never remember anything. Although there was one time I do recall, during a sleepover when I was about ten. I woke up to find the other girls huddled together, whispering. When I asked what they were doing, they giggled and said I was crying in my sleep, talking to my 'daddy'. I was so embarrassed I never slept over at Caitlin Stevens' house again.

Rachel said she never remembers anything after she's been sleepwalking. So I wondered whether she could be the one who took the shoes – mistakenly, of course – while having an episode. Who knows what goes through her head when she's like that?

But I checked her room and zilch. Nada. They're definitely not in there, unless there's a secret trapdoor hidden somewhere.

The most likely scenario is that I've simply misplaced them. The nights when I'll wake up at two a.m., still wearing my clothes and my shoes, face down in the middle of my bed with no memory of how I got there. Yeah – it's possible I've done something while dead drunk. I'm the one who knew exactly where they were, anyway. Who else would make a beeline for the shoes, touching nothing else? Whoever took them knew where to find them. But if it was me who moved them, why aren't they anywhere in my room?

Without those shoes, I have nothing. No evidence, no proof, no names . . . except for one.

My only other lead in connecting Mark to what happened That Night is this Sophie girl that Mark was supposedly involved with, but what am I supposed to do without her last name? If I were still living with Mark, I could go through his phone, look for a contact with that name. I temporarily unblocked him on Facebook and searched through his friends list (he only has a few, he's never on there – too good at covering his tracks) but no joy.

All I know, if Bruce is telling the truth, is that this girl is – or was – involved with Mark. She's young, blonde, and she was there with Mark that night at the party around the time he went missing. Therefore, it's likely she saw something.

I'm running out of time, my only piece of evidence is missing, and I have no leads.

Sophie.

Sophie.
Sophie.
Sophie.
Run, Sophie.

I'm interrupted by a knock at the door, but the sound fades behind the whooshing in my ears.

'Run, Sophie!'

Images flash in the forefront of my mind: Mark's face, twisted with rage. A crumpled body, face down on the ground. Looking down at my stomach. Blood.

'Don't fight me,' a man's voice − Mark? − hands on my body. Pain.

'Run, Sophie!' A girl, her voice high-pitched, hysterical.

Another knock at the door startles me from my trance.

'Mary! Are you in there?' The door opens and Ben steps through, his face drawn and pale.

'What is it?' I say, my heart pounding.

Ben's eyes are haunted. 'It's Rachel. There's been an accident.'

Chapter Thirty-Three

The sky erupts the second we get out of the car and we run across the car park, shielding our faces. Ben and I are soaked by the time we reach the front desk where a stout, solemn-faced woman with wiry grey curls greets us. 'Can I help you?'

Ben has been unusually quiet throughout the car trip, so I step forward and say, 'We're here to see Rachel Cummings. She's a patient here.'

'Visiting hours finished at eight-thirty.'

I glance at my phone. 'But it's only just before nine. Please, we're her friends. She's in Emergency.'

'Emergency?' The woman shakes her head. 'Sorry, family only.'

'But she doesn't have any family,' I say, unexpected tears springing to my eyes. 'Can't you let us see her?'

The woman hesitates and Ben slants me a curious look. Then, sighing, the woman says, 'Down the hall to your left. The fellows over there might let you in if you're lucky.'

I release the breath I've been holding. 'Thank you.'

Ben and I walk at a fast pace, our footsteps echoing in the quiet corridor.

'She was unconscious when they put her in the ambulance,' Ben murmurs. 'You might want to prepare yourself.'

I shiver and Ben slips an arm around my waist.

'Why didn't you go with her?'

Ben shrugs. 'They said I could ride with them or come separately. I wanted to find you first. I've sent Cat a text but she hasn't replied.'

We reach Emergency and, in contrast to the eerie silence of the hallway, there's a flurry of activity. People in white coats scurry in and out of the electronic doors, lights flash and there's the constant, low murmur of voices. The sharp, astringent scent of disinfectant fills my nostrils.

We reach a desk where a lady with long, silvery-blonde hair hovers. 'We're here to see Rachel Cummings.'

'Okay then.' The lady taps at her keyboard, a large solitaire diamond ring flashing on her left hand. 'They've moved her to ward two.'

My heart lifts. 'Does that mean she's okay?'

The woman smiles, revealing a gap between her top teeth. 'It's certainly a good sign. Are you family?'

'Yes,' Ben asserts, before I can say otherwise. 'Where can we find her?'

The lady looks at her watch. She hesitates, then leans forward, lowering her voice. 'In the north wing, room thirty-four. You'll have to make your way to the other side of the hospital, I'm afraid.'

'That's fine,' Ben says, flashing a smile. 'Thank you.'

The noise and commotion of Emergency behind us, we find the north wing and make our way through the deserted corridors. It feels like a different hospital here; some of the fluorescent lights are out and one is flickering, casting shadows on the bare, white walls. We pass a solitary desk manned by a bored-looking nurse who simply nods at us as we pass. We spot the sign for rooms twenty-five to forty and follow the hall until we find thirty-four.

I hesitate in the doorway.

'It's okay.' Ben places a hand on my back. 'I'm sure she's fine.'

There's no one around, so we step inside. It's dark, save for the flickering light from the television on the wall, and contains nothing but a tired-looking armchair and two single beds side by side. One is empty, and Rachel is in the other. She's on her back with her eyes closed and her hands clasped over her chest like she's praying. Rain teems outside the window.

'Maybe she's asleep,' I whisper.

'Rachel?' Ben calls softly.

Rachel doesn't stir.

'She looks okay, don't you think?'

'I can't tell,' I say. 'Where did you say she hit her head?'

Ben taps the base of his skull. 'On the back, here. When the car hit her, she just kind of flew to one side and then fell backwards onto the pavement. I heard the crack when she hit her head.' He closes his eyes briefly. 'It happened right outside our building. They must have cleaned the blood off her. The back of her head was covered in it.'

Goosebumps rise on my arms and I rub them, feeling cold despite the humidity.

'It happened in slow motion, just like they always say. I could see it coming – saw the car heading straight for her. It was like I knew what was going to happen but I couldn't move fast enough to stop it. By the time I yelled out, she'd already been hit. Then the fucker just drove off. I didn't think fast enough to even catch his number plate.' Ben sighs and shakes his head. 'I feel like such a dickhead.'

'What?' I say, incredulous. 'Ben, it's not your fault. Like you said, it happened before you could react.'

'Yeah.' Ben sounds doubtful. 'The thing is, Mary . . .' Ben's eyes, lit bright in the light from the hallway, find mine. 'It kind of looked like the car was *aiming* for her.'

The temperature in the room seems to drop. '*What?*' I whisper, hugging my arms to my chest.

There's a rattle and a squeak from the hallway and I glance over Ben's shoulder to see a silver trolley being wheeled by a tiny, dark-haired woman in a blue uniform. She disappears around a corner, and when I look back, Ben's staring at something behind me.

'What is it?' I feel the back of my neck prickle.

'Someone was staring at us.'

'What?' I look over my shoulder, but the corridor is deserted.

'There was someone there, in one of the doorways.'

'It's probably just a patient,' I say, but I move closer to Ben.

'Yeah. This whole accident business has got me paranoid.' Ben's brief laughter is unconvincing. He strokes my arm, slips his hand into mine and squeezes. 'I wonder when she'll wake up? Maybe we should just go.'

We turn at the same time to see Rachel sitting upright, two eyes gleaming in the dark.

Chapter Thirty-Four

'Rachel!' I drop Ben's hand and clap mine across my chest. 'You're awake.'

Rachel nods slowly.

'How are you feeling?' Ben asks, stepping further into the room.

I follow him and stand by Rachel's bed. I can see her better here; her cheekbones look hollow and there's a streak of dark blood through her light hair.

Rachel looks from Ben to me as if trying to figure something out. I wonder if she saw us holding hands. She already knows he was in my room the other night. 'I'm okay,' she says, voice hoarse as if from disuse. 'Just a bump on the head. I'm a bit groggy from the meds, though.'

'I saw what happened,' Ben tells her. 'I'm so sorry. If I'd been faster—'

'It was so strange,' Rachel interrupts, staring into the middle distance. 'One second I was crossing the road, the next I woke up in hospital.'

'I'm so sorry,' Ben says again. 'I should have come with you, been there when you woke up. I didn't think it would take so long to get here.'

Rachel raises her right hand. It's only then I see it's connected to a tube that runs to some sort of machine with blinking lights. I can just make out the outline of the tattoo on her wrist. 'Don't worry about it,' she says. 'It's no one's fault. Except maybe the arsehole who hit me.' She laughs but it's more of a wheeze. 'The doctors say I'm really lucky. The blood made it look worse than it was. I just needed a couple of stitches. They think I've escaped concussion, but they're keeping me in overnight as a precaution.'

Relief swells inside me. 'Thank God. We were so worried. We came straight here, but traffic was crazy and then this lady was saying that we might not even be able to see you . . . She was all "family only", but then . . .' I stop, biting my lip.

Rachel's expression is solemn; she looks so unlike herself. 'Thanks for coming,' she says to me, then turns to Ben. 'Both of you.'

'Of course,' I say, smiling at Ben. 'Ben lied so we could get in to see you.' I turn back to Rachel, but she's staring at the wall. 'Are you okay?'

Rachel blinks. 'Yeah. Just really tired.' She lifts her head, winces, and rests it back on the pillow. 'My head feels fuzzy. Probably the painkillers.'

'Yeah, they'll knock you around,' Ben says. 'You should get some rest.'

'Yeah,' Rachel sighs and her eyes slip shut. 'You guys go home, I'm just going to be sleeping anyway.'

'Are you sure?'

Rachel keeps her eyes closed. 'I'll be fine by tomorrow, I'm sure. I'll see you guys then.'

I hesitate, darting a glance at Ben.

'Do you have your phone?' he asks Rachel.

Rachel nods towards the chair, clothes draped over the arm. 'In my jeans pocket.'

'Call one of us when you need me to come pick you up, okay? If you run out of battery, I'm sure they'll let you use the phone here.'

'Thanks, Ben,' Rachel whispers. She looks at me, then at him and her lips turn upwards a fraction. 'You're a good guy.' Her eyes slip shut again.

'We'll leave you to it.' Ben reaches out to squeeze Rachel's arm. 'See you very soon. Rest up.'

As we're leaving, Rachel calls out, 'Mary?'

I turn back and see a glimmer of something in her eyes, something I didn't expect. Desperation. 'What is it? Are you okay?'

'Let's talk. When I'm out. Okay?'

I watch her closely, wondering what's made her so afraid. 'Of course.'

We say our goodbyes and I look over my shoulder one last time before leaving the room. Wrapped up in her white gown, so small even in the tiny bed, Rachel looks like a child.

I shiver as Ben and I step into the empty corridor again. It's creepy with no one around. The north wing has the air of a ghost town.

When we get home, it feels like we've been gone for days. It's pitch-black and we go about flicking on lights, turning on the TV for some background chatter. It's as if neither of us wants there to be silence.

My phone buzzes and I check it. 'Cat's not back until tomorrow,' I tell Ben. I feel a pang in my stomach. Cat and I haven't spoken since our fight the other morning. 'She left her phone at work and she's texting from her friend's phone to say she's been drinking, so she'll crash there. That means she doesn't know what's happened.'

'Leave it 'til tomorrow, then. No point worrying her now. Rachel's okay, anyway.'

'Yeah.' I smile. 'That's thoughtful of you.'

Ben's watching me, something like hope in his eyes.

Feeling nervous, I pull at a loose thread on my T-shirt. 'I'm not really hungry. Are you?'

Ben shrugs. 'Not really. I could use a drink, though.'

I try to disguise my relief. 'Yeah, me too. After all that.' I grab us a bottle of Merlot and two glasses, and Ben sits down on the couch, patting the seat beside him. He stretches one arm out, like he's about to give a one-armed hug. I smile and sit, leaning in, and he wraps his arm around me. It feels natural, safe.

We sip our drinks and Ben strokes my hair gently as we watch an old episode of *The Simpsons*. It's safe viewing, comforting. An ad for pizza delivery comes on the TV and my stomach grumbles. 'Ooh, pizza! Let's get some.'

Ben laughs. 'Guess you were hungry after all.'

'Guess so.'

Ben's eyes twinkle as he looks at me. 'Mary, Mary, quite contrary.'

A surge of adrenalin makes me flinch.

'Mary?'

I shut my eyes, pushing away the bad thoughts.

'Hey. What's wrong? Come here.' Ben pulls me against him, kisses the top of my head. 'You looked like you thought I was going to hit you.'

I don't say anything. Silence yawns between us for a minute and then Ben's arm tightens around me. His voice is soft when he speaks. 'You know, that offer to talk . . . or, well, listen. It doesn't expire.'

I lift my head and find Ben watching me uncertainly. He's so kind, so *good*. It makes something ache inside me.

'I don't want to talk,' I say.

Ben swallows. 'Okay.'

I raise my knees and twist sideways so I'm kneeling on the couch. Leaning in, I touch my lips to Ben's. His mouth is soft and tastes of wine. I pull back and he leans closer, cupping my face, kissing me in a way that makes my eyes sting with tears.

The pizza forgotten, we undress each other and make love right there on the couch, his heart thudding against mine, his breath hot in my ear.

Outside the window, the rain picks up, beating against the pavement, drowning out the sound of the ocean.

Chapter Thirty-Five

12th December 2016

Rachel's back home. I picked her up today and now she's in her room, resting. She was right, they only needed to keep her overnight and she seems fine now, except for having to wear this plaster thingy on the back of her head. And there's the stitches, but they'll come out in a week.

I wonder what she wanted to talk to me about, what had her so worked up. I guess I'll find out when she's recovered. I keep thinking how frightened she must have been when she woke up in hospital. It's terrifying what can happen in a split second. Lives can be irrevocably changed, or taken away. Nothing is permanent. No one is safe. And I'm no exception.

I don't know what to do anymore. I'm at my wits' end.

I'm not sleeping, I can hardly eat. I'm on my second wine and its only lunchtime.

The shoes haven't shown up and I have no leads on Sophie. The cops won't listen to me and I can't prove Mark's threatening me. What use are they, if they're powerless to help someone in danger? What use are they if they won't look into testimony from an eye witness? I mean what's the fucking point of them?

Some might think it's surprising that they haven't found out what happened to Tom yet. But I don't. I dredged up some articles on the case and they were rife with reports about police incompetence, justice not being done for Tom. But then people just stopped talking about it. Like that Zak's manager guy Bruce said, they found juicier things to sink their teeth into. Tom was just some druggo from a poor family, not a missing toddler or a beauty queen murdered in a crime of passion. No one cares. Not least his family, who, according to media coverage, weren't even at the funeral.

It's not the first time the police have failed me. I haven't written about this yet because, unless I have to, I prefer not to think about it. When Mum and Dad disappeared, it was big news. I don't think it was so much to do with the fact that they were minor celebrities in the mid-nineties — their wines outsold all the major national names and were highly sought-after overseas — but more to do with the fact that everyone wanted to know what was going to happen to Sylvia and Alan's poor, devastated daughter. Everyone wanted a piece of the story, to burrow their way into somebody else's drama.

Because people are like that, aren't they? They're voyeurs, desperate and hungry for stories to make their own lives seem less pointless. Because that's all we do, really. Tell ourselves – and each other – stories. Hello, reality television? Facebook? Instagram? It feels like people are more interested in the drama than in justice. Sometimes I think our culture of the spectacle isn't so far removed from mediaeval times. Though instead of people's bodies being mutilated for entertainment, their souls are on show. I'm not sure what's worse.

So, after the hype died down, and some up-and-coming model went missing, people stopped caring about my parents. The cops stopped looking. And now, five years later, I'm pretty sure that if they weren't dead then, they are now. All because of complacency and incompetence, sheer incompetence.

I'm not going to let it happen again. I've finally had the chance to get my facts straight since finding out about Sophie. I've written down the new things I've remembered from that night. If I can fill in the gaps, maybe I'll remember something of value.

1. Someone screaming, 'Run Sophie!' – it was a female voice, I think. Could it have been a friend of Sophie's? Does that mean someone else was a witness to what happened, or did this happen at a different point in the night? Surely if someone witnessed a murder they'd have told the police. Unless Mark got to them first. What if it's not just me who's in danger?

    And Sophie – she was there, she saw things. She must have. According to Bruce, she was with Mark when he went missing – that fits exactly into the time frame *when Tom was killed. Plus, I heard someone calling her name, telling her to run. What if Sophie's in danger too? Unless she's still with Mark, in which case he'll have her under control. He'll be keeping her quiet.*

Who is Sophie? And where is she?

2. *The bloodied brick Mark was holding was the murder weapon, because although no weapon was ever found, the nature of Tom's injuries revealed the cause of death.*

3. *I remember a man's voice saying 'don't fight me'. And I was in pain . . . I don't know if the two are connected. Maybe someone was attacking me — Mark? Is that how I got the blood on me?*

And there's another thing, a feeling I get in my body when I think back to that night. Fear.

Who was I afraid of? And why?

It feels hopeless. I keep thinking myself in circles. Even if I remember what happened, the police don't care what I think I saw. I have no evidence. They don't believe that I was even there; they think I'm crazy, that I'm making it all up about Mark. They don't see that he's a con man, that I've been conned and so have they.

Well, if the police won't help me, it's time to do what I should have done a long time ago. It's time to take matters into my own hands.

My phone buzzes and the base of my skull prickles. I know who it is before I even check.

I'M IN SYDNEY. COME MEET ME.

A different number, again. All capitals. Not a question, a command. *Come meet me.*

I burn inside. He thinks he can order me around? He doesn't know I'm on to him; I know his tricks and they won't work anymore. I know more than he thinks.

The wine gives me Dutch courage and I do something without thinking. I text back.

Who is this? Jake, Jon or Raj?

I wait, blood roaring in my ears. The text he's written has come up green on iMessage, so he's probably using some old, disposable phone, which means I can't tell if he's read my reply. A minute passes. Then three, then ten. I don't know if I'm afraid or excited. My heart is hammering behind my ribs.

'Hey you.' I turn to see Cat hovering in the doorway. Her hair is damp and she's wearing a light robe and a hesitant smile. 'Can we talk?'

I swallow, try and fail to arrange my features in a neutral expression.

Of course, Cat notices. She's by my side in an instant, looking at me with concern. 'What is it? What's wrong?'

I retrieve my phone, hold it up. 'Mark.' I shrug, aiming for nonchalance. I don't feel I can let myself be vulnerable in front of Cat anymore. Something's changed between us, and it can't change back just like that.

Cat sighs, leaning against the door frame, one hand on her hip. I notice her hair's growing out even more, blonde

239

roots creeping through the black. 'What's he saying this time?'

'He's in Sydney. He wants to meet.'

Cat releases a slow breath. She puts a finger to her lips, catches my eye with a look that's almost sheepish. 'Have you considered it?'

My jaw drops. '*What?*'

Cat holds up her hands. 'Sorry, you know I didn't mean . . . not *alone*, obviously. I'd come with you, or you can take Ben for protection. Somewhere public with lots of people around.'

I can't process what I'm hearing. This is the last thing I'd expect to hear from someone who knows what I went through with Mark. Someone who's meant to be keeping me safe. 'What *for* exactly?'

Cat avoids my eyes. 'You're suffering, Mary. I know I fucked up, I shouldn't have said anything to Ben behind your back. I'm sorry. But I'm worried about you . . . Yes, Mark's a bastard and I know what he did to you, but don't you think you might be . . . I don't know.' She exhales harshly. 'Overthinking things?'

I can't believe what I'm hearing.

'Hear me out,' Cat rushes on, as if she knows she's crossed a line. Again. 'I've just been thinking maybe Mark needs to hear it from you. That it's over, I mean. That could be the underlying problem . . . maybe he just doesn't *get* it. Maybe he doesn't believe you're not coming back, that this won't all go back to normal. You left a couple of times before, didn't you? And you went back. Maybe he figures this is the same. And, if you tell him face to face . . . it could be your chance to stand up to him. You could look him in the eye, tell him in no uncertain terms that you're never coming back. Maybe *then* he'll give up.'

My body feels cold. She doesn't understand. 'He's dangerous,' I say in a flat voice. 'You know what he's done.'

Cat doesn't say anything. Silence hangs between us, heavy and uncomfortable. Her eyes stray to the window and her hand fidgets against her thigh, making the chunky bracelets on her wrist jangle. 'It's just . . . you've tried the police. They looked into it . . .'

'They didn't . . .'

'And the only thing making you think that Mark . . . you *know*,' she sighs, 'is your memory of that night. And, I'm sorry to say, but you know what you can be like. When you've been drinking . . .'

My face burns.

'What if it's not a memory? What if it was a dream . . .? All this talk of the murder, all those pictures in the paper, it's bound to be putting images in your head. And all the booze, lately . . .' She lets that sink in. I thought I'd been hiding it. But she knows.

'We've been friends forever, M. And we've always been honest with each other, haven't we?'

I don't reply.

'Look. Rachel's . . . troubled. I get it. And I'm sure she's

241

nice enough, under all that. But *you don't need this*. You can't save everyone, Mary. I know you just want to help, you were like that as a kid. Even with pets, you always picked the sick ones. It's like you gravitated to them. Look what happened with Mark . . .'

I inhale sharply.

'I'm sorry, I . . . that was harsh. I didn't mean . . . Fucking hell. I know this is hard. It's only natural, after all you've been through . . .' Cat crosses the room and slips her arm around me, pulls me into a hug. It feels forced, awkward. Her hair smells of coconut and cigarette smoke and I wonder if she's been at the pub. 'I'm not going to make you do anything you don't want to do, okay? But your aunt made me promise to look after you and, so far, I'm doing a shit job. Don't make a liar out of me. Please? Just go see Doctor Chang. For me?'

She pulls back and looks at me, stroking my arms, her brown eyes full of pity.

I want to hit her.

'I'm sure he'll be able to help with all this; he'll know what to do. And maybe he can even help you remember some things. And then you'll know for sure what happened.'

I don't want to hear this. I don't want her hands on me; I want to push her away. But I don't, because she's right. Not in the way she thinks. She thinks I've lost it, that the psychiatrist will 'fix' me. But maybe he can help me in another way.

242

'Okay,' I say, forcing a smile. 'I'll book an appointment for as soon as possible. I promise.'

The relief on Cat's face is almost comical.

I'm true to my word. After checking on Rachel who's still resting in her room, and forcing down some food, I call Doctor Henry Chang's office and speak with the receptionist. The soonest available slot is just under a week away, but it will have to do. I'm only making the appointment so I can get the prescription for my meds, anyway. I won't need the session. Because I'm making other plans. Without meaning to, Cat has given me a brilliant idea. Dangerous, but brilliant.

As I stretch out on the couch, letting the plan take shape in my mind, I glance at my phone. No reply from Mark. My lips twitch in a smile as a surge of power fills my chest. This has never happened before. I've done something I wasn't able to do in all the years we were together.

I've got to him.

Chapter Thirty-Six

I dream in black and white. *Cat and I are at school, rehearsing for the play that's opening tonight. She's Romeo, I'm Juliet. We're doing the balcony scene.*

I'm not sure how it ended up this way, and I don't remember choosing roles. I do know Cat's unhappy about it though. Who wouldn't be? I don't tell her, but I think it's fitting. She's so much taller and broader than I am, more solid, more into sports and with an attitude that befits . . . well, a guy.

The boys from our 'brother school', Helfield Boys' Comprehensive, have paid a special visit to watch rehearsals. It's a novelty, having boys here. I'm wary and on edge, as I always am around boys, but the rest of the girls don't seem to share my uncertainty. I'm embarrassed for them with their hapless flirting and lack of shame. The boys aren't even that great.

I know Cat's hating that she's dressed in slacks and a vest, her long hair tied up and hidden under a cap, her breasts strapped to her chest, while I'm decked out in a mediaeval-style frock with a plunging neckline. I catch Adam Benson staring at my chest and it makes my stomach feel funny. I glance back at Cat and she's glaring, her face pinched with stress. Her eyes glint in the lights.

Suddenly the sky is black and dotted with stars. I've got a plastic cup in my hand and there are people around me, hot bodies packed close. Music whines from a dodgy set of speakers somewhere nearby. We're at the after-party, someone's backyard – Megan Keeler, I think – and Adam's at my elbow, watching me like a salivating dog. It's as if he thinks I can't see him.

I take a sip from my cup. The sweet and sticky liquid has a harsh aftertaste – bourbon. I slug it down, relishing the burn.

Next thing, I'm in the bathroom, fluorescent lights blinding. Cat's tear-streaked face is in front of me, her eyes red-rimmed, cheeks smeared with black. Her blonde hair hangs limply around her face, the single dyed-red streak like a smear of blood at her temple.

My heart is pummelling my ribs. What's she saying? I can't hear her for the white noise in my ears. Then the sound comes on, like someone's flipped a switch.

'You had to do it, didn't you?' Cat's voice is deafening.

I want to ask her what she's talking about, but my voice won't work.

'You had to go and kiss him. Adam Benson, of all people!'

'What? I didn't . . .'

'But you did, though, didn't you?' Her eyes, like daggers, send

246

*a shiver down my spine. 'You couldn't stand that he liked me
and not you. You couldn't let me have him. You couldn't just let
me have* one fucking thing!'

I wake to see a magpie sharpening its beak on the railing
outside the glass sliding doors. From my horizontal position
on the couch, I watch as it angles its head from side to
side, eyes gleaming like onyx. Aunty Anne adores the crea-
tures. *Such intelligent birds*, she says. I've always found their
intense, narrow stare unsettling.

The magpie stops, tilts its head and fixes its glassy eyes
on me. I get a strange little shiver. The bird stares for a
moment, then hops onto a neighbouring roof. I'm seren-
aded by one of the most distinctively Australian sounds;
magpie feet on aluminium like pattering rain.

I'm alone with my thoughts. Fragments of a dream are
caught in my mind like flies in a web. Nameless, shapeless
doubts claw at the inside of my skull. I feel like I'm missing
something. Something big.

I grit my teeth, squeeze my eyes shut in an attempt to
force clarity. Things feel different with Cat now. And it's
not just that she broke my trust. It's more than that. There's
something . . . *familiar* about this feeling. I can't help but
wonder, has it always been this way between us and I've
just been oblivious?

There's one thing I can't get past: she doesn't believe
me about Mark. She thinks I should *meet with him*, for
fuck's sake. My supposed best friend, and after everything

247

he put me through, everything he's *done*, she thinks I'm imagining things. She thinks I'm mad.

But Rachel is different. She's seen things, knows things. Cat can never understand. Rachel *gets* me. Gets *it*. And Cat's jealous – that has to be it. She's always been a little jealous, hasn't she? And now there's the Ben thing, and my friendship with Rachel. She can't stand that I might need someone other than her. Well, what does she expect, when she has so little faith in me? If Cat can't handle that I've made another friend, that's her problem.

One of the flies stuck in the web of my mind starts to buzz. I shut my eyes, remembering.

You can't save everyone, Mary. I know you just want to help; you were like that as a kid. Even with pets, you always picked the sick ones. It's like you gravitated to them. Look what happened with Mark . . .

I sit up straight. Wasn't Cat one of the 'sick ones'? Wasn't she that sad, loner kid with no friends before I came along? My mind shuffles through memories like a stack of cards. Cat's clueless comments about Mark. The look on her face when she twigged something was going on between me and Ben. Rachel's warning, that night in her room. Cat's face smeared with mucous and mascara, her mouth open in a silent scream.

You couldn't just let me have one fucking thing!

Could Rachel have been right about Cat all along? That pedestal Cat's put me on has always stood just a bit too high. Wasn't she always a bit possessive at school?

A bit . . . controlling? The way she copied my clothes, got mad at me when I wore my eternity necklace from Mum instead of my half of the 'Best Friends' necklace she bought. A silver heart split in two; I had 'best', she had 'friends'. How she didn't like me having other friends. That time she screamed at me because I went to the movies with Cally Watson and didn't invite her. When I think about it, that's pushing the friendship a bit far. Isn't it? Is it normal to want someone all to yourself? To expect exclusivity?

I trust this woman with my finances. My secrets. My past. How easy it would be for her to screw me over.

My skin itches, as if irritated by some invisible insect. I run my nails over my forearm, my eyes drawn to the bright red lips on the Rolling Stones poster hanging on Cat's bedroom door. My stomach flutters, like I'm about to step out on a high ledge. Do something I'll regret. But I can't help it; my feet carry me across the living room to Cat's door. Before I can open it, something on the floor catches my eye: a photo. Even from my standing position, I can see it's been torn in half. The side that's left is of Cat, smiling at the camera, teeth glinting from the flash. I crouch down to pick it up.

It's from years ago, back when she'd lost all the weight and was still blonde. I remember the exact moment it was taken – we were lying on our backs on the freshly mown grass at my parents' house, my arms raised above us holding the camera, both laughing as we tried to pout for the photo, but eventually we gave up and smiled.

We had escaped out there for the afternoon, drinking too much wine and sneakily smoking cigarettes. The other half of the photo is gone, but I can fill in the blanks. I had that photo pinned up in my bedroom for years.

I turn it over and a strange feeling washes over me. The world tilts – only a fraction, yet suddenly I'm seeing it from a different angle.

On the back of the photo, one word is scrawled.

SLUT.

Chapter Thirty-Seven

13th December 2016

I remember it like it was yesterday, dream about it in all the vivid detail of a flashback. The vines reflect the light of the setting sun, gleaming like golden thread woven through the landscape. I pluck a single sun-ripened grape from a cluster, pierce the taut skin with my teeth and taste its nectar, tart and sweet.

Cat sits cross-legged beside me, biting her fingernails. She's tried to quit the habit three times now to no avail. I can't remember a time when her nails weren't gnawed to the quick.

'You really shouldn't,' she says.

I pop another grape into my mouth. 'Shouldn't what? Do this?' I collect a handful of grapes from the wicker basket and pour them into my mouth, watching Cat's reaction out of the corner of my eye as most of them spill out of my mouth and fall to the ground.

She tucks a strand of pale blonde hair behind her ear, folds her arms across her chest. 'That's such a waste. Stop messing around.'

'I'm not messing around. I'm enjoying myself. There's a difference.'

I look at my friend and I wonder, in a moment of clarity, whether she ever enjoys herself.

'Are you still going to dye your hair black?' I ask as I spark a cigarette. I splutter on the exhale; I still haven't got the hang of it.

Cat sighs audibly, looking cross, but she doesn't comment on my actions. 'Thinking about it,' she grumbles.

'You should. You'd look badass. You should do it before Megan's birthday. Can you believe she'll be legal before us? You know she got held back at school when she was in Year Six. That's why she's turning sixteen this year.'

Cat doesn't say anything.

We're silent for a while as I smoke, coughing on every second drag. I'm not sure why I'm doing this. I know Mum wouldn't be thrilled, but she couldn't say much because I've caught her having a sneaky fag now and again. With Dad, I can never be sure what he'll be cool with. Part of me wonders if I do these things because my parents don't give me many rules, and I wish, in a way, that I had some way to rebel.

Cat doesn't seem to share that desire.

'Are you still planning on doing it with Ethan?'

'What? Oh.' I wrinkle my nose. Ethan Yeats, the boy I'm supposedly dating. Only I haven't really seen him in three weeks and on the rare occasion he actually texts me, it's with a dick pic. I have no intention of sleeping with him. I'm not sure I want to sleep with anyone. The idea of sex just seems so . . . aggressive.

Still, I don't want to lose face, so I shrug and say, 'Sure, I guess.'

I take a gulp from the stolen bottle of last year's Riesling – a good year, Dad says – and blow a plume of smoke between the vines so my parents don't see it.

'You should be careful. Use . . . you know. Use, uh . . . protection.'

I smirk. 'You really do take my parents too seriously,' I say. I put on a sing-song voice, echoing my mother's words as we left the house earlier. 'Look after my girl, Cath-er-ine!'

'Shut up,' Cat snaps, her mouth pursed like she's tasted something sour. And I'm reminded of how shirty she's been lately, how nothing I do seems to impress her anymore. I wonder what's bothering her. Whether it's me.

I sip and smoke and stare down the path between the grapevines that stretch endlessly into the distance.

'Give me that.' Cat snatches the bottle from my hand and for a second I think she isn't going to let me have it back. But then she looks at it funny, squares her shoulders. She presses the mouth of the bottle to her lips, hesitates only briefly before tipping her head back and taking a long swallow.

★　★　★

253

The sun has nearly set. Cat and I lie on the freshly mown grass in the back paddock, staring up at the clouds. We're not being careful anymore. Not bothering to hide. We finished the wine and lost the bottle somewhere on the way back to the house, then decided it was a good idea to lie down and catch the last of the amber rays of sun. I can feel the warmth on my face, see the shadows lengthen and loom around us, the temperature drop to tolerable.

Mum's singing in the tasting parlour, loudly and off-key, and Cat and I loll our heads to the side so we're face to face, our noses almost touching, and dissolve into giggles.

At last she stops, or maybe she's gone to the other side of the house, who knows. Now all we hear is the evening breeze whispering through the vine leaves.

'I love it here,' Cat says to the sky. 'You're so lucky, you know.'

'You always say that,' I say, annoyed. It makes me feel guilty when she says it, like it's my fault or something. Like I chose my parents on purpose.

'I'd never get away with this at home. Never ever ever. Your parents are so cool.' Cat's voice is wistful. She's drawing invisible circles in the sky with her index fingers, her collection of silver rings glinting in the fading light.

I don't say anything. She doesn't know that sometimes my parents fight. That having 24/7 access to wine isn't always the best — or safest — thing. It makes me realise I don't tell Cat everything. Does that mean there are things Cat keeps from me, too?

254

'It's always kind of been about you, hasn't it?' Cat's voice interrupts, and my thoughts trickle away like spilled wine.

'What?'

I feel Cat's hand clasp mine, and even though it's hot and sticky, I don't pull away. 'I mean, more you than me.'

'What?' I repeat, and giggle, partly because the grass is tickling the back of my neck, partly because it's hard to follow what's going on. My thoughts are murky, like muddy water.

'I don't mind usually,' she says in a whisper, like it's a secret. Her breath tickles my ear and it kind of feels nice. I lean closer. She smells of coconut. She always smells of coconut. 'You're more interesting than I am, anyway. But sometimes . . .' She doesn't finish her sentence and the words hang, unspoken, in the air.

'You're interesting, too,' I say, partly to break the silence but also because that's the nicest thing I can think of to say.

'I'm not.'

'You are!'

'I'm not.'

'Okay, you're not.' I laugh, but it comes out as more of a snort.

Cat doesn't respond. I feel bad, but I don't know what else to say. And I think for a second. Is she right? Is it about me all the time? Do I let her have a say? It's hard when she's always so interested, always asking questions. Hard when she doesn't talk about herself much. And I forget to ask, I suppose. Or maybe because she doesn't like to say, I've stopped pressing her.

My eyes suddenly feel gritty and I rub them with the heels of my palms. Am I missing something? Is there something Cat's trying to tell me? The thoughts slide over each other, slippery like eels, and I can't grasp them, so I let them slither away into oblivion.

The sky darkens as the sun drops behind the hill. A shadow moves in my peripheral vision.

My father stands by the house, in the shade of the veranda. He's watching us. He knows we're here, but he doesn't call us in. Doesn't tell us off. He just stands there. And it makes me realise . . . I grasp at another thought, but it wriggles away. He does that a lot. Doesn't he?

Through the haze in my mind, the darkness that's falling, I can't tell whether it's Cat he's watching, or me.

Chapter Thirty-Eight

I've emerged from a booze-free sleep feeling stronger, more on top of things. My plan is brewing, evolving, and when it's fully formed I'm going to speak to Rachel. She'll believe me, and she'll want to help. I know it. Then I'll show Mark. Show Cat. I'll show them I'm not the girl I used to be.

The houseboat bobs in its usual place, unseeing eyes staring out as I jog past. I avoid looking at it, increasing my pace as I near the northern end of the beach. There are fewer people here and the shore widens and rises in low dunes. To my left there's a nature reserve, dense with fir trees, linking the foreshore to the mountain. Beyond it is a sandy crest, rising above the sea.

I don't usually come this far. I was thinking of taking the track that runs through the reserve, but when I stop and stare into those trees, my heart leaps into my throat. Something primal inside me is transmitting a message – *Turn back. You don't want to go in there.*

An image flashes in my mind – running, tripping, crashing through trees. A voice, snarling. *Get up, you stupid bitch.*

My body goes cold. I can hear the words so clearly. Is it real? Am I imagining it?

Get up, you stupid bitch.

My pocket vibrates and I nearly jump out of my skin. Breathing deep, I snatch up my phone. There are two messages.

Don't forget that doco on at 8.30 on SBS tonight. And congrats on your appt. w/ Dr Chang next wk! So proud of u. C x

I shove down a flash of anger, check the next message.

MARY, MEET WITH ME. PLEASE.

Please. It's ridiculous, but I get a thrill. Begging now, are we? I feel that surge of power again. I had it all wrong before. Yes, I had reason to be afraid. I still do. But what I didn't realise is that Mark's scared too. I know what he did. And that gives me power. I feel the balance shifting, raising me up. Crushing him down.

And then it comes to me. That's it, the final piece in the puzzle, the plan emerging, fully-fledged, ready to take flight.

I get a shiver. It's dangerous. Exciting. I've got reason to drink tonight. It's a celebration. A victory.

★ ★ ★

'All I Want for Christmas' whines out from the tinny overhead speakers and Christmas baubles gleam in the low lights. We're in one of the older local pubs – what passes for old in Sydney anyway – and even though it's Monday, it's packed to the rafters. The rowdy patrons at The Alice are in holiday mode, flushed with cheer and house-made cider.

It's too crowded and noisy, so once we've bought drinks I steer Rachel outside. There's a beer garden out the back, crammed with smokers, candles flickering on the low brick walls beneath a veil of smoke. A path veers off to one side, so we slip down there where it's quieter.

'How's your head?' I ask.

'Better. I've taken off the bandage now, and the stitches were dissolvable.'

'Good.' I try to smile. 'Good, I'm glad.'

'What is it you wanted to talk to me about?' Rachel says.

I close my eyes, and open them again when I feel Rachel's hand on my arm.

'It's okay. I know it's hard,' she adds. 'That's why I've waited so long.'

'What do you mean?'

'You had to be ready.' Rachel's eyes are dark pools. She's so close, I can smell the wine on her breath. 'Who is it? Who is it that hurt you, Mary?'

I breathe slowly. Rachel's not like Cat, I tell myself. She'll understand. She'll believe me.

'You can tell me,' Rachel whispers, stroking my arm.

'Nothing you can say will shock me, I promise you. Here . . .' She lifts the wine bottle from the cooler and tops up my glass. Her smile is encouraging. 'Dutch courage.'

My temples throb, though I've barely had anything to drink. 'My ex,' I say, before I can lose my nerve. 'He's like yours.'

There's a pause and then Rachel nods, once, as if she was expecting it. Her eyes are on my face. 'Oh, Mary.'

'So I know you understand. You've asked if I was in any kind of trouble.' I swallow. 'Well, I am.'

Rachel leans in, her hazel eyes glittering gold in the light coming from the beer garden. 'What kind of trouble?'

I take a long pull from my wine glass and set it on the wall beside me. 'Mark. My ex. He . . . he killed someone.'

Rachel gasps.

'And now he's after me.'

Rachel presses two fingers to her lips, her eyes round and fixed on mine. 'You're sure about this?'

'You have to believe me, Rachel. No one else does. Not even the police. But I know what he is, and I know what he's capable of. He has . . . aliases. No one knows the real him because he's an expert at hiding, at protecting himself. And he's done this, I know it.' There's a frisson running through me. As the words tumble out, I feel lighter. The way I did when I first met Rachel.

Rachel's face is close to mine. There's a hardness in her eyes that wasn't there before, and something else.

Something fierce. 'I believe you, Mary.' She takes my hands in hers and squeezes, hard. 'I had a feeling it was something like this. Something big. It must have been so terrible, keeping it to yourself.'

I choke against an unexpected sob. 'The police don't believe me, Cat doesn't believe me, so I thought you might not either. I didn't know who to trust.'

Rachel strokes my palm with her thumbs. 'They don't know you,' she says. 'They don't understand you like I do. They can *never* understand. I've seen what's out there.' She pulls my hand to her chest, presses it to her heart. 'Of course I believe you.'

A tear slips down my cheek. 'You don't know what that means to me.'

'Yes, I do. Because you did the same for me.' She smiles. 'God. You must be so scared.'

'I was. I am. But not for long. I have a plan.'

Rachel leans in, a strange intensity in her eyes. Somewhere in the distance an ambulance siren wails. 'Tell me,' she whispers.

I don't know if I feel sick or high or both. 'He's been texting. Making threats, saying he's coming to get me. I ignored him, thought I could go to the cops and they'd do something. But they didn't.' I take a breath. 'They won't. So it's up to me.'

'What are you going to do?'

'I'm going to take care of him myself.'

'You mean . . . *kill* him?'

I'm thrown for a second. Kill Mark? The thought is so ludicrous I almost laugh. But then I see it. Mark's face, distorted with fear. Smashing his skull in with a bat, over and over.

'No, no. Of course not,' I say quickly, looking over my shoulder. 'I was thinking I could meet with him, get him to confess to what he did. I could bring my phone, have it recording in my pocket or something. I used to do that sometimes, only he'd always find it later and erase the evidence. But he won't do that this time. We'll be somewhere public . . .'

'It's dangerous.' Rachel's chest is rising and falling rapidly, as if she's scared. Or excited. 'I'll come with you.'

'I was hoping you'd say that.' I exhale, relieved. 'We have to work out the details, but I think we can do it. If I get a confession, the police will have to listen to me.'

Rachel's nodding, her eyes gleaming in the low light. 'Yes. Yes, they'll have to, won't they?'

'I'll send him a text then. Arrange somewhere to meet tomorrow.'

We don't speak for a minute, thinking ahead to what must be done. The merry sounds of music and laughter seem to come from a different world. A world of normalcy, friends and laughter, a world I'm not a part of.

But I will be. Soon.

'You'd better drink up, then,' Rachel says, raising her

glass. She smiles, teeth glinting in the low light. 'Big day tomorrow.'

I lift my glass to meet hers. The glasses clink like the chime of a bell, sealing our fate.

Tomorrow, everything changes.

Chapter Thirty-Nine

'Lick.'

My tongue follows the curve from my thumb knuckle up to the base of my forefinger. My senses are heightened, my breath hot against my skin. I watch as Rachel does the same. Her pink tongue darts out and runs along her wrist, leaving a wet strip behind. There's something mesmerising, even seductive, about the action.

I shake my head; my mind is slipping. I can't let it, I need to think clearly. I need just enough for courage, not to cloud my judgement. I need to hit that sweet spot.

'Sip.'

I throw back the cool liquid, wince as it burns its way down my throat and pools in my stomach. Rachel's eyes hold mine as she takes her shot.

'Suck.'

I mirror her movements as she presses the lemon wedge between her full lips and sucks, a single tear trickling down her cheek. I'm nowhere near as collected; I cough, splutter and make a grab for the iced water.

Feeling like I'm in a trance, I stare at Rachel as she stares at me. A slow smile spreads across her face.

'So?' she says.

'So.'

'What do we have?'

I show her the blank screen, the cursor still flashing, willing me to type something.

Rachel reaches for my phone. 'May I?'

I hand it to her and she stares at the screen for a moment before tapping at it with her fingernail, her head tilted to one side.

She licks her lips, shoots me a coy smile. 'Gimme a sec.' She salts her wrist again, licks it, and downs the second of our two-for-one tequila shots. Without so much as a grimace, she drains the lemon wedge of its juice and places it on the table.

I leave my second shot where it is. I need my wits about me.

Rachel's focus has narrowed; she taps the screen in silence for thirty seconds or so. Then she smiles and brandishes the phone in front of my face.

'Wait, I can't see.' I take the phone, start to read.

OK, I'll meet you. See you at the lookout spot at the southern end of Halo Beach at four o'clock tomorrow. Xx

My heart skips a beat. 'Kisses?'

'Trust me, it's perfect.'

'It's short.'

'It's to the point.'

I bite my lip. 'Do you think he'll come?'

Rachel's eyes glitter. 'Of course he will. He's desperate, Mary. Remember, you have the power here.'

A shiver moves through me, like an electrical current. Maybe I'll have that drink after all, I think, eyeing the shot glass. Rachel's right. For the first time, the power is mine.

Rachel places a hand over mine. 'You're ready for this?'

I think of the look in Mark's eyes when he spat in my face.

Making me ride in the back seat of the car like a dog.

Washing the blood – Tom's blood – from my body, alone and terrified.

I think of his mind games, his threats.

I think of what he has done, what he will do again.

'I'm ready.' My thumb hovers over the phone. 'No. Wait.'

Rachel looks alarmed. 'What? Why?'

I smile, take her hand in mine. I bring it close, so her thumb is next to mine. 'Together.'

Rachel smiles back, warm and bright.

And, together, we hit SEND.

Chapter Forty

There's a man outside my window. He's whispering to me, whispering my name. The wind is whispering too — telling me secrets, things I'm supposed to understand, to remember, but I don't.

Something isn't right. I'm afraid, but there's something else. A wrongness, buried deep. That unpleasant tingle, like when a spider crawls over your skin. I want to run, to escape the feeling, but my legs won't move. I'm paralysed.

He's not outside anymore. He's in the doorway, his bulk filling it, blocking the light from the hall. This man is not a stranger. I know him. I crave him. I fear him.

'Mary, Mary,' he whispers, and I can hear the sing-song sneer in his voice, the rasp of his ragged breaths. 'What am I going to do with you?'

Only when he steps into the room, coming to me slowly, slowly, it's not Mark's face I see.

It's my father's.

I wake suddenly, gasping air into my lungs. All I can see is white. I scrabble desperately until I emerge from the sheets, breathless.

The bed creaks and something warm brushes my leg. I jolt before realising what it is. The air rushes out of my lungs in relief and the fear, the confusion, is replaced by another, much more pleasant, feeling.

The muscles in Ben's smooth brown back shift as he rolls over to face me. Last night comes rushing back; I sneaked into his room, crawled under the sheets, kissed him until he woke.

'Hey, gorgeous,' he says in a husky voice, face breaking into a smile. 'You're still here.'

My chest swells with an emotion I can't name. I don't think I've ever felt it. 'I'm here.' I smooth down a tuft of his hair, trailing my finger over the stubble on his cheek. Memories of what we did come flooding back and heat rushes to my face.

Ben's eyes soften as he looks at me, holds my gaze. He gently clasps the base of my skull and pulls me down into a soft kiss. I don't think twice about the fact that I probably still taste of tequila because I'm enraptured by his lips that move to my cheek, my ear, my neck and then he pulls me down beside him and wraps me in his arms and blows raspberries on my shoulder until I giggle.

The air has cooled overnight and Ben's body heat is like a beacon. I don't feel shy. I don't hide. I lean into him, relishing the feel of his skin on mine, nuzzling my face to his neck. He sighs.

This is new, rare. The absence of uncertainty, that gut-wrenching push and pull. It's unfathomable. Where Mark was sharpness and ice, Ben is softness and warmth. My life hasn't shown me security like this. Yet somehow – immediately, with my gut – I sense it here.

My thoughts crystallise. This is how it's *supposed* to feel. This is how it's *supposed* to be. And I want it with a ferocity that shocks me. I want it and I'm going to fight for it.

'What do you want to do today?' Ben mumbles into my hair. 'I was thinking we could go to lunch or some-thing. Maybe that new pub by the water?'

When I don't answer, Ben pulls back and strokes my arm.

'What is it?'

I hate having to do this now. Spending a normal day with Ben, going to the pub, lazily strolling home. It sounds like heaven. But there will be time for that later. I'll make sure of it. 'I have plans with Rachel.'

'Right.' Ben's gaze drops to the crumpled sheet.

'No, listen. Ben,' I say, cupping his cheek. He looks up, surprised. 'I want to, I really do.' Excitement bubbles up and I'm grinning. 'You don't have to worry. I'm sorry

I've . . . I'm just sorry, okay? I'll open up. I want that. I want to share with you. I want to try.'

Ben stares at me in silence for several beats until panic creeps in. I've been too hasty. I've misread his intentions. But then he grins. 'Mary,' his voice is hoarse. His eyes hold mine. 'I don't care what's happened, whatever it is.'

'I know,' I say. 'But I want to tell you. And I will . . .'

'I'll be here. When you're ready.'

I'm smiling so hard it hurts. We stare at each other for several rapturous moments until there's a knock from down the hall. It's Rachel at my door.

'Ugh. Sorry.' I untangle myself from the sheets, get out of bed and dress quickly, tingling under Ben's watchful gaze.

Before I leave I look over my shoulder and pause for a moment, drinking him in.

'I'll see you later,' I say with a smile.

I hope to God I'm telling the truth.

Chapter Forty-One

The wind whips our hair in all directions and I'm wishing I'd brought a hair tie to keep the lashing strands out of my face. It's not unusual for the weather to fluctuate at this time of year, but today is something else entirely. The wind blowing off the water is ice-cold and the air feels heavy with moisture. I bury my hands in the pockets of my hoodie, my fingers finding the cold angles of my alarm. It feels like a touchstone.

'Trust the weather to be this shit today,' Rachel mutters, pulling the hood of her jumper over her head, her feet crunching in the wet, shell-heavy sand. A grey, tattered rucksack bounces on her back, the handle of a baseball bat protruding from the zipper. The sight of it makes my stomach clench. This wasn't part of our plan, but I tell myself Rachel's just being cautious. 'How are you feeling, Mary?'

I shrug.

'It's good to be scared,' she says. 'It'll make your reflexes quicker.'

This statement frightens rather than reassures me. I think of Mark's pleading message, trying to recapture the power I felt only yesterday. It's gone.

'See that houseboat?' Rachel's saying, jerking her head to the right. There's an energy in her today – she's restless, on edge. 'I used to fantasise I had one of those growing up. That I could go wherever I wanted, live wherever I wanted. And if I didn't like a place anymore, I could leave. Just like that.'

I look at the houseboat, creaking back and forth, staring out with its unseeing eyes. I shiver. Those were almost my exact thoughts when I first noticed it.

'What was it like, Mary?'

'What?'

'What was it like? I mean, you had a boat like that, didn't you?'

'Huh? No, I . . .' I look at the houseboat more closely, tripping over something on the sand then righting myself.

'Sorry,' Rachel's staring ahead and I can't see her face. 'I thought you told me about it once. But I must have been mistaken.'

Frowning, I crane my neck to see the boat until we round the turn leading to the bush track, and it's out of sight.

If it were warmer, the leafy foreshore would be crowded

on a Sunday afternoon. Instead, only a few people are scattered about; a frazzled young couple coaxing their screaming toddler into a car, a group of teenagers smoking by the entrance to the bushwalk at the mouth of the woods. Magpies warble in the trees overhead, something rustles in the bushes as we pass.

My stomach is full of bricks. I feel sick. 'Rachel,' I say, my feet stopping of their own accord. 'I'm not sure about this.'

Rachel's head whips around and the fire in her eyes makes me flinch. 'You're not giving up now!' She moves towards me. I step back and her eyes soften. 'I'm sorry. I'm sorry, Mary. I know this is hard . . . harder for you. But you've come too far to give up. You know you need to do this. You *need* to, Mary.'

I look in her eyes. There's compassion and conviction and something else. Determination. Isn't that what I want? To be strong, and to stop running? I nod. 'Okay.'

Rachel takes my hand. 'Come on.'

I put one foot in front of the other, run over the plan in my mind. I can do this. I *have* to do this.

The sounds of human voices disappear and soon all I can hear is the squelch of our shoes and the patter of rain. We're nearing the crest of the craggy hill that looms above the open sea, our arranged meeting place. Public, so safe enough, yet isolated enough for a confession. I can't see anyone, but I feel a presence, like someone is watching.

'I'm going to have to disappear,' Rachel says.

'What?'

'Before he sees me. He has to think you're alone. Don't worry, I'll be right nearby. Watching.'

I pull in a shaky breath. It's happening. 'Yeah. Yes, okay.'

We approach the crest. I don't know how long I've been walking, it feels like an eternity, when there's pressure on the small of my back, nudging me forward. 'Go.' I look over my shoulder but Rachel's gone.

'Mary!'

I freeze. Nothing could have prepared me for his voice.

'Mary!' He's striding towards me – where did he come from? – hair damp and stuck to his head, his mouth stretched in a lopsided grin. Those ice-blue eyes bore into me. 'Hey.'

It's as though I'm watching him on a screen. 'Wait . . .' I say, but I don't know what for, and he stops a metre from me, brow creased, eyes moist as if with tears, but it's probably just rain.

'I've missed you.' His voice breaks on words that would once have made me weak. Behind him the sky is clearing, it opens like a halo above his head. He's only a few metres from the edge of the crest that rises above jagged rocks and stormy sea. He looks lost.

I twitch, instinctively wanting to reach out to comfort him. Muscle memory. But my brain catches up and I dig my hands into my pockets. My fingers find my alarm, then my phone. I inch my thumb along the screen to the right spot and press. *Record*.

'Haven't you missed me?'

I glance behind me; there's a thatch of bushland nearby and one massive tree. Maybe Rachel's hiding behind there.

'Mary.' The softness, the uncertainty, in his voice doesn't suit him.

I swallow, hard. 'You hurt me, Mark.'

He frowns. 'I hurt you?'

My spine straightens though my knees are jelly. 'You know you did.'

'*I* hurt *you*?'

A bitter laugh escapes. He's trying this old routine, even now.

'Mary, I don't know what to say. I don't know how you can think that.' He edges towards me, his eyes wide and sincere. 'Everything I did was out of concern for you. You know how you can get . . .'

I tremble, swallow against a lump in my throat. He'll never change. He can't see it. What I did for him, what I would have done – anything, *anything*. Now it's too late. What he's done can't be glossed over, can't be turned back on me. The damage is permanent. It can't be erased.

'I know what you did.' My voice sounds small, pitiful. I raise it. '*I know what you did.*'

Mark's searching my face, the picture of confusion. He does it so well. 'What are you talking about?'

'That night. I know what you did. Tom Forrester . . . I *know*.'

Understanding dawns on Mark's face. I watch as

confusion turns to shock, then to derision. 'Oh, you're funny – *hilarious*.' He looks almost amused, but the glint in his eyes is my warning. I step back.

'I remember. I saw you. You did it. I saw you holding the brick. It was covered in blood.'

'You're crazy.' His voice is dangerously soft. He takes a step towards me. 'You have no idea what you saw.'

I fight the urge to run, reminding myself Rachel is close by.

'You don't remember a thing. You were fucking high, fucking drunk. You and your imagination . . .'

My fingers clench in fists. I don't know if I'm shivering from the cold or shaking with anger. 'Just admit it, Mark. Or should I say Jon? Raj, maybe? Who were you that night?'

Mark laughs. 'You think you're clever, don't you? You think you've got it all figured out.'

'We both know it was you. Why don't you just admit it?'

'You don't know anything,' he sneers. 'I told you to forget about it. For your own good, Mary, you should just forget about Tom Forrester.'

'I can't!' My voice breaks. 'I have to know. Tell me . . . did you do it?'

Mark shakes his head. 'When are you going to learn? When are you going to learn to listen to me?' There's something in his eyes that resembles pity. 'My Mary. Mary, Mary, quite contrary.' He holds out his arms, takes another step forward.

Before I can even shout 'No!' there's a loud *thwack* and suddenly he's on all fours at my feet. My lungs seize on a gasp as Rachel swings the baseball bat again, bringing it down onto Mark's skull with a solid *crunch*. He lies face down on the grass, motionless, dark liquid pooling around his head.

Rachel wipes her brow with the back of her arm, looks at me, then back at Mark. She nudges his ribs with her toe as if testing his weight. 'Arsehole.'

Time slows to a halt, staggers, then speeds up again. All I can hear is the sound of my own breath.

Rachel looks over her shoulder, drops to her knees and places both hands on Mark's chest. She grimaces as she pushes him with all her might, but he is a dead weight. The next thing I know, she has grabbed my wrist and I'm down there, on my knees.

'Help me, Mary.' Rachel's voice is eerily calm, her face a mask as she stares down at the back of Mark's head. The rapid rise and fall of her chest is the only thing betraying her panic. Or is it something else she feels?

I'm not sure what she's asking of me. But, somehow, I don't hesitate. My vision is glossy through the tears, and I focus on my hands splayed over his leg, the feel of his coarse, wet jeans as I grab them with my fingertips. Together, we roll him, over and over. Until he reaches the edge of the crest.

The rain picks up. I don't even hear the splash.

Chapter Forty-Two

The rhythm of the train is like a heartbeat. It sounds over my raging pulse, rocking me to and fro like a mother nursing her baby. Only the rhythm cannot comfort me. Nothing can.

It's been over an hour. We're somewhere on the central coast, just across the water from Sydney's northern beaches, from home, but I haven't been paying attention to the stops. I'm numb. Then I'm jittery, seasick. Then numb again.

I close my eyes, trying to shut out the images. Mark's face. The blood, so much blood. Rachel on her knees. What she did. What *I* did.

Help me, Mary.

A surge of nausea has me clamping my hands to my mouth. I gag, swallow, slam my eyes shut and will myself to hold it in.

Rachel doesn't seem to notice.

I try to focus on something, anything. Out the window, through the mist, ancient mountains rise above the grey sea like sleeping dragons. The sky is grey too, the same melancholy shade, and storm clouds roll through, menacing.

Rachel won't stop moving. Her ankles are crossed, her foot bouncing, bouncing, bouncing. We haven't spoken since Sydney. She's chewing her nails, peeling off half-moon slivers, pulling them from her mouth and throwing them on the floor.

Watching her is making me nervous and my stomach is as violent as the sky. I avert my gaze to the only other passenger in the carriage; an obese middle-aged man sprawled prone across a three-person seat, head thrown back, snoring. The sound is awful and he looks disgusting, a huge green glob of snot hanging from his nose vibrating with each snore.

Nausea rises again. I'm about to run for the loo when the train begins to slow and Rachel gets up. 'We're here.'

Light rain is falling when we step from the carriage, each pulling our hoods over our heads. There haven't been many houses along the way and there are even fewer here. Beyond the tiny, deserted platform there's only bush, and beyond it I can hear the crash of waves on the shore. 'Where are we going?'

Rachel doesn't respond, she just throws a peculiar smile over her shoulder. I'm shivering now, though it's humid here, warmer than it was in Sydney. The storm seems to have followed us, purple-grey clouds hang low in the sky and there's a faint rumble in the distance.

I follow Rachel out of the platform and into a clearing where a narrow path winds into the bush. We don't speak – the only sound is our feet crunching along the undergrowth. The path is well-trodden, which is a small comfort. I have no desire to be in the middle of nowhere right now.

After a few minutes, a house appears through the trees. Although it's not really a house – more of a cabin, built in the style you'd expect to see in northern Europe rather than the New South Wales central coast. It would be pretty if it wasn't so dilapidated.

Rachel continues along the path until we reach the front door. There's something familiar about the cabin, something I can't place. She opens the door – it doesn't appear to be locked – and walks inside. I follow.

We enter a spacious living area, decorated sparsely, not much but a dusty six-foot faux Christmas tree in the corner near a stone fireplace. Plastic chairs – the shabby, broken kind you see lying by the side of the road during council pick-up – are arranged in a semicircle, pointed at a space where a television should be, but there is only a hole in the wall with some power cords sticking out. Empty McDonald's wrappers, beer bottles and crisp packets litter the room, hinting at squatters.

What once might have been a beautiful space is now covered in dust and cobwebs, dank with the smell of mould. It bears all the signs of a scene hastily abandoned. Rachel never mentioned anything like this. Why has she brought me here? What else has she got planned?

Something slithers down my spine; a creeping sense of déjà vu.

The floorboards creak as we cross the room. We pass through an arched doorway and into a kitchen that opens onto a wooden deck, a layout not dissimilar to our place back home. The room, though small, gives the illusion of space, light-filled and open. The island in the centre is only half constructed; bricks and tiles lie scattered on the floor. Beyond the glass sliding doors, left open, I can hear the sea.

'What is this place?'

Rachel doesn't answer, she just dumps her rucksack on the island, riffles through it and pulls out a bottle of amber liquid. Bourbon.

I look through the open doors at the churning sky. It's not raining, but it's dark for the time of day. The rhythmic crash of the waves beckons me. The deck planks feel unstable under my feet, and I tread gingerly until I reach the rickety railing. The house has been built into a cliff face. Below, the grey sea laps at the rocky shore.

It's a long way down. If you fell the wrong way, you wouldn't survive the landing. Before I can even think of Mark, my body goes cold all over — for another reason. I've been here before. I know it, in my bones.

'Here,' Rachel appears beside me with a plastic cup. I can smell the bourbon and the sickly sweetness of cola.

I take the cup and gulp from it though my stomach churns. 'I've been here before.'

'Yes.'

I stare out at the rolling ocean, wondering what it would be like to plunge into its icy depths. 'Do you think he's dead?'

Silence. Then the click of a lighter as Rachel lights a cigarette. I didn't even know she smoked. 'I don't know. I think so.'

I close my eyes, see the image of Mark's face gushing blood. I can't think about it, can't think about what she did. I was wrong. Wrong about everything.

'We have to call the police.'

'I'd rather die.' Rachel looks fierce. She inhales aggressively on her cigarette, stares out into the distance. For a second it's like I don't know her, have never seen her before.

'Can I have one of those?'

Rachel hands me the cigarettes and I pull one out with shaking fingers, flick the lighter several times before it ignites.

As I cough on the first drag, something occurs to me. 'Why'd you bring a bag?'

'What?'

'That bag, why'd you bring it?'

Rachel shrugs. She's not jittery anymore, though she's

eyeing me warily. She puffs on her cigarette, sips her drink. 'To carry the bat and stuff.'

'Bullshit.' The sharpness of my voice startles me. 'You knew we were coming here. That's why. What else is in there?'

Rachel sighs. 'Just some supplies. A few clothes, toothbrushes. Booze.' She gives me a weak smile.

'You planned this. You . . .' I bite back the ugly, unfathomable words. *You killed Mark.*

'He was going to hurt you. I couldn't let him do that.' Rachel flicks her cigarette butt over the railing. 'Don't think he wouldn't have killed you if he had the chance. Like he tried to kill me.'

'He what?'

Rachel snorts. 'Getting hit by that car was no accident. He wanted to make sure I didn't get to you before he did.'

I shake my head. What she's saying sounds crazy, but what part of all this was ever sane? I don't know what to believe anymore.

'Why are we here?' Somehow, as I ask, I know I already have the answer.

Rachel gives me a sad smile. She takes our cups into the kitchen. When she returns, they are both full.

There's a chunk missing from the rotting balcony railing, as if something has fallen through it. Beyond it, in the distance, something bobs on the water's surface. That's our beach, over there, across the water. I can see the fish and chip shop, can just make out the abandoned houseboat, the one with blank eyes that stare at me as I pass.

Our very own boat, a voice says in my mind. *We can spend nights there in summer, take it to the cabin on holidays. So much quicker than driving or the train. And so much fun!*

My heart pounds. Now I see it, caught on the edge of one of the broken rails, red and white and fluttering in the wind. *Police tape.*

I pull hard on the cigarette, my head spinning. I close my eyes as my body shakes. 'Oh my God.'

Rachel puts a hand on my arm. 'It had to happen this way.'

The Christmas tree. The unfinished kitchen island. The rickety wooden deck. The houseboat.

I whirl around, stare hard at the bricks littering the kitchen floor. They were redoing the cabin. Renovating. *'We'll build a kitchen island, fix up the deck.'* There were arguments about the patio furniture, the colour of the lounge-room walls. I was here. I was here that Christmas with my parents.

A strange sound, like a whimper, fills the air. It takes a moment before I realise it's me.

White Christmas playing on the television in the background. The clink of ice in glasses. Shouting. Me on the floor, hands over my head, crying. My mother's voice.

'What did you do to her? What did you do to our baby?'

Chapter Forty-Three

'How are you feeling?'

Someone is speaking to me. I blink and see Rachel's face come into focus. There's a pain in my chest, making it hard to breathe. My head is thick with sleep, my mouth pasty like I've eaten chalk.

Rachel is smiling sadly as she brushes a strand of hair from my face. 'You've had a shock. You needed some rest.'

'Where am I?'

'You were feeling tired, so I took you to bed. I brought clean sheets and everything.'

I look around. I'm in a small bedroom, as run-down as the rest of the house – damp and dusty, sagging walls, nothing but an old vanity dresser with a broken mirror and the bed I'm in.

'I just passed out?'

Rachel looks sheepish. 'I knew it would be a shock, coming here. I gave you some of your meds. In your drink. I thought it would help.'

I look at the girl sitting on the edge of the bed, her skin smooth as glass, those kitten-round eyes in her child-like face. This girl killed Mark. She drugged me. She knew about this place and planned to bring me here.

She's insane.

Under the covers, I reach for my pocket and realise I'm no longer wearing my hoodie. My phone and alarm are gone. *Fuck.* I glance at the door. Somehow I know it opens to the hall, which leads to the living room. I could probably make it from here to the front door in ten seconds.

'Rest some more,' Rachel says. 'There's no toilet paper and I didn't have room for much food. There's a little shop around the corner – thought I might pop in before it shuts. You're okay to stay here, aren't you? It'll be safe. I won't be long – ten minutes, tops.'

When I find my voice, it comes out in a croak. 'Okay.' I rest my head back on the lumpy pillow, close my eyes until I hear her stand, walk down the hall, open and close the front door.

I throw back the covers and stand so fast my head spins. My eyes dart around the room and land on my hoodie hanging on the back of the door. *Thank God.* I grab it, plunge my hands into the pockets. There's no phone, but there's something else – something small, hard and familiar, buried deep. Rachel must have missed it. I grab the alarm and shove it in the pocket of my jeans.

I'm about to run for the door when I see the rucksack, fallen over on its side, contents spilling out. Bold letters catch my eye – a name written in bold, black text. *Sylvia Baker.*

I know I should go as Rachel will be back any minute, but I crouch down and snatch up the newspaper.

A tragic Christmas for the Baker family.

My eyes skin the column of writing and pick out the words: *Sylvia Baker kills husband Alan Baker, then herself, in a murder-suicide.*

Blood pulses in my ears.

I scroll further down: *Teenage daughter sexually abused by father.*

My heart stops. The world goes quiet.

What did you do to our baby?

With a strangled sob, I drop to my knees.

I don't know how long I've been kneeling. The room has grown dark. It can't have been too long; Rachel's not back.

I remember now. I remember it all.

All those nights. The fear. The shame. The secrets.

That Christmas. The screaming. Wood splintering. The splash. Then another. Silence.

I have to get out of here.

But why did she bring you here? a voice asks.

I need to leave. Run. Alert the police.

What does she know that you don't?

I grab the rucksack and turn it upside down. A large notebook, some clothes and a hip flask tumble out. There's something else in there, bulky and heavy. I shake the bag and a pair of red shoes hit the floor. *Clunk, clunk.*

I'm shaking uncontrollably. It was her. *She* took the shoes. *Why?*

I grab the notebook and flip it open. I'm assaulted by photographs. Tens of them, hundreds, in varying sizes and shapes, some cut from magazines, some from school yearbooks, some taken as recently as last week.

All of them are of me.

Hands trembling, I turn the pages. There are photos of me sunbathing as a teenager on the beach. Me on the balcony in the Fitzroy apartment. One of me sleeping in the Sydney flat. Me posing with Megan Keeler in our school uniforms, lips pushed forward in a duck pout – she's printed it from Facebook. Several of me and Mark: one of us kissing, one of me naked, sprawled prone on the bed. One of me wearing the flimsy silk dress and red shoes I was wearing That Night. How did she get hold of these?

I turn the page and the room grows darker still. Newspaper and magazine articles about my parents – their careers, their vineyard estate, their achievements, their failures. Paedophilia rumours, divorce rumours. Murder. Suicide.

I pull out a newspaper clipping which is coffee-stained, its edges worn. *Alan and Sylvia Baker: MISSING. Last seen at family holiday cabin on the NSW central coast.* I squint at the pixelated photo. It's this cabin. My parents were last seen here. My chest is tight. *Rachel knew this all along?* It's hard to breathe. Yet I can't stop looking.

There are more pictures of me, and some of Rachel. A page torn from my school yearbook. There's me, coming first in the cross-country marathon. And Rachel – it's her, I can tell – in the choir photo, blonde hair cut short with a crooked fringe, grainy in black and white, barely recognisable. How did I not know we went to school together?

I find a few clippings on the Tom Forrester case wedged between the pages. *Murderer never found* underlined in red pen like blood stains. Angry red lines slash an 'x' through Tom's face, as though he's a mistake in an essay.

There's the other half of the photo I found near Cat's door. Me smiling, one eye squinting, my left arm visible as I'm angling the camera above us. I think of the ugly word scrawled across the back of the photo. *Slut.* It was Rachel who wrote that, not Cat.

Another photo – a recent one of Mark kissing a girl who I think, at first, is me. But it isn't.

It's Rachel.

'Fuck.' I run an unsteady hand over my face. It's too much. My parents, Mark, *this*. 'What the fuck. What the *fuck*?'

Something compels me to keep looking. There are photos of me and Rachel. Some of us stuck together from different photos. Our faces, cut in half, spliced together.

Rachel's head on my body. One word scrawled above her head, over and over and over.

Sophie.

Sophie.

Run, Sophie.

It was her. It was Rachel all along.

Chapter Forty-Four

I can't swallow. Can hardly breathe. I've reached the end of the scrapbook but there's still more . . . a couple of lined A4 pages folded in half at the back of the book.

I unfold them with trembling fingers. There's a date scribbled – 7.12.16, a week ago – at the top of the page, the writing ill-formed and messy, as if written in a hurry. It looks like a letter – though it's not addressed to anyone. Either way, I know it's meant for me.

You'll find out if I'm not careful. And it's not like I don't want you to – eventually, of course. I don't want there to be secrets between us. We've had more than our share of lies and we both deserve better than that. But I didn't want you to find out like this. This wasn't how I planned it.

I wasn't going to tell you about me and Mark. I didn't think it was necessary, but I know better now. You need to know everything, from beginning to end. No secrets. No lies.

I've fucked up so badly. I should have known. In fact, I did know, but I did it anyway. Why? Why? I could ask myself that question a million times and still never truly understand. All I know is I loved you too much, if that makes any sense at all, and even though I know better than I did before, even though I know you're not someone to envy but someone to pity, I couldn't help it. All those years of yearning . . . when the chance came to pretend, to be you for just a second . . . it was too irresistible. It was a mistake, and I regret it — I promise you I do. The only consolation is that I learned things about you. And about him. Enough to figure out what needs to be done.

I want to explain; I want you to understand, though I have no excuse. It first happened at that dingy place you went to together sometimes, usually on Wednesdays when it was less crowded. The underground place with the neon pink light above the door and nothing else to mark its existence. It was easy to follow you in, and I did it often — the lights were so low in there, dim-lit like a brothel. Yes, that's right, I would know — with those cheap red beehive-shaped candle holders on every table and hundreds of old black and white postcards tacked to the walls. You'd order those tiny $7 pizzas that came *out on scratched wooden paddles — a red wine for you, Jack Daniels for him, and I'd sit in a corner, pretend to wait for someone and watch. Just to make sure you were okay, I'd tell myself, but of course it went a bit further than that. Proven by what I did one night when he showed up there alone.*

I didn't know what he was like back then. I swear it. Not the extent of it anyway. Of course I didn't, or I'd never have done what I did. My visits never went further than a bit of eavesdropping in the beginning, and things seemed okay then. Like I said, I was checking on you. Ever since what happened to your parents, that diagnosis that Doctor Sarah gave you (I booked an appointment with her a couple of times, lifted some info off that dinosaur of a laptop of hers afterwards. She really needs to put a password on it), I figured it was my job to look out for you. Not like fucking condescending Cat, or your well-meaning but useless aunt. What the fuck have they ever done for you? Pretend everything is fucking fine? Never let you talk about shit, never let you figure out the truth so you can properly heal?

I don't blame Doctor Sarah. At least, not fully. You were getting better for a while, making progress — everyone could see that. But something must have happened because you stopped going to see her, and that's when things spiralled out of control. Not all at once but slowly, slowly, until the old you was almost gone. Was it him? Did he stop you going back? Stop you from being the real you and facing the real facts? It must have been — because he wanted to keep you. And for that to happen, for him to keep you compliant, he had to keep you blind.

He's good, I'll give him that. Not at sex — too rough, and not in a good way. But controlling enough that it's exciting, at least. You know what I mean, of course. (Or was it different with you?) Rough enough that it feels like you're being properly fucked. But that's where the good points end, and there's only so much mindless jackhammer sex you can take before it gets boring. He's too inconsiderate, too sloppy. After trying to impress the first few times, he shirks the pretence, caves in to his selfishness.

But it was exciting that first time. I'm sorry, admitting it is terrible, but it's a relief, too. Like I said, I don't want there to be secrets between us. So, the truth: it was exciting, thrilling to be in the bed where you slept, to smell you on the sheets. I could pretend. I could pretend I had everything, that I lived in this flash apartment, that I had a bank account full of money, that I was loved by this dark and sexy man who was nailing me into the bed.

But things are rarely how they seem and he didn't turn out to be that great, did he? The sex was crap, wasn't it? Let's call a spade a spade. Someone who doesn't give a fuck about others, who can't put themselves in someone else's shoes — what chance have they got at being good at something as intimate as sex? He's better at the mind-fucking. He puts more time into that and invests more energy, because it serves a purpose. Serves him. With the sex? He'd already got what he wanted.

I suppose it started when I'd ask questions about you. Maybe it made him question himself, to consider for a moment what he was doing to you (if he has any shame, that is). Maybe he was just bugged by my questions. Who knows? But once he'd let the mask slip it never took much to set him off, did it?

It wasn't the physical stuff that was the worst thing. It was the psychological abuse – the way he made me feel. That's the ultimate control, isn't it? Grinding someone down until their self-worth is dust. Until they believe those carefully constructed lies. And one of the best tools? Turning it all around on you. Blame and shame. You don't realise how easy it is until it happens to you. It's so subtle you don't even notice it's happening. You already think you're shit, so someone pointing it out gently, making it sound like concern – well, you just lap it right up. And once that pattern's in place, the more obvious stuff can be glossed over with excuses, undermining your memory of it. 'You were so fucked up you can't remember what happened.' 'You were the one throwing punches.' 'I wouldn't have done it if you weren't flirting with that bartender.' 'Maybe next time you'll know not to get me so worked up.' 'I was jealous because I love you so much.'

And of course it worked wonders on me, because

I'm riddled with shame. Me with even more cause than you, after what I'd done. And didn't he get away with shit once he figured out he could point out what I was doing to you — I was a whore, of course, never mind that he was the cheater. Gaslighting. Google it; the fucker is textbook.

But while people like that might be cunning, they're not smart. If they were smart, they'd be decent people and live a decent life. Live with some fucking self-respect. Nope. People like him are missing part of their brain or something — they'd rather waste time figuring out how to wrought the system than earn an honest living.

See, the idiot gave me a heads-up. The way he spoke about you, like you were some puppet he could control — it was sickening. This one night, high as fuck, he told me everything. With this shit-eating grin on his face like he was proud of it. Like I was supposed to be on board with his scheme to use you up and spit you out. Like I was supposed to think he was clever.

That sob story about his brother killing himself? I'm sure he told it to you, too. Yeah, that's a line. Don't get me wrong, his brother did top himself. And Mark found him. I googled it — it was in the paper that year, so his story checks out. But that's his MO. That's how he gets girls into bed. Players' handbook 101, right? I feel so pathetic that I bought it. And, along with it, all the bullshit that was somehow excusable because he had this one bad thing happen to him. We all have bad things happen to us at some point, don't we? And we don't use it to manipulate others to get what we want. We don't use it to excuse our shitty behaviour. He's a coward and a liar and a cheat and I hate him as much as I ever hated my foster father.

He'd have proposed to you. Ha, did you know that? I don't think you did. I don't think you have any idea that was coming. He'd have proposed and, if you said no, he'd have blackmailed you into it. Use that night Tom was murdered to threaten you, hold it over your head so you'd give in. And you know it's not because he loves you. I'm not saying it to hurt you, because you know it already. You've got something else that matters much more to him than that. Thank fuck you figured it out in time. Just.

That night when he let his guard slip? That's when the light bulb went off. That's when I knew what he was. And what I needed to do.

That – amongst other reasons – is why I can't let him find you. Not until I've done what needs to be done, anyway. Not until I've figured out a plan. I can't let you find out about us, or about that night, that way – and he'd use that, say I tricked him into it all somehow. That I was to blame for everything. I'll have to go back to the apartment to get those shoes because you can't find them. If you do, and you take them to the cops, you'll find out everything else. And it's too soon for that.

I will tell you everything. But the time has to be right. You deserve a second chance at life, and I'll make sure you get it. Make sure those fucking enablers in your life stop letting you live a lie. Forget fucking Cat. You need me. You need me to show you the truth, and be there for you when you finally understand.

There's a smudge at the bottom of the page – a signature of some kind? – that looks like a snake. Or a letter.

'S'

The front door slams and I jump, the notebook falling to the floor.

'Fuck!' I run to the window and try the latch but it's rusted shut. I scan the room frantically for a weapon, but it's as bare as a prison cell.

Footsteps sound in the hallway seconds before Rachel bursts through the door. She smiles, holding up a bag. 'You're up! I got candles as there's no power here. Oh, and some wine . . .'

I back up towards the window until my back is flush against it.

Rachel frowns. 'What's wrong?' She looks down to where her belongings are scattered on the floor. 'Oh.'

I scan her face, trying to read her expression, but it's like I'm looking at a complete stranger. Suddenly everything flickers like a television screen with bad reception.

I blink, shake my head. The colours are leaking from reality and it feels like I'm underwater.

I sink to my knees, cradling my head in my hands. What's happening? The world's gone black and white and fuzzy around the edges, I can feel the darkness beckoning.

I'm on my back now, I'm not sure how. I feel no pain, only the pull of unconsciousness as Rachel stands over me, looking down with a peculiar smile.

Chapter Forty-Five

'Are you awake?'

I rub my eyes and turn towards the sound of the voice.

'Mary?' Male laughter, warm lips on my forehead, my cheek. 'Wake up, sleepyhead.'

I yawn and blink as my eyes adjust to the light. Ben's face comes into focus; he's smiling down at me, frail morning sunlight framing his messy hair like a halo.

I feel a rush of warmth in my chest. And then, just as quickly, I go cold all over. I sit up in bed, my eyes darting around the room. *My* room, back in the apartment. How can that be?

'Where's Rachel?'

Ben eyes me curiously. 'I don't know. Does she work on Fridays?'

'No, it's just that we . . .' The words die on my lips as

it hits me. We never met with Mark. Never went to the cabin. Rachel isn't some deranged killer.

It was all a dream.

I fall back against the pillows, relief bursting out of me in a bark of laughter.

Ben looks down at me with a bemused expression. He lifts a strand of hair that's fallen across my face and tugs it. 'What's so funny?'

I shake my head, basking in the wonderful feeling of relief. I'm going to tell Rachel it's a stupid idea to meet with Mark, that I'll just keep trying the cops. That's the smart thing to do, isn't it?

'Mary?'

I giggle. 'Sorry. It's . . . Oh, never mind.'

Ben chuckles as he shakes his head. 'You're a funny one.'

'Oh, hey. Do you want to try that new pub by the water?'

Ben's face lights up. 'I was going to suggest that!' He throws back the covers and hops out of bed like an exuberant child, already tugging his shorts on over his boxers.

I watch the muscles in his back working as he pulls on his T-shirt. He has a tattoo on his shoulder I haven't noticed before. Some kind of Celtic symbol, hard to see from here. It looks familiar, though. I narrow my eyes. Didn't Mark have a tattoo like that?

'What are you waiting for?' Ben is saying. 'Get up, you stupid bitch.'

My skin goes cold. 'What did you say?'

When Ben turns around, Tom Forrester's face is staring down at me. 'I said, *Get up, you stupid bitch.*'

Light sears my corneas when I open my eyes. I scream.

'Oh dear,' Rachel says, her face coming into focus. She's kneeling over me with a torch in her hand, her brow knitted. Golden hair hangs over her shoulder in a gossamer curtain. She turns off the torch, clicks her tongue. 'You must have had a reaction to the meds. Are you not supposed to mix them? I'm sorry about that. Your pupils are fine now, though. What are you on again?'

I try my voice but it comes out as a gurgle.

'Sorry, what was that?'

'You . . . drugged me?' My head is clouded, my brain heavy. 'Again?'

Rachel looks hurt. 'I never *drugged* you. Honestly, Mary, what do you think of me?'

I don't know what to think. It's a struggle to sit up, but I manage. 'How long have I been out?'

'Nearly twenty-four hours.'

I jolt. 'Fuck.'

'You must be hungry. Are you hungry, Mary?'

My stomach rumbles, but it's nausea I feel. 'No.'

'You should eat something. I've made . . .'

'No!'

Rachel looks shocked, then her face hardens. 'I'm sorry, okay? This hasn't been easy on me either. I didn't want . . . I honestly didn't know you'd be out for so long. I only wanted you to relax, so I could explain . . .'

'Relax?' My voice is shrill. Adrenalin fires through my weakened body. 'You're kidding, right?'

Rachel glares. 'This was the only way. I've only done this for your sake. You have to trust me.'

My eyes wander to the photos and newspaper clippings littering the floor. '*Trust* you?'

'I've only ever wanted what's best for you. I think deep down you know that,' Rachel says quietly.

I stare at her, trying to make sense of her face. Trying to reconcile this strange person with the girl I thought I knew. 'Cat will be wondering where I am. So will Ben.'

Rachel shakes her head. 'No. They won't. I texted them from your phone saying we were going away for a few days. You know, to get some headspace. Cat didn't think it was a great idea, but that's probably because she's not my biggest fan, is she?'

When I don't respond, Rachel frowns and sighs.

'I suppose you're thinking she was right about me now.'

Dear, dependable Cat. She tried to warn me. Why didn't I listen? What have I done? I run a hand over my thigh, feel the shape of the alarm through the denim. I squeeze my eyes shut and press, hard. *Please let this work.* 'I don't know what to think,' I say. 'I mean, what the fuck? What the *fuck*, Rachel?!'

'Calm down,' Rachel holds up her hands. She smiles as though everything is fine. As though *I'm* the one who's crazy. 'You've had a shock. It's understandable. If you let me explain . . .'

'Explain? Explain what? I trusted you. I thought you were trying to *help* me!'

'I *am* trying to help you,' she snaps. 'I'm trying to protect you.'

I gape at her and she glares back.

Then she takes a deep breath and smiles. 'I can explain, from the beginning – I promise. It will all make sense then. Can you at least let me do that?'

I shake my head, almost laugh. What choice do I have? 'Sure,' I croak. 'Sure, why not?' I curl my fingers around my alarm. The cops will be here soon. Let her tell her sob story. It will be the last lie she ever tells me.

I'm foggy-headed and a bit unsteady on my feet, but I follow Rachel into the kitchen and sit on one of the stools by the island. Though it's still light enough outside to see, the sun will be setting soon. Rachel lights a candle, opens a bottle of wine and fills our plastic cups to the brim. I shake my head at the insanity of it all. I'm about to drink wine with a killer.

'I'm not going to hurt you, Mary. You can relax, okay?'

Words evade me. I nod, though I don't believe her. I've seen what she's capable of.

'Okay,' Rachel gives me a secretive smile, as if this is a girls' weekend and we're playing truth or dare. 'Good.'

'Why am I here?' I ask. 'What does it have to do with

the night of Tom's murder? I saw the articles. What do you know about it?' I have a feeling I already know.

Rachel doesn't say anything for a moment, but then she asks, 'What do you remember, Mary?'

I scoff. 'Why don't you tell me what you remember?'

Rachel looks around, gestures to the balcony. 'What do you remember about what happened here?'

I close my eyes against an unwanted memory. My father's eyes wide with fear. The screaming. The splash.

'Mary?'

'I remember what happened,' I say, my voice barely a whisper. 'I remember what my *father* . . .' My voice breaks on the word. 'I know what he did. What Mum did to him because of it.'

Rachel exhales as if she's been holding her breath. 'That's good.'

I eye her sharply.

'Not good, exactly. Of course it's not good. But it's progress.'

I narrow my eyes. 'Why does any of this even matter to you?' I ask. 'Why do *I* matter? Just help me understand that much, at least.'

Rachel brings her cup to her lips, takes a long pull. *This ought to be good.*

'I guess it first started at school,' she says eventually. She's quiet for a moment, staring thoughtfully through the glass doors. 'You were different to the others, especially to me. You had everything. You know that, don't you? I mean, you literally had *everything*.' She laughs without humour.

I watch her, one hand on my pocket.

'It wasn't just that, it was other stuff too. Who you are. Or who you *were*. Before, I mean,' she sighs, twisting a strand of hair around her finger. 'Everyone liked you. You didn't even have to try. It wasn't just because of your parents, all that money and fame and shit, although that's what I wanted to believe then. It was more than that. At school, you didn't give a fuck what anyone thought. You always had some smart-arse comeback. You were funny, smart, pretty . . . All the guys thought you were *so hot*.'

Her words conjure a vague memory of that version of me; the one I lost to grief and abuse. The one I wanted to be again. Is that really how people saw me?

'They never even noticed me. Neither did you, of course. You don't remember me, do you?' she asks.

I avoid her piercing gaze, thinking of the grainy picture of the girl with untidy hair and an awkward smile. It's hard to believe they're the same person. 'No,' I admit.

Rachel's laughter is short and sharp. 'Nobody noticed the girl who cut her own hair, wore second-hand uniforms and couldn't afford a mobile phone. I only got into that school because they felt sorry for me – did you know that? Did you know they have a scholarship programme for kids like me?'

I shake my head.

'Well, they do. My foster parents . . . Marnie and *Steve*.' She spits the name. Her eyes glitter. 'They couldn't afford shit. Don't know why you'd take on a kid if you couldn't

afford it, if you didn't give a *fuck* what happened to them.'
There's a bubble of spit in the corner of her mouth. She
wipes it away.

'I wanted to be like you. I wanted what you had. I
wanted to *be* you.' She gulps her wine and sniffs. 'I took
it too far. I know that. Don't think I don't know it, that
I haven't realised. I have. And I'm making up for it, I swear.'

I clutch the cup that's growing warm in my hand.

'It was such a strange feeling; it was like I loved you
and hated you at the same time, you know?' She looks at
me as though she expects me to understand, and looks
away when I don't respond. I see it now, how broken she
is, like an injured bird. Yet it's hard to believe, even now,
that she's capable of killing.

'I used to sit behind you in registration. My name came
right after yours . . . Baker, Cummings.' She smiles wist-
fully. 'You always had this curl of hair on the back of your
neck when your hair was in a ponytail. Right here . . .'
She reaches out and I jerk away from her hand.

She gets this lost, hurt look. Then her expression darkens.
'Do you remember getting suspended from school? I
thought that was *so cool* when I was fifteen. Some girl
called you a slut and you let her have it. Wasn't the first
time, either. They said you had anger issues. Sent you to
the counsellor. Remember that?' She snorts. 'But then you
started ditching school, not showing up for classes. I
wondered where you were. I worried. After I found out
what happened to you, what your dad did . . .'

I flinch.

'They were just rumours, but *I* knew they were true. I'd know the signs, wouldn't I? I wasn't jealous then. Not after that. I couldn't believe I hadn't picked up on it before . . . hadn't realised how similar we were. I'd thought you were so perfect, but I was wrong. And suddenly, I understood. I've always had it in me, too. The anger. It never goes away. I started to realise we weren't so different after all, that we had a lot in common. All your confidence, that bravado – it was just an act. And that made me love you more.'

She smiles at me, a strange, wistful smile.

'The Mark thing just happened – I didn't plan it. I want you to know that. I would never, *ever* hurt you on purpose. I was looking out for you. I watched you sometimes – not in a sick way, not in the shower or anything. I just wanted to check what you were up to, make sure you were okay. When all that stuff happened with your parents . . .' She trails off, inhales sharply through her teeth.

I close my eyes against a thrust of pain.

'That was so fucked up, and it changed you. You changed.' She looks at me, hard. 'That was when I started to worry about you. I was planning to bump into you somewhere, start chatting over a drink, try to get to know you. I knew we'd understand each other. I thought I could help.

'It was totally by accident that I ran into Mark when he wasn't with you. It was at that underground bar in Fitzroy you guys used to go to. I knew you were seeing

313

him, I think it was around the time you guys were moving to the coast. I asked about you, said I knew you. It was nice to hear him talking about you. I liked it. I could believe we were really friends.'

A clap of thunder sounds in the distance as the last of the sun's rays disappear over the horizon. The candle blows out and the room grows darker.

'I didn't mean to do it, Mary. But when I had the chance . . . when I let myself imagine it was me he wanted, over you . . . over *you* of all people!' She laughs. 'I felt like I'd made it. I had what you had. I had your *boyfriend*.'

Chapter Forty-Six

'What then?' I say. 'What about *that night*? You were there, weren't you?'

'I was with Mark that night, yes. But not because I wanted to *be* with him. I didn't. I shouldn't have let it get that far – it was stupid, selfish. I'm ashamed of it.'

She relights the candle and I watch as the jaunty light dances over her face. 'But I know now it happened for a reason. It gave me the chance to get closer to you, to understand what he put you through. See, that night I had a plan. I knew you were going to be at the party and I was going to take the opportunity to talk to you, to convince you to leave him.' Her eyes narrow and she snatches a cigarette from the crumpled soft pack on the island.

'Mark wouldn't leave you.' She sticks a cigarette in her

mouth and lights it. 'I'd already tried to convince him, but he wouldn't. I knew by then what he was doing to you. Because he was doing the same to me. The whole lot – hitting, name-calling.' She laughs bitterly. 'You saw the bruises.'

Something twists in my gut.

'But it's the gaslighting that fucks with you most, isn't it? When they make you think *you're* crazy, convincing you it's all you when it's *them* all along!' She explodes into peals of laughter that reverberate off the walls.

'He's like a dog with a bone when he wants something, isn't he? He won't let up. And he wanted you. I couldn't let that happen, couldn't let you get sucked back in.' She drags long and hard on her cigarette, blows a pale rope of smoke towards the ceiling.

'It wasn't that hard to track you down. I got your details from the school records and called Aunty Anne – she's lovely, isn't she? Clueless, but lovely. I gave a fake name, said I knew you from school. Don't be angry with her, Mary – she didn't tell me anything. She's so protective of you. You're lucky to have her. Anyway, she wouldn't tell me where you lived, of course, but she let slip that you'd gone to Sydney. When I stalked you and Cat on Facebook, I saw Cat's post about signing the lease. You couldn't see the street number in the photo, but I recognised the area. It's a pretty recognisable beach. You didn't really think that through, did you?'

She pauses for a moment, exhaling smoke thoughtfully

as she runs a hand through a length of fine hair. Her fingers snare on a knot.

'Cat made it easy when she posted about wanting a roommate. I'm surprised Mark didn't find you himself. Cat blocked him on Facebook, I'm guessing, and she's smart enough not to have given away any details online. But she wasn't careful enough. She doesn't understand, does she? Doesn't give people like him enough credit for being the scum they are. She tried to get me to stay away from you. Me! As if *I* was the one who was the problem and not her! As if you're not allowed to be friends with anyone else! You know why I feel that way about her now, don't you? She doesn't get you, Mary. She just. Doesn't. *Get* you.'

I say nothing and Rachel runs a hand over her face, looks suddenly tired.

'She didn't recognise me, of course. I knew she wouldn't; I was invisible to the pair of you at school. At least this time that worked in my favour. But, in the end, it was me who fucked up. Mark wasn't giving up and I gave us away. I was careless, I'll admit it. I'd turned off location settings on my phone, changed the number, but I should have straight up got a new one. He'd found some way to track the phone itself – fucked if I know how that works, but technology makes it easy for stalkers these days.

'So to pre-empt things I got in touch with him, thought I'd try to keep him at bay. He wasn't having it – he was obsessed. He'd have done anything to get you back. Mainly to save face, of course.' She laughs bitterly. 'So I became the enemy. For one thing I'd left him, and you know how he *hates* to lose. But on top of that he thought I was going to mess things up for him. He knew I was a little . . . *preoccupied* with you. I wasn't the best at hiding it. He thought I was going to tell you about us, that it would ruin his chances of getting you back. He wanted me out of the picture.

'Whether he meant to kill me with that car or not, who knows? Maybe he saw me and just lost his shit. He doesn't care about people – psychopaths don't. They'll do anything and everything to get what they want and whoever gets in the way is just collateral.'

I watch Rachel stub her cigarette out on the bench. When she lifts her head, her eyes are hard. 'I tried everything, but it was you he wanted. He'd never leave. Not because he loved you, but you know that already – people like that aren't capable of love. They're opportunists. They take what they can get, when they can get it and it's all for one purpose – to serve themselves.'

I stare at the liquid in my cup, feeling sick.

'It wasn't just your money, though he knew he had a sweet deal with that. It wasn't just that you were arm candy, making him look good. Any bitch with a pretty face and money could've given him that. But you were different. You and your . . . condition.'

I glance at her sharply. 'Condition?'

'He said once he could do things and you wouldn't remember, because you don't remember things. You don't remember sometimes, do you?'

'I remember now,' I tell her. 'I remember enough.'

She shakes her head. 'Not everything — not yet. But you will, soon enough.' She sighs. 'Cat told me everything about your parents, about *you*. She made me promise not to talk to you about it . . . not to *upset* you.' She gives a scornful laugh.

'Everyone was lying to you, Mary. Everyone thought they were doing the right thing, *protecting* you, but I thought you deserved to know the truth. That's why I brought you here. I wanted to help you. Believe me. That's all I've ever wanted. I know what it's like not to remember . . . to have a part of yourself you don't trust . . .'

Something rises in me: a strange, sick feeling.

'It happens to people like us. When someone hurts you like we were hurt, sometimes the only way to cope is to block it out — so you can forget. So you can pretend it didn't happen.'

Though it's humid, I feel cold all over.

'Don't you ever have gaps . . . periods of time you can't recall? Aren't there things you wish you knew but can't remember?'

I shake my head angrily. '*Stop it!* I don't want to hear this. This isn't about *me*. This is about *you*. What happened that night, Rachel? Or should I say *Sophie*?'

Rachel's eyes widen. Then she laughs, a short, sharp bark.

'You can cut the bullshit. I *know* you're the girl I've been looking for — the one who was there that night, with *him*, when it happened. That's why you took my shoes, isn't it? Because that blood would have been pretty fucking incriminating. You took them to protect yourself. I know it now, so don't bother trying to deny it. Just tell me what you did.'

'For fuck's sake, I was protecting *you*!' Rachel's voice is sharp, almost a shriek.

I shrink away from her.

She shakes her head, her eyes unfocused as she stares into her cup. 'I had to. In case you remembered and gave it away. In case the cops figured out the truth.' She sighs, a world-weary sound. 'You've got it all wrong. He was attacking you, Mary.' Her voice is hoarse, the way she says my name is drawn out, strange.

My head aches. I'm tired of mind games. 'For God's sake . . . What do you mean?'

'Tom. I saw what he was doing. And I . . . I was so *angry*. He was *hurting* you . . .'

'Tom? *Tom* was hurting me?'

Pain, splintering through the back of my head. Fear.

'Get up, you stupid bitch.'

Rachel nods. Her eyes are wet.

My heart pounds. 'Did I see what happened?'

Another nod.

I screw my eyes shut, grit my teeth. 'There was blood on me, where did it come from?'

Rachel gives me a funny look. 'I told you,' she says in a quiet voice, speaking slowly, 'I went looking for you.

320

By that stage you'd been missing a while, and I knew you'd had a lot to drink earlier. I was worried. Mark was high as fuck and angry, he kept saying you had his drugs and he wanted them. I wanted to warn you . . .'

I nod. I remember him harassing me about some eight ball I couldn't recall ever having.

'I went looking where Mark said he'd left you. I could hear voices in the distance. When I found you . . .' She pauses, swallows. Her eyes dart away. 'I only saw the end of what happened, but I could figure out the rest. If I'd only got there a minute earlier . . .' she trails off.

The room grows darker.

'I called out to you, but you ran.' Rachel's voice is barely audible now.

Sophie!

The waves hiss and crash against the shore below, the ocean whispers its secrets. And then it hits me, like lightning, sending shockwaves through my body.

'I know what you did. And I don't care. I only ever wanted to help you. I wanted to save you,' she whispers.

Run, Sophie.

'But it was too late.'

Through the ringing in my ears, there's the whoosh and suck of the retreating tide. Soon the shore beneath will be washed bare, with only a scattering of shells and seaweed left behind. Soon it will be nothing but a graveyard.

A sharp keening breaks the spell. I can't pinpoint the

sound; it seems so far away. Then suddenly it's here, right nearby – the sound vibrating inside my head. Someone screaming. *Me*.

My surroundings come back into focus – darkness, candlelight, the cool night breeze on my skin. I'm shivering, panting. My throat feels raw. Rachel stands before me, her mouth wide. She's saying something, shouting maybe, but I can barely hear her over the roar of blood in my ears.

'It's okay. Please, calm down . . .'

I look around. We're near the edge of the deck now, though I don't know how we got here. I'm standing near the broken railing, hands clenched at my sides. My chest is tight. My head throbs.

'Just come back from the edge. Please. Come on.'

There's a rhythmic pummelling over the whispers and the waves. Footsteps on the front path, several pairs.

The cops have come. Adrenalin spikes in my veins. They can't find me – not now.

I turn and grip the rotten, splintered wood of the railing and look down. The sea is black tonight. Only the tips of the waves are illuminated by silver light. My heartbeat roars louder than the waves and I feel like I'm down there, like I'm drowning in the deep, cold water.

The footsteps grow louder; they're getting close.

I take a step towards the edge. There's a crunch as the rotting wood disintegrates under my foot.

'No!' Rachel shouts. I look over my shoulder and she's

staring me dead in the eye. She reaches out a hand, speaks calmly, softly. 'Come back here where it's safe. It will be okay, I promise. Nothing bad is going to happen, I'll make sure of it.'

There's a loud knock at the door, a booming voice shouts, 'Hello?'

I look down at the water and back to Rachel. 'How can I trust you?' My voice trembles. 'I can't even trust myself.'

Rachel smiles, her eyes never leaving mine. 'Because you have to. I can help you. I can make things right.'

The door rattles and the house shakes; a plank breaks away from the deck and falls to the ocean below. Any second the door will cave in.

'It's the police! Open up!'

The clouds overhead have parted and Rachel's round eyes gleam in the silvery light. 'We're even now, can't you see? We've both fucked up. But we deserve a second chance. I can give us that. But only if we're in this together.'

I look down at the churning black sea. My head swims. I feel faint.

'Please,' Rachel says, her voice mingling with the whispers of the waves. 'You have to trust me, Sophie.'

Chapter Forty-Seven

Four months earlier

20th August 2016
12.48 a.m.

I don't remember having a single drink and yet I'm stumbling in my heels, my stomach churning with acid. Mark's holding onto my arm; he's practically dragging me. 'Pull yourself together,' he mutters. 'Bruce will be here any second.'

As if on cue, a beat-up, pale blue Ford pulls up at the curb and a fat, ginger-haired man of about fifty gets out. 'G'day,' he greets Mark, then nods at me.

'Sophie,' I say, reaching out a hand. Mark slaps my hand away and glares at me. I'd forgotten – I'm not supposed to use my real name.

'Got a niece named Sophie,' Bruce volunteers, although no one asked.

'You don't say.' Mark has that sneer in his voice he gets when he thinks someone's a waste of skin. He puts his arm around me and pulls me close, marking his territory. Bruce merely smirks.

They make the exchange, looking over their shoulders like the shifty bastards they are, then Mark and I trudge over the sandy foreshore, back towards the party. He's looking at the goods, muttering to himself about how he got screwed. He's always like this right before he gets a hit. I don't know why he doesn't just do it now.

I slip in my heels and grasp his arm for balance. He swears angrily and shakes me off, so I stumble and land on my knees.

'Hurry up,' he snaps.

I get to my feet and hurry after him, anger fizzing inside me.

'Shouldn't use that old fucker, he's useless,' Mark complains.

'Beggars can't be choosers,' I mutter, and, without warning, Mark turns and whacks me across the face with the back of his hand.

'No one asked you, did they? Dumb bitch.'

My cheek burning, I stand there as he storms off, lighting a cigarette as he goes, putting his phone to his ear. When he speaks again, it's in a soft voice. He's suddenly calmer, warm even. He doesn't look back.

It's enough. It's enough now, I tell myself. While I still burn inside and out, I make a decision. It's now or never. Fuck it that I don't have any clothes – I've got money. I'm the one with money – not him; *he* needs *me*. Ha! Imagine the look on his face when he realises I'm not coming back, when he realises he'll have to come up with a way to pay the rent. And he's forgotten I still have that eight ball in my purse. He's going to be sorry.

But my triumph is fleeting. The familiar quiver of fear creeps through me as I think, *Where will I go? What will I do?* I've alienated myself from all my friends. I barely speak to Aunty Anne anymore. Cat's been off the radar for months.

I'm alone.

I shiver, suddenly cold. Picking up my pace, I head back towards the party. I shouldn't be out here – it's dark and no one's around. Just as I'm thinking this, I hear footsteps behind me.

I whirl around to see a shadow move amongst the trees. There's the sound of twigs breaking and then a figure appears – a guy, younger than me, with long hair, wearing a T-shirt and jeans. He walks towards me. 'Hi.'

I take a step backwards.

The guy smiles; all I can see are his teeth in the dark. 'You lost?'

'Uh, a little.' I glance over my shoulder, take another step backwards.

'Are you heading to the party?' he asks. He steps further

into the light cast from a street lamp and I can see his face. He's young, lanky, with a friendly, open face.

I sigh with relief. 'Yes! Yeah, I'm on my way back there . . . I am a bit lost, actually.' And more than a bit drunk.

'I'll walk you,' Lanky Guy says, pointing ahead. 'It's just up there. I know the place well.'

'Thanks so much,' I say, turning to head in the direction he points in, but I stumble and fall in my shoes.

Lanky Guy catches my arm and steadies me. I sense that he's surprisingly strong – his hands are huge and calloused, his grip tight. I know I'll have bruises tomorrow. 'Careful,' he laughs. 'I want you in one piece.'

'Sorry,' I say, then think that's a weird-arse thing to say, isn't it? I'm starting to feel dizzy and I want to go home. I just want to sleep.

'Actually, I think I'll just go somewhere and get a taxi,' I say. 'I'm not feeling well.'

'It's too late for that,' Lanky Guy mutters.

It's then that I get a swirl of dread in my stomach. I don't know where we are and I don't know where we're going. I can't hear the ocean anymore.

I try to pull away, but Lanky Guy grips me tighter. Panic blooms.

'Please, I just want to go home.'

Lanky Guy doesn't say anything and that frightens me more. He faces straight ahead, pulling me along as I stumble and trip. It's darker here, so I think we're in a park, or maybe a reserve. There's a clearing and a building of some

328

kind – it looks like a house until we get closer, and I realise that it's a church, still under construction.

'Please.' The word comes out as a sob.

'Shut up,' he hisses, looking around before hauling me by the arm and into the half-built structure. There are objects in the way and I keep tripping over things, hard things, on the ground. Bricks.

Lanky Guy shoves me hard against the wall and my head cracks against the cold bricks. Shoving his forearm against my throat, pinning me in place, he reaches down, then lifts his arm again. Something glints in the moonlight. The blade of a knife.

'Don't fight me.'

My body gives an involuntary jolt.

'I said *don't fight me.*' I can't see his face clearly, but I can hear the hate in his voice. 'You got that?'

I nod dumbly and he grunts, letting go of me for a moment. Without the support of his arm, I wobble and slip, landing painfully on my tailbone. My hand touches something cold and hard. Something with sharp edges.

'Get up, you stupid bitch.'

I hear a belt buckle clinking and it triggers a memory. Some ancient thing, buried deep, surges to life. My father's face flashes in my mind and rage comes in a white-hot burst. As I shake my head, desperate to blink it away, I am back in the church and he is leaning towards me. My fingers close around the object beside me and I swing my arm upwards until the object connects under his jaw, snapping his head back with a *crack*. He wails and pitches forward, the knife clattering to the ground, and I duck out of the way just as he falls to his knees. He's making a horrible sound, like he's choking, and the next thing I know I'm holding the brick above my head, standing over him, chest heaving.

What am I waiting for? I turn to run, but then something closes around my ankle and pulls me to the ground. I scream and yank my leg back, but his grip is steel. Swivelling my body, I raise the brick and slam it down on his skull. This time there's a sickening crunch.

Something comes over me – it's like I'm in a dream. Anger squeezes like a fist inside my chest and I don't stop. I can't. I keep pounding the brick into his skull, striking him again and again and again. My ankle is released. He is slumped face down on the ground. He doesn't move.

There's a rustle in the bushes nearby and I turn my head sharply.

A girl's pale face, illuminated by moonlight, stares out at me from the darkness. I stand in shock, my breath loud in my ears. At first I'm not sure I'm seeing straight. But then the girl snaps out of her trance and steps forward.

A wave of panic hits me and I turn and run, tripping over the uneven ground, heading towards street lights in the distance.

'*Wait! Please wait, it's okay!*' the girl's voice calls after me.

But I don't stop. I follow the lights until I reach a road, and there are houses and I can hear the ocean again. I run towards the sound, towards where I think the house was, where people are, throwing glances over my shoulder, waiting for the stranger to appear. I reach the shore, my heels sinking in the sand. Then I realise I'm still holding the object – a brick, wet with blood – and terror seizes me.

What have I done?

Dizziness takes hold, the world sways. I stumble along the sand, towards the sound of people partying. The lights are closer now and there's some kind of low wall next to me. I drop the brick and hold onto the wall to stay upright. I can hear music and laughter; it can't be far, maybe someone will come. Maybe someone will find me.

And then someone does come, materialising from the darkness, running towards me. It's Mark, his face like thunder in the glow of a street lamp.

There's someone else coming – a girl, running, pale hair flying. The girl from the woods.

Mark kneels in front of me, picks something up from the ground, and stares at it. The brick.

'Run, Sophie!' the girl shouts.

The ocean roars in my ears, my eyes slip shut and all I see is blackness.

Chapter Forty-Eight

11th January 2017

Dear Journal,

This is the first time I've written in you, but it feels like we know each other quite well. I've been getting to know you over these pages. Mary was quite the writer. It's a shame you'll have to burn once I've written your final entry.

We haven't officially met, but you know a version of me. My name is Sophia Baker. Sophie. And this is my story. The real story.

When I was a little girl, we lived in a big, beautiful house and I had everything I ever wanted. I was spoiled, *most people would say. Pretty and privileged. From the outside, my life was idyllic.*

My family lived in a grand old house in Melbourne and were the proud owners of a sprawling vineyard in the Victoria countryside. My mother was a chef turned celebrity-chef after she published a string of popular cookbooks. My father was a successful businessman who bought several wine brands producing some of Australia's most acclaimed wines.

We went on overseas trips every school holiday, attended media events, picked grapes, dined in Michelin star restaurants and drank mouth-watering wine long before I was legal. Dad travelled a lot for business and Mum and I spent hours creating recipes and filling our home with wonderful aromas.

But from when I was very young, Mum suffered migraines. Ever since I can remember, after a busy day in the restaurant or a photo shoot or television appearance, she would eat dinner, pop a pill and go to bed. And later, my father would come into my room. He'd read me fairy tales and sing nursery rhymes from my favourite book. He'd tell me that all the princes in all the world could come to my rescue, but there was only one man who truly loved me, who would truly protect me.

Mary, Mary, quite contrary. That one was my favourite. I'd ask him to sing it to me again and again, shivering under the bedclothes as the inevitable drew nearer, praying I could delay it. And then he'd close the book and place it on the nightstand. He'd turn out the light.

It went on right up until the Christmas just after I turned fifteen, when we were staying in the cabin by the sea. That was when my mother found out our secret. Her sleeping pills hadn't done the trick — or she'd forgotten to take them, perhaps. She saw the empty space beside her, thought she'd find out where her husband went at night.

For all our sakes, I wish she'd never found out.

After she struck him, he fell backwards. His arms flew out and he grabbed her by the wrist. They both fell over the edge of the deck. To this day, I can hear the screams. I ran to the edge, stared down into the rolling grey sea, but it was too dark. I couldn't see a thing.

I didn't speak about what happened that night. It wasn't that I chose not to — I couldn't because I didn't remember. Or Mary didn't, I should say. Apparently, when Aunty Anne arrived for Christmas and found me hiding in the cupboard, I didn't say a word. And I stayed silent for two whole months.

I can still see the inside of my wooden cell; it is etched into my memory. I traced the splintered wooden interior with my fingers as the light rose and faded through the crack in the doors, murmuring the old nursery rhyme over and over. Mary, Mary, quite contrary. *I suppose that somewhere along the line, as the minutes and hours ran together, the name stuck.*

As Doctor Sarah explained, now that I've remembered, now that I am Sophie again, she can tell me more about my condition. As Mary, I was too fragile. Doctor Sarah feared I would be unreceptive, that it could do more damage than good. But now I know. Dissociative Identity Disorder, *they're calling it. Gradually, in order to block out and separate myself from all the bad things I'd seen and experienced in my life as Sophie, I took on a new identity. I became Mary.*

Memory is a fickle thing when it comes to the average mind, but in the mind of a DID sufferer it's another thing entirely. I've had plenty of time here in the clinic to google the crap out of my condition. It's fascinating, in a morbid way. There are personal accounts on various sites and blogs ranging from people blacking out multiple times a day (that's all they remember – it's the people in their lives who have to deal with their other identities) to people fully becoming another person with no memory of their previous life. Some people have multiple personalities – one lady had eight! – hence the old term 'multiple personality disorder'.

My case is unusual. Mary seemed to remember our childhood, our teenage years, our family, Doctor Sarah, Aunty Anne and Uncle John. She remembered things from before she became Mary. But she'd blocked out the bad parts, invented a different version of her life, her childhood, where she was happy, carefree, confident. She chose to see our life the way it appeared from the outside rather than the way it really was. Her – my – our brain's way of coping with the unthinkable.

Of course, some things couldn't be ignored – like the fact that her parents were gone. So she invented some story that they went missing – which sounds mysterious really, almost romantic – rather than the truth. Because, let's face it, anything is better than the truth.

I suppose Mary could have carried on that way forever. Perhaps I would have eventually been eradicated. I don't know – I don't think it works that way. Because if it did, we could all be anyone we wanted. If we didn't like who we were, we could literally become someone else. Erase the past, create a new identity. The ultimate self-reinvention.

But as Doctor Sarah says, our memories have a way of coming back to us when we least expect it. Our psyches can't protect us from the truth forever.

I don't share Mary's memories. Sometimes I have dreams so

vivid they feel like memories and I wonder if they're hers. Sometimes I have flashbacks – see images of things I'm sure I've never experienced. Many sessions with Doctor Sarah and the psychiatrists here at the clinic have taught me that Mary didn't share my memories either – not consciously. That's why there were gaps – those blank spaces. That's why she didn't know about the things I've done.

So fifteen-year-old me became Mary, once I started talking again. I started going to therapy and I met Mark and . . . well, I've read Mary's entries here. We both know the rest. At times I'd switch to me again. I have memories of Mark, of the kind of man he was, of the things he did to me. To us. I remember our apartment. I remember parties. I remember the aftershave he wore. But Mary stayed with him for three years, and the memories I have make up all of a few months, tops. They're just snippets, snapshots of a life someone else lived. Mary's journal entries are all I have of the life she led in my body.

I remember the first time I, Sophie, 'met' Mark. Waking in an unfamiliar bed with a stranger next to me – naturally, I freaked out. He thought I was taking the piss, that I was pretending to be someone else on purpose. Once he figured it out, he wasn't happy. But being the opportunist he is, I guess he found a way to take advantage of the situation.

Mark preferred Mary to me. He told me. He'd be angry with me, shouting at me to fuck off, fuck off, fuck off and I couldn't understand why. I can now. Meek, trusting Mary who'd had a nice childhood and did what he said was infinitely preferable to her rage-filled, fucked-up alter-ego. Plus I suppose she stuck around

337

longer than I did, was more 'stable'. I'd wake up thinking it was Sunday when it was Thursday, wondering what the hell had happened, angry and confused and scared, and he couldn't stand it.

He stayed because of the money. He sought me out when I left because why wouldn't he? He had a nice little arrangement going. It was the perfect situation for a guy like him.

Anyway, back to the story. So, on the night of Dealer Dan's party, Mark disappeared after we scored the drugs from Bruce (Mark was with Rachel, I now know. Turns out he was cheating – no surprises there) and Tom Forrester held a knife to my throat and tried to rape me. So I killed him. Simple as that.

Was it an accident? In the dead of night, when I can't sleep with the thuds and screams coming through the wall, I can't be sure. And I suppose no one will ever know, because Rachel told the police it was Mark who did it. Her and me? We were just innocent bystanders. Only we know what really happened. Only we know what I did.

I'm not like most people in here. I cop 'princess' a lot, amongst other names I won't mention. But – aside from this one girl who gives me the finger every time she sees me – once people find out what happened to me, why I'm here, they all get this same look. A combination of pity and perverse fascination. I'm not sure how that makes me feel.

They're all suffering from severe mental illnesses, of course, but most of them are actually okay. They know what it's like to have seen or done horrible things. To suffer in ways most people will never have to imagine.

Maybe they wouldn't be so sympathetic if they knew the

truth. If they knew what I did, and that I'm not sorry for it. How differently would that night have ended, how many lives might Tom have gone on to destroy if I hadn't done it? It was self-defence. Him or me. Why would I be sorry?

I've seen first-hand how powerless the authorities are to help people like me. I've lived through the consequences of complacency and incompetence. I've seen how they violate the victim who's already been violated enough, conspiring to expose them as liars, whores, as willing participants in their own assault. It becomes about the crazy bitch attacking the helpless, confused man, not the abused woman reaching the end of her tether and lashing out in self-defence.

It would be us on trial, not them.

Now, more than ever, I wish Mum were here. The grief Mary didn't let me feel has poured out in a deluge and it just keeps coming. I grieve my father, too. That surprised me at first, but apparently it's normal. It's not because I miss him or forgive him or want him in my life. I think it's because it's the opposite of that. My grief for him is tainted, more violent, because I both hated and loved him; the fury and the guilt threaten to suffocate me.

Doctor Sarah says I may need to grieve my father three times. Once for the man he was – a man who hurt me when he should have protected me. Once for the man who died that night by the sea. And once for the father I wished he'd been – a man who would nurture and love and protect me. The kind of hero every daughter dreams of: someone who champions her rights, not someone who steals them from her.

I can see that Doctor Sarah's right. She usually is. I hope when that final phase of grief has passed, I will be at peace.

Rachel was the first one to visit me here, after Aunty Anne. I didn't recognise her, not exactly, but she seemed familiar, like an old friend or a distant cousin. I thought she was a nurse at first, dressed in white with her gentle smile, fair hair backlit like a halo.

When it was just the two of us, she explained what happened. She brought me this journal from my bedroom in the apartment we shared. She told me to read it when I was alone, and hide it. She explained exactly what she saw That Night – what she did for me. I'm not sure that I deserve her loyalty.

Rachel said that after I realised what I'd done, who I was, I turned pale and passed out. I must have panicked and pressed my alarm at some point because the cops turned up at the cabin. But Rachel had a story ready to tell them that would save me, not implicate me. She even put herself in jeopardy. She told them Mark had attacked me on the cliff and would have killed me if she hadn't stepped in. He was swinging a baseball bat wildly, and she was trying to wrestle it off him. All it took was one final tug from him, and as Rachel let go of the bat, he lost his footing and stepped backward, off the cliff edge. We escaped with our lives. He wasn't so lucky.

I don't know what really happened; it was Mary who saw, not me. But I backed up Rachel's story, no questions asked. I owe her that much. Because of her, I'm free. Or, at least, I will be soon.

It's funny the way two people come together in life, sometimes. As far as I can gather, Mary and Rachel barely knew each other. Mary doesn't mention her much in this journal. She's practically a stranger. But because of one man, we are bound forever.

It's all worked out pretty nicely, I guess. Mary's journal entries support Rachel's testimony. The blood on my shoes was Tom's, which proves I was there and backs up Rachel's claim that Tom attacked me before Mark killed him. Turns out the pair were affiliated – drug dealing, of course, which gives Mark further motive.

I sometimes wonder how things would have turned out if it weren't for Rachel. Would I be in this place? Or would they have locked me away somewhere a million times worse?

I don't mind it here, most of the time. It's funny, but the insomnia, the anxieties, even the anger I lived with all my life, like I was hardwired that way – it's all lessened. Maybe it's peace of mind. I have my life back, and now everyone knows the kind of men they were – my father and Mark. They got what they deserved. And I've got my whole life ahead of me.

I've had some other visitors, which has been nice. Aunty Anne comes a lot and she brings me home-cooked meals because the food is terrible here. This guy called Ben came about a week ago and apparently Mary was involved with him. He seems nice enough, kind of sweet but not much to look at. I don't remember him at all. Poor guy, he looked devastated. Mary hasn't mentioned Ben much in her journal. I wonder how close they were, what he meant to her. Maybe I'll get to know him, over time.

Cat's visited more often than anyone. After hearing her side of the story it's painfully clear how devoted she was to stick by Mary – me – all this time. Despite the things I did to her over the years. Dumb kid stuff, admittedly, but still hurtful. Like going after boys she liked, because I knew she liked them. To prove to myself that I was better, that I could win. I cringe to think of it. Back then I had so much to prove — all that hidden shame and self-loathing, all that anger with nowhere to go. It's a wonder I had any friends, and somehow I've ended up with two: Rachel and Cat. Fierce, devoted Cat, who made it possible for me to break free and move on, who — under Doctor Sarah's strict instruction — went to great lengths to make sure the 'Mary' delusion went unshattered. Everyone knew — Ben, Rachel, Gia. Cat told them, to protect me. To make sure I was safe. Until I was ready to understand.

That's why it such a shame that, after everything, someone else succeeded where she failed. The new girl was the one who broke through, who got me where I needed to be. Because for all the psychoanalysis the professionals and the do-gooders threw at me, Rachel was the only one who truly understood. Maybe that's why Cat and Rachel never visit together, and don't speak of each other much.

I'm getting used to the routine here. I like knowing what's going to happen every day. It's a comfort. Security. My meals are brought for me, I can watch all the films and read all the books I want. They even let me cook sometimes, under supervision. I might learn to be a chef, like Mum.

In some ways I actually like being in this place. There's no ocean, no roaring waves to taunt me with their whispered memories. And if I play my cards right, someday soon, I'll be out of here. I can go anywhere I like, start afresh. Maybe Rachel will come. I've got money, I can head north, find myself a little place of my own. Far from the sea.

Acknowledgements

There are so many wonderful people to thank:

Agent-extraordinaire Lorella Belli, for believing in this book and in me. You hadn't even read the entire manuscript when you jumped in with an offer – and it's been a rollercoaster ever since! I feel extremely privileged to have you in my corner. Thank you for everything.

Rachel Faulkner-Willcocks, for being such a zealous advocate of *The New Girl*. I'm so grateful for your faith in this story.

My brilliant editor, Katie Loughnane, who has been such a passionate and enthusiastic supporter. You've understood the heart of the story and have made me feel comfortable placing my work in your (very capable) hands – thank you so much for that.

Jade Craddock for her exceptional copy-editing skills,

Bella Bosworth for proofreading, and Alison Groom for the stunning cover design.

And, of course, enormous thanks to the entire 'dream team' at Avon! I couldn't have hoped for a better home for my book. You've given me a wonderful introduction into the publishing world and I am so grateful for your unparalleled energy and hard work. Every one of you is a star!

My mentor, Laurence Daren King, who guided me through a thorough re-write and helped me turn a decent book in to one that had agents grappling for it. Thank you for everything you've taught me.

Harry Bingham for seeing potential in this manuscript and steering me towards the right agent. I have learnt so much from the information and resources you provide aspiring authors with.

Huge thanks to my talented friend and fellow author, Sarah Epstein, who has been there since the very beginning. You've supported me in countless ways and I don't know what I'd have done without your advice, guidance and friendship.

Heartfelt gratitude to Sonia – without your care and support, I wouldn't be where I am today.

My wonderful family-in-law – Mai, Kjell, Kjell Magne, Dagfinn, Henriette and Lene for your enthusiasm, support and for being my international cheer squad! Tusen takk alle sammen.

My mother, Judy, for reading to me as a child and

ensuring that I was always surrounded by stories. You planted the seed that became a life-long love affair with books. I am so lucky to have such a selfless, loving parent. Thank you.

My grandparents, Marjorie and Arthur, who worked so incredibly hard to provide for this family. Everything I have, I owe to both of you.

Thank you to my aunt, 'Tilynn' Lynn Day, who has been such a special part of my life – and an endless source of information and enthusiasm for all things literary!

My stepfather, Andrew Mack, for being someone who understands the insanity of the writing process! You have been ever-ready with a listening ear, an appropriate article or the loan of a book. Thank you for the support.

My baby son, Milo, who has opened my mind and my heart in ways I hadn't imagined possible. I couldn't love you more.

And last, but far from least: thank you to my wonderful husband Vidar, who has been there for every step of this journey – plotting, conjuring, dreaming, commiserating, hypothesising and (finally!) celebrating. You've experienced every moment with me and I am infinitely grateful for that. Thank you for understanding the way my mad mind works and for making me feel like the most important person in the world, every single day. This achievement belongs to you too. I love you.